SAVING HER TARGET

DARE TO SURRENDER
BOOK THREE

DANIELLE PAYS

Saving Her Target
Copyright © 2020 by Danielle Pays

Edited by: Jen McDonnell, Bird's Eye Books
Cover by: Maria @ Steamy Designs

www.daniellepays.com

Chapter One

I want to lick every tattoo off your body.

Zach Brannigan stared at his phone, shaking his head. Why the hell had he given his number to the blonde last night? Now he had to deal with her flirty texts trying to get him to go out.

Nope. Not interested.

That was his last thought before someone tackled him to the ground.

What the fuck?

It was the middle of the day, and he'd just gotten jumped? Adrenaline coursed through his veins, and he was ready to gain control and pop back up when he heard the familiar click of cuffs around his wrists.

Panic set in.

"Carl Marucam, you are under arrest," a woman said.

Carl? Who the hell was that? Then he remembered Carl had been the guy looking for William Chanler a while back.

As he was hauled up, he looked for the male officer that took him down. The only person he could see was a woman who in no way could have taken him down. She wore a black pantsuit and was at least six inches shorter than him. Her frame was petite, but she must be all muscle to take him down the way she had.

"Shit," Chase blurted as he approached.

That's when Zach took a longer look at his captor. He couldn't hide his grin even if he wanted to. She was stunning with dark hair cut short and piercing blue eyes. How the hell had she taken him down? Most men couldn't; he had to have a good hundred pounds on her. But while he was grinning at her, she was glaring at him. Yet, even with a glare, he felt a stirring in his pants that he quickly willed away. With his hands cuffed behind his back, he would have no way to hide his attraction.

"That's not Carl," Chase said.

The woman looked Zach up and down. "Dark hair, tattoo sleeves, beard."

Yep, that about described him.

"Hi, I'm Zach Brannigan. What's your name?" He was still grinning like a fool.

"Is your wallet in your back pocket?" Chase asked.

He nodded.

Chase pulled it out and handed his license to the officer.

Zach took advantage of his chance to take in this beautiful woman as she studied his ID. Finally, she shook her head and turned her gaze to his. The moment their eyes locked, he swore he saw her lip quirk up briefly.

He wanted to know this woman.

"I'm sorry, Zach. You matched the description for a wanted man."

He had to know her.

"I'd love to be *your* wanted man," he purred.

He'd make fun of any of his friends for behaving this way, but what the hell.

"Really?" Chase said, shaking his head.

Yep, he'd catch hell for this later.

The woman suppressed her smile, but he saw it. Her lips curled up a bit.

"You're a good-looking guy, you shouldn't hide it under all that fuzz," she said as she unlocked his cuffs.

Ah, she was warm to him.

"Is that so?" he asked. "When you're done here, you should come into my pub and tell me more about it."

"Your pub?" she asked.

He tossed his thumb over this shoulder. "Brannigan's Pub back there is my place."

Her eyes swept up and down his body, and damn if he didn't stand a little taller under her stare.

"Thanks for the offer, but I need to get home and clean my carpets."

Carpets? What the hell?

He couldn't remember the last time a woman

turned him down. Hell, *they* approached *him*. Of course, the fact he lived in a small town that was home to so few single men helped that out. This woman clearly was not from Fisher Springs.

Chase doubled over in laughter at his suffering.

The woman turned to his amused friend. "Officer, contact me if you hear from Carl."

"Will do," he said.

The woman walked away, and Zach's mind raced with the interaction. The woman was tough and hadn't succumbed to his charm. Who the hell was she?

"What's her name?" he demanded.

"Agent Jessie Doyle. She's with the FBI. But don't get excited." Chase clamped his hand on Zach's shoulder. "She has no reason to come back to Fisher Springs."

Zach crossed his arms and grinned. "I'll give her a reason." Then his grin fell as his eyes caught on a man on the opposite side of the street. "Hey, is that Joey? I haven't seen him in months."

Chase glanced in the direction Zach was looking. "Joey!" he called.

The man waved, but didn't stop.

"I have to say, I'm not a fan of his blond hair," Zach said. "Looks like he's still using. I hope Dunin can help him. Hey, before I forget, do you have a business card from Agent Doyle?"

Chase laughed and slapped Zach on the back. "No, I don't. Nick might, though. I gotta go. Lunch is waiting for me. See you later."

The moment his friend was out of sight, Zach grabbed his phone and shot a text off to Nick, hoping he would give him the number and no grief.

Stepping inside his pub, he almost tripped over the boxes surrounding the bar.

Damn it!

He had to take deep breaths to calm his anger. This wasn't the first time his manager, Adam, had the liquor delivered through the front door. And as last time, Adam was unpacking the boxes, placing the bottles anywhere they fit.

"What the hell is going on here?" Zach asked.

Adam turned, and the color seemed to drain from his face. "Shit. Sorry, boss. The delivery came. I wasn't expecting you in so early."

No, he obviously wasn't, since he was doing something Zach had already asked him not to do once before. Zach scratched his beard while he stared at the kid.

Adam was in his mid-twenties but seemed younger than his years. Zach was trying his hardest to teach him anyway, because after working hard for six years, he thought he deserved a vacation. And he wasn't going to get one if someone else couldn't run this bar. But then something like this would happen and make Zach wonder if that trip to Hawaii would remain only a dream.

"Adam, I appreciate your effort, but the delivery was supposed to go in the back. We only bring out what we need. If you pack the shelves, you're asking someone to run off with a bottle."

Adam's mouth fell open as he stared at the boxes, then the shelves. "I didn't even think of that."

Of course he didn't.

"Please move the extra inventory to the back. I'll be in the office making some calls."

Zach closed his office door. He had nothing he had to do, but he needed to get away from Adam. He liked the kid, but he had really hoped he would have learned a little faster. Maybe he had to let this go; Adam was a great bartender, and worked well with the vendors.

He sat back in his desk chair, and his thoughts shifted to Jessie. He couldn't remember the last time he had been drawn to a woman like that. Hopefully, Nick would come through with her number.

Checking his phone, he growled when he saw the detective's response.

Nick: *Sorry, can't share FBI numbers for personal reasons.*

Zach: *I have a real FBI emergency here. Serious, I need her number.*

Nick's response was fast.

Nick: *An emergency in your pants doesn't count. Nice try, though.*

Bastard.

Zach tossed his phone on his desk. Then he chuckled. He knew how to get that card. Nick might be one of his best friends, but his fiancée Lauren and Chase's girlfriend Harmony were the ones always trying to set him up. One mention to them about Doyle, and he was sure Lauren would get him the number.

Nick: *Don't think of getting it from Lauren unless you are planning to ask her to break into the Fisher Springs Police Department to get it.*

Damn Nick. Well, now he'd have to take it up a notch. He was meeting with Lauren next week—he'd ask for her help then. As his accountant, she was taking care of all his books, and considering how sad those were right now, a happier topic of conversation might be good.

Unless something changed soon, that new bar in Davenport would put him completely out of business. Bucky's Bar. He couldn't stand the name. And what in the hell were they doing that was drawing all of his customers away?

Hell, he should go there and see for himself. That's why he'd hired Adam as the manager, after all, so he could have a night out once in a while.

His mind drifted back to Jessie. While she rebuffed his advances, the quirk of her lips and the way her eyes moved over his body told him she was interested. Damn, if only Chase hadn't been there, she might have been more receptive. Unlike the women that hit on him at his pub, he wanted to get to know Jessie. Now he just had to figure out how to get the personal number of an FBI agent. It couldn't be that hard, could it?

Chapter Two

A sudden knock made Jessie jump. She glanced up to see Carter standing at her door. Thankfully, it wasn't Dillon.

How she'd ended up in the same office as her ex was something she didn't understand.

Dillon had been one of her instructors in Virginia when she first joined the FBI. They'd started off as friends, and then one night, she was feeling a bit homesick, so he whistled a song and danced with her.

She knew dancing with her instructor was crossing a line, but he really seemed interested in her and he was attractive. Then he kissed her, and she was hooked. Their relationship developed quickly after that.

He was often busy, but she'd thought everything was good between them—until she found him in his office whistling the same song and dancing with another student. She listened at the door and heard him say almost word for word what he'd said to her that first night. It turned out he didn't have tennis every Tuesday and cross fit every other day. The reason he could only see her on Wednesdays and Saturdays was because he had other recruits to fill all his other days.

When they'd begun dating, he'd told her she couldn't tell anyone, that his job would be at risk if his superiors found out he was dating one of his students.

Well, she'd finally learned why he didn't want her talking.

After training, she had been transferred to Richmond, and thought she'd never have to see him again. Then he started showing up at her apartment on the weekends, begging her to come back to him. She refused and thought that was the end of it. Especially when she found out her request to transfer to Seattle had finally been approved; she'd been so happy to be near her family again.

The last six months in Seattle had been great, aside from the first month when she discovered Dillon had transferred to Seattle as well sometime before her. Never did it cross her mind that Dillon would leave Quantico. Why would he give up his cushy teaching position? Unless someone had turned him in.

"Jessie?"

Great. She'd spaced out in front of her boss.

"Sorry, Carter. Can I help you?"

"Yes, can you come into my office?"

She studied the man, trying to gauge his mood. While she had recently wrapped up a multi-state case, she'd also let Carl Marucam slip through her fingers again a couple weeks ago.

"Sure," she said then rose to follow him.

Carter had the largest offices. When he was promoted last year to Assistant Director in Charge, he was moved into the corner office with windows on two walls. Most of the building was dark, and everyone subsisted on the fluorescent lighting. But not Carter; he had bright, natural light and plants.

Carter sat down and motioned across from him. "Please sit."

Well, shit.

Carter usually paced as he discussed cases. Sitting was reserved for reprimands or demotions.

"I wanted to talk to you about a new case," he said.

"New? You don't want to talk about the Marucam case?"

Carter laughed. "No, I read your report. Good work. The Billings office is working on it now."

"Billings... as in Montana?"

"Yes, we have reason to believe that he's hiding there. But I called you in here because I have a new case for you." He tossed a file down.

She opened up the familiar manila folder and quickly scanned the file log and then leafed through the documents.

"A distribution company?" She glanced up.

Carter had turned away and was staring at his computer. "Yes. Hawthorne Distribution delivers liquor to numerous bars, restaurants, and country clubs, mostly in Washington, Oregon, and Idaho, but they also supply elsewhere too. We believe they are being used to launder money."

As she dove further into the file, she saw what appeared to be stock photos of men loading boxes onto a truck.

"Why do you believe that?"

"Because we have someone on the inside."

She set the file down and leaned back into her chair. "An informant?"

Carter waved his hands. "I know you had bad luck with one in the past—"

"Bad luck?" She narrowed her eyes. "He shot me."

"This one is different. Trust me."

Jessie ground her teeth. "What makes him different?"

"This person provided sufficient evidence to indicate that Hawthorne Distribution is laundering money for the Bannon brothers. The Bannon family is known around here for dealing meth—unfortunately, they've managed to keep their hands clean. If we can find out exactly who in Hawthorne is in on the money laundering, it might create an evidence trail to the Bannon brothers."

That got her attention. "Whoever it is, is an insider? Are you sure?"

Carter nodded.

"Then why do we only have stock photos in

this file?"

"We need to obtain the real photos. Those are from the company website. If the informant tried to get photos inside the warehouse, he would be risking his life."

"Why the hell would he risk his life to help us?" Carter held out another folder.

She grabbed it and quickly read through it. A young boy, age sixteen, had been charged with murdering a federal agent.

"The DA wants to charge him as an adult," her boss explained. "We made a deal. If the informant's information is good, then this kid will do some time in juvie and be released at eighteen."

"Less than two years for murder?" Jessie asked, curiously.

"Truth be told, there's some ambiguity about why the agent was on their property. The kid said he thought the agent was an intruder. We don't want to put the agent's partner on the stand. He's currently working undercover. This deal is in the best interest of the FBI as well."

"Does this mean this boy is part of the Bannon family?"

"No. Jessie, trust me," Carter pointed to the file. "This is good information."

"All right." Now was not the time to argue. "What exactly do you want me to do?" she asked.

"Meet with Agent Mitchell Blaese on Monday. You'll be partners on this investigation. He's familiar with the Bannon family history."

Familiar?

It was possible but unlikely. Blaese had only been an agent for a couple of years, and she couldn't imagine they would assign junior agents to any Bannon case. He was green. Unfortunately, rumor had it he was trying to land the promotion that had recently come up, the same one she wanted.

Just her luck, she had to seriously compete against a man with much less experience than she had.

"Has he worked on a case involving the family?"

Carter chuckled. "No, but I had him read them all. Don't worry. He's a good agent."

She nodded, wondering if Carter would say that about all his agents. She hadn't met Blaese personally, so she had to trust her boss on this one.

"For now, go home," he said jovially. "Take the weekend off. You deserve it."

"Thank you. I'd love that."

Carter laughed. "I'll bet. It looks like they worked you hard in Richmond. Hopefully, you'll find things nicer here."

Jessie stood and was almost to the door when she saw Dillon walk past through one of the windows. Carter appeared to be in a good mood so if there was ever a time to ask, it was now. She turned around. "Carter, I do have one question. I was surprised when I discovered that Dillon, I mean *Agent Harris* works out of this office. He was one of my instructors during the new recruit training."

"Yes, I'm well aware. You can thank Agent Harris for your transfer here. He pushed hard for you, explaining your family was here and that you had struggled with homesickness during training."

What. The. Fuck? "He said I struggled?"

Carter laughed. "Don't worry about it, Doyle. I've seen your work. I'm no longer concerned about you."

"You were concerned?"

Well shit, maybe the rumors about Blaese competing for the same promotion were founded. If Dillon had soiled her reputation, she'd be easy to beat.

"Agent Harris told me all about how you leaned on him when he was there. I'm sorry if you think he overshared."

"Why is he here? Why did he leave Virginia?"

"Well, you should probably ask him that, but I will tell you it was his request. Now, go, enjoy your weekend."

Jessie walked out of Carter's office in a daze. She'd broken up with Dillon last summer. Why the hell had he transferred to the office she wanted and told her boss lies?

Before Carter could change his mind, she returned to her office and shut everything down.

It was only five pm. That meant she could go to the happy hour her friend Sam regularly set up. After missing the last several, she was surprised her friends still talked to her.

* * *

As soon as she walked into the bar, Sam shouted to her. Jessie turned to see the petite brunette waving to her. She'd been jealous of Sam's hair since she met her. It was long and wavy and always looked like she just walked out of a salon. Opposite of her super straight hair she wore short to avoid dealing with.

"Over here!"

She made her way to the table. The bar was dark but crowded.

"I'm surprised to see you," Sam said.

"Carter told me to take the weekend off. I got out of there before he could change his mind."

Sam also worked at the FBI Seattle office. But somehow, despite the hours, she managed to have a life outside of work.

"About time you got out. Kaila should be here any minute."

The Corner Bar was their usual hangout. It was a typical sports bar with photos of athletes on the walls, and often, hockey was playing on the television screens.

"Hey, your brother's playing tonight. *Damn* he's fine. Why haven't you set me up with him yet?" Sam asked, staring at the television.

Jessie glanced up and couldn't hold back her

smile. All four of her little brothers played hockey. Silas, the oldest, played professionally. The others hoped to as well when they were old enough.

She shook her head. "You'd tear my brother apart. He's a softie."

Sam laughed. "I don't see anything soft on that man. Damn."

Jessie covered her ears. "Gross. I don't want to hear about my brother's body. Besides, I thought you were seeing someone. Are you finally going to give up some information about him?"

Sam smiled. "It's casual. He's great at sex, but he's not interested in an actual relationship."

"I'm sorry. That sucks," Jessie said.

Sam shrugged. "It's fine. He's been very clear about it. No harm, no foul."

"Hey, girls," Kaila tossed her backpack on the table and sat in the remaining chair.

With her long, blonde hair and long legs, she was the opposite of Jessie in many ways. Kaila was feminine and never went out without lipstick and high heels. She was Sam's friend, but had quickly become Jessie's friend too.

"How'd you get out early?" Jessie asked.

Kaila worked for the King County Sheriff's Office, and usually couldn't make it to happy hour either.

"My lucky day. How the hell did you get off early?"

"Reward for wrapping up my last case."

A waiter dropped off two margaritas and a beer.

Jessie grabbed the beer and smiled at Sam. "Thank you for remembering."

Sam had ordered Jessie a margarita the first time they'd gone out, but as hard as she'd tried, she couldn't drink it. Too much sugar. No, she was a beer girl.

"Did you order these?" Kaila asked Jessie.

"No, I did," Sam answered. "And if you two stood me up, I'd be crawling back to my condo, drunk off my ass." She laughed. "Now that the drinks are here, no work talk." She turned to Jessie. "What I want to know is if you're seeing anyone yet. It's been long enough, we need you to get out there already."

Long enough. Sam was right in that regard. But after finding out her ex had bad-mouthed her, Jessie didn't exactly feel confident about jumping on the love train any time soon.

"I have no interest in dating ever again," she said.

She'd told Sam and Kaila that her last boyfriend had been cheating on her. That was as much detail as she was willing to give. Fortunately, they didn't press for more.

"What happened to you sucks. But don't you get horny?" Sam asked.

Jessie spit out the sip of beer she was taking. "It's always about sex with you, isn't it?" She wiped her mouth with a napkin.

"Of course it is. But seriously, there isn't any man out there that you look at and wonder what it would be like to share a night?"

An image of Zach Brannigan popped into her head. Why the hell did she even remember his name? And why the hell hadn't she been able to forget those blue eyes that had bored into her as if seeing her soul?

God, listen to me. Seeing into my soul.

He'd said enough that she knew his type — arrogant, cocky, thinks he's God's gift to women. Just like Dillon. She wasn't going to fall for that again.

"Ah! Look at that smile! Jessie, what's his name?" Kaila leaned forward, excited.

"It's nothing." Jessie waved her hand dismissively, but she couldn't help her lips from turning up at the corners.

"Nothing my ass," Sam said. "Spill."

Knowing they weren't going to let up, she told them all about how she had tackled him and then when he showed interest, she said she had to clean her carpets and left as quick as she could.

Kaila threw her head back and laughed. "You told him that? The poor guy. I wish I could have seen his face."

"He did look a little hurt. But that could have been because of the officer laughing next to me."

"There were witnesses?" Kaila slapped the table. "Oh, that's too funny. Terrible, but funny."

"I'm pretty sure they were friends. He was probably teased about it later."

Sam leaned forward. "What did this guy look like?"

Jessie bit her lip as she imagined Zack. How would she describe him?

"I guess he's a cross between Jake Gyllenhaal and Adam Levine but better looking than either of them. He has these piercing blue eyes and tats covering his arms."

"He sounds yummy. Does he have a beard?" Kaila asked.

"Unfortunately, yes," Jessie said.

"I don't understand how you can't love beards on men." Kaila shook her head. "They can be so sexy."

"I just don't."

"What's his name?" Sam asked.

"Zach Brannigan."

Sam smiled.

"What?"

"You remembered the guy's name. You like him."

"Well, it doesn't matter. I'll never see him again. He lives in Fisher Springs."

Kaila laughed. "That's not that far, only a couple hours away."

"Exactly. And with all the free time I don't get, there's no point in even thinking about him. Besides, he's not my type. He's a cocky playboy."

"Well, you don't have to date him. A playboy could be fun for a night," Sam said, waggling her eyebrows.

Jessie rolled her eyes. "Even if I wanted to—and for the record, I don't—how would I go about that? Track the guy down and say *hey, come to my place for a night, and then we'll never speak again*?"

"Damn, you're bad at this, aren't you?" Kaila asked.

Jessie drank down the rest of her beer, thinking about her lack of dating experience. Dillon had been her first serious boyfriend. She'd dated a couple of guys in college, but it hadn't been anything lasting.

Now she had Dillon on her mind.

Did Sam know him or that he helped get her transferred?

No, she couldn't ask about him without these two interrogating her, and her history with Dillon was the last thing she wanted any of her coworkers knowing about.

"I haven't really had many boyfriends. It hasn't been a priority." Jessie shrugged.

"Okay, we are going to need more drinks. We will help you figure out what to do about this guy," Sam said. "And by 'figure out,' I mean where, when, and how you will do him." She winked.

Jessie would let them plan, since they seemed to enjoy it, but there was no way she was tracking Zach Brannigan down.

Chapter Three

Zach walked into the grocery store and practically ran into someone as his phone buzzed in his pocket. Zach pulled it out and stared at the screen, letting out a sigh.

"Hey, texting that blonde still?"

Zach glanced up to see Chase Harvey standing in from of him wearing a shit-eating grin.

Chase had seen him flirting with the blonde a few weeks ago in his pub and assumed he'd taken her home. He hadn't. She'd seen his tats, and he could see in her eyes he was another bucket-list fuck for a woman like that. No thanks. Been there, done that.

"No, it's my mom. I should call her."

It was true that he should check in. He'd let a few weeks go by and hadn't responded to her calls. He knew she'd ask how the business was doing, and that was one question he didn't want to answer right now.

Then he noticed Chase was wearing a baseball jersey and tight pants.

"Are you on a baseball team or something?" he

asked.

"Softball. The King County Sheriff's Office has a team, and they let me play on it."

"How did I not know this?"

"It only started back up recently, and I only got in a couple of games last year."

"That's cool. Who do you play?"

Chase shrugged. "Other law enforcement agencies' teams. Today we are playing the Seattle FBI office."

Well, that was interesting.

"Any chance it's co-ed?" Zach asked.

"It is. But that doesn't stop them all from being assholes."

Zach couldn't stop the grin spreading across his face. He had no luck getting Jessie's number from Lauren. Apparently, Nick had it under lock and key at the police station. And he couldn't find anything personal about her while searching social media.

"Take me with you. I'll be your biggest cheerleader."

Chase frowned. "You want to watch me play softball?"

"Sure. I'd love to watch you play. And who knows, I might see Agent Doyle."

Chase tipped his head back and laughed. "Nick told me you asked for her card a couple of weeks ago and he said no. I guess you really have it bad if you are willing to stalk an FBI agent."

He crossed his arms. "Yeah, that was a dick

move by Nick. And I'm not *stalking*. I thought it would be nice to go to a softball game, ya know, get some sun. If I see her, I see her."

"Uh huh. Well, if you really want to go, grab something to drink. We need to get going."

Zach grabbed a large bottle of water and met Chase in the checkout line.

"Does Nick play too?"

Chase laughed again. "No, I guess you haven't seen him throw a ball?"

"No. That bad?"

"Yep. He said he played hockey."

Zach thought of his friend Nick. He was a big guy. "I can see that."

After they made their purchases, they stepped outside.

"I'll follow you to your place so you can park your truck. I'll drive us there. It's between here and Seattle," Chase said.

After the five-minute drive to his place, Zach got into Chase's truck and enjoyed the ride, listening to the radio.

Zach couldn't remember the last time he'd been out of Fisher Springs. At first, he was nervous to leave, worried he'd run into some old family member. But the odds were slim. They had rarely ventured out of Idaho all those years ago; no reason to think that had changed. And even if he did run into someone from his past, they might not recognize him anyway. He'd changed a lot since he left at eighteen.

Chase parked the car, and they walked to the field.

"Take a seat over there." Chase pointed to the left, at a set of bleachers currently occupied by several women and even more toddlers.

Zach glanced at the other set of bleachers and saw several men quietly staring at their phones. "But that side looks better," he pointed.

"That's the FBI side."

Zach scanned the FBI dugout but didn't see Jessie. It was still a bit early, so he wasn't going to lose hope yet.

"I'm going to warm up. Have fun. Good luck if your agent is here." Chase patted him on the back and walked away.

Zach walked around and took in the park. There were bathrooms a few yards away and more parking. Just as he was about to turn back to the field, he caught a glimpse of a familiar brunette.

Jessie Doyle walked out of the bathroom wearing a baseball shirt and jeans that were both sculpted to her body. With each step, he couldn't help but watch her tits bounce. She was talking to two women and didn't see him until he was right in front of her.

"Agent Doyle. Nice to see you again."

Her head snapped up.

He raised his hands to shield himself. "Please try not to tackle me, if you can help it."

Her two friends' eyes immediately went to his

tats, then his beard.

"Is this Zach?" one asked her.

He couldn't contain his grin. "You told your friends about me? I knew we had a connection."

Jessie closed her eyes, took a breath, and then opened them and looked directly at Zach with a smile.

He had to give her credit, if she was embarrassed, she hid it well.

"I mentioned that I took down a large man, yes."

He stepped closer, forcing her to look up. "Is that all?"

She balled her fists and glared at him. "Yes."

"Then how do they know my name?"

Her mouth fell open into a perfect O, and his thoughts instantly turned dirty.

"Hi, I'm Sam and this is Kaila," Sam said pointing to the blonde.

"Nice to meet you," Zach said.

"Jessie, I'm impressed. He has to be at least six foot three and over two hundred pounds," the tall, blonde said.

That was surprisingly accurate.

"I've taken down bigger," Jessie said as she side stepped past him.

"I hope you have more game than that," Sam said to Zach.

Her friends followed Jessie back to the field as he watched, dazed.

More game? Hell yeah, he had more game. He

was going to win her over.

After a few hours of watching Jessie, he wanted her even more. She was fiercely competitive, but she was also damn good. She and Chase were the best players out there, that was for sure.

But his favorite part was after he took off his jacket. He caught Jessie glancing over a few times. Or really, more like she was checking him out.

In the bottom of the ninth, tied with two outs, Jessie was now up to bat. On the first pitch, she swung and hit it hard. The ball flew to the back fence line, and she easily rounded the bases before they got it back home, winning the game.

Some tall guy shouted in Chase's direction. "Sorry you guys lost. Again."

A few others laughed.

"We won't lose next time. Count on it," Chase yelled back. Then he spotted Zach. "Ready to go?"

Zach shook his head and pointed toward Jessie. Chase grinned. "Good luck."

Zach approached the FBI dugout, where Jessie stood with her back to him talking to her friends.

"You played great out there, gorgeous."

She swiveled around, and he stuttered to a stop. She was breathtaking. Her dark hair offset her ice-blue eyes. She had a cute upturned nose. Even her lips were perfect. But what he really liked was she had a small mole on her cheek. Something about it was sexy as hell.

Her eyes roamed down his chest. When she glanced back up, heat emanating from her eyes. "Gorgeous? I don't take kindly to pet names."

He stepped as close as he dared and noticed her breath hitch. "Something tells me you do."

Her nostrils flared as she glared at him. Then she looked past him, and the color drained from her face. She stepped back.

"Not something you'll ever find out." She stared him down.

"I think I will," Zach said.

Jessie shook her head. "You see, that right there is the problem."

"Problem?"

"You think you can charm me, and I'll fall at your feet? I hate to break it to you, but you aren't God's gift to women, even if you seem to think so."

Well, damn. He couldn't hide his grin. "You seem to have some strong feelings toward me."

She arched a brow. "Strong? Yes. I don't like your type. You're a playboy, Zach Brannigan, and I'm not interested."

"I think you are, and for some reason you're putting up all your defenses. The question is why?" he asked.

Someone whistled a song in the distance behind him. The anger in Jessie's eyes dissipated as she looked toward the sound. It was replaced by something that looked a lot like fear.

"I have to go." She pushed past him, and her friends stood there stunned.

Damn, this wasn't going as he hoped.

He turned to see what she could have seen. A man was watching him.

Who the fuck is that?

"You really like her, don't you?" Sam asked.

"What?"

She was smiling. "I've never seen her thrown off by a man like she is around you."

What the hell?

"Thrown off? She played a great game of softball, turned me down with ease, and walked away. If anything threw her off, it was that guy." He turned to nod at the man, but he was gone.

"She hides it well, but you had an effect on her."

"Here." The other friend handed Zach a piece of paper from the clipboard she was carrying. "That's the softball schedule. Jessie always plays. You know, in case you wanted to run into her again."

"Why would you give me that?" he asked.

"She needs some fun. But if you screw around with her head or her heart, you answer to us. We know where to hide bodies so they won't be found."

"Uh…"

What the hell was he supposed to say to that?

Sam rolled her eyes at her friend. "Stop being

so dramatic." She turned to Zach. "You hurt her, we hurt you. Simple."

"You got a pen?" he asked.

Kaila handed him a pen. He wrote his phone number and a note for Jessie. "Can you give this to her? Ask her to text me."

The woman smiled. "Will do."

"Kaila! Sam!" Jessie called from the other side of the field.

"Busted," Sam laughed.

"Good luck," Kaila said.

He watched Jessie as her friends crossed the field. She held his gaze. He couldn't resist. He winked. She rolled her eyes then turned and walked with her friends to the parking lot. A few more steps away, she glanced back again. He caught the smile she tried to hide.

A big hand clamped down on his shoulder. "Wow, you have it worse than I realized." Chase was beside him, grinning.

Unfortunately, his friend was right. Now he had to hope her friends were right too.

Chapter Four

Two days later, and Jessie could not get Zach out of her head. Well, him and Dillon. *If looks could kill.* But Dillon had no right to give Zach any looks.

Seeing Zach had caught her off guard. She'd been so busy trying to make sure she was nowhere near Dillon that she practically walked into Zach.

The man was just as attractive as she remembered. The way he watched her the entire game was intoxicating. But she had to remember Zach was not her type. He was arrogant and thought she should fall for him because he'd hit on her. No thank you.

Dillon had whistled that familiar song while watching her today. It was disturbing. Why the hell had he come to the game anyway? He hated softball. But Carter plays, so perhaps he was trying to kiss up to the boss.

She hoped like hell he wasn't there for her.

That was even more evidence that she should stay away from Zach, no matter how charming he could be. Listening to her heart had gotten her in trouble last time.

But her friends wouldn't shut up about Zach after the game. She finally accused them of sounding like a high school clique. That shut them up. If there was one thing they all had in common, it was that they'd all been on the wrong side of the cool girls in high school.

Her friends didn't understand why she didn't date. Even after she'd told them her ex had cheated on her, they figured enough time had gone by, and the way to resolve her issues was to get back out there. According to Sam, she should have had many rebound fucks by now.

Truthfully, Jessie had thought about it, but anytime she'd gone out, and a man had shown interest, she'd immediately looked for clues that he was lying. It was exhausting.

She had trusted Dillon blindly and gotten burned. She couldn't do that again. She shook it off. It didn't matter. Seeing Zach at the game was a fluke. The odds of it happening again were low. Although, she did pull up the calendar to see if they would be playing the same team anytime soon. Sadly, no. And that left her feeling disappointed.

All the more reason she shouldn't see that man again.

However, there was nothing wrong with fantasizing about him. When the sun had come out and he'd taken off his jacket, she couldn't stop staring. He'd been wearing a Henley tee that stretched across his pecs. When she'd first tackled him on the sidewalk, she could feel he was muscular, but *seeing* his muscles bulge under his shirt… Yep, she'd be fantasizing about that image for a while. And in her fantasy, he kept his mouth shut.

With her mind on Zach, she arrived at Hawthorne Distribution's main office faster than expected. Taking a deep breath, she got out of the car.

All she had to do was go in and meet with the sales team. They were ready for her, she was certain. She had contacted them and sold her story about her plan to open a new chain of bars and needing a regular distributor to provide the alcohol, and they'd asked if she could come in and meet with them. Of course they did; she'd made sure to include the fact she wanted to stock top-shelf liquor.

A few raindrops started to fall, so she picked up her pace to the doors, which opened automatically and let her into a large lobby area where a young woman sat behind a desk.

"Can I help you?" she asked.

Jessie plastered on her game face and stepped forward. "Yes, I have an appointment with Tad Mora to discuss a possible distribution contract."

"And your name?"

"Jacki Alexander." That was her usual undercover alias.

The woman smiled and picked up the phone. "Jacki Alexander is here to see you."

The room was large, but she noticed that there was only one door, and it was closed behind the reception desk. The walls were covered with larger versions of the same stock photos she'd already seen, showing men wearing smiles as they unloaded Hawthorne Distribution trucks.

"Ms. Alexander?"

Jessie turned around to find an older man in a business suit. His look screamed *salesman*. He was what she expected.

"Yes," she replied.

"Let's go back to my office."

She followed him through the door and down a long hall. It came to a T, and they turned left.

Tad led her into a small, grey office. There was one light overhead, and the space was nearly barren except for a desk and laptop. The room was more dreary than her department's interrogation room, and that was saying something.

"I understand you are interested in a contract for several bars, is that right?"

Showtime. She leaned forward. "Yes, that's correct. I'm shopping around a few distributors, but I'd like to get a contract in place by the end of this week."

Tad turned his laptop around and proceeded to go through a slide presentation explaining why their company was the best.

"If you would like to move forward, we require our customers to fill out an application. It asks for more details about your needs as well as a quick background check."

Jessie nodded. After researching several distribution companies, she'd expected this. "Yes, I'm interested," she told him.

"Great, I have your email address, so I'll forward you the link for the online application. If you fill it out today, I should be able to get you set up by the end of this week."

"That sounds great."

Once Jessie was back to her car, she let out a sigh of relief. She knew she'd pass the application process with flying colors; the tech department had set up her fake businesses and had all the paperwork filed where necessary. It was what came next that would be the hard part.

The week progressed slowly, with Jessie spending a great deal of time in stake-out mode, watching the distributor's warehouse from as far as her binoculars allowed. After hours of observation, she knew nothing more than she did on Monday.

Fortunately, she didn't have to drive all the way out there today, which was a relief. Maybe she could meet Kaila and Sam for Friday happy hour again. She'd already briefed Carter on what she had discovered so far. Which was nothing, really.

She'd taken photos of the boxes going out of the

warehouse, but there was nothing unusual about any of the activity. She had to wonder if her time wouldn't be better spent watching the activity at the bars and restaurants where the deliveries were made.

Her phone rang, startling her.

"Doyle," she said when she answered.

"Come to my office. We need to discuss the Hawthorne case." Carter ended the call. No hello, no goodbye.

When she walked into his office, she could feel the tension in the air. He was sitting at his desk, bent over his laptop.

"Come in and shut the door," he said.

After closing the door, she sat down in the chair across from him.

He leaned back and shook his head. "The distribution company emailed today to say they were sorry, but they cannot work with you."

She sat up straight. "What? Did they say why?"

Carter let out a loud sigh. "They said they couldn't handle the size of your business at this time. It's bullshit. I spoke to our informant. Apparently, the company only takes a small number of applicants whose background checks come back clean. Instead, they seek out clients who have something in their past they can use against them."

Jessie jumped up and paced the room. "And we are just now finding this out? That would have been great to know last week."

Carter closed his eyes. "I know."

"So, now what? I can't go back in there. Do you have a plan B?"

Carter was quiet for a moment. The key to their entire operation was getting a contract with the distribution company and getting someone on the inside.

Jessie's mind was racing. "We can try to get an agent hired in the warehouse," she suggested. "Then we can increase surveillance."

Her ideas weren't any better than the original plan, but nothing else came to mind.

"We've had a couple guys inquire about work, and both have been turned away. It's not looking like we'll be able to get someone inside," Carter said.

"Then have another agent apply, like I did."

Carter pursed his lips. "After I learned what happened, I asked tech to set up Agent Blaese, and he'll apply next week. But I'm afraid we don't have time to wait for that. The Director is coming in Monday and wants an update."

"I'm sure he will understand we need more time."

Carter stood up and walked over to a mini refrigerator next to his file cabinet. He pulled out a can of Pepsi. "You want one?" he offered.

"No thanks."

"The director has wanted me gone for a while. I'm afraid he'll use this to get me transferred."

Transferred? Carter may not be the best, but at least he was fair. Who knows what a new boss would be like.

"Well, we could try something else. I was thinking instead of watching the warehouse, I might follow the delivery truck to a place or two."

"Find out who their customers are?" Carter asked.

"Watch the deliveries. There's nothing unusual at the warehouse, so what if Hawthorne Distribution is unaware, and it's only some of the drivers that are moving the money?"

Carter smiled. "That's a good idea. Also, we can run our own checks and find out which of their customers would be most willing to help us out."

She was in for another working weekend, she knew it.

"I need you to start on that today," Carter continued. "You can leave right away. I'd like a long list of their clients by Monday morning, and as much background information as you can dig up."

This was partly why she didn't have a life, her weekends rarely seemed to be her own. Hopefully, she could gather enough information today to justify taking tomorrow afternoon off. There was another softball game, and that was one thing she didn't want to miss.

"I'm on it," she said as she stood up.

"If you find anything promising, send it to me right away." He punctuated his demand by opening his soda can.

Jessie made her way to her office to shut down

her computer before heading out.

"Do you have a minute?" Sam asked.

"Actually, I'm on my way out." Jessie glanced up and noticed the huge grin on her friend's face. "What's going on?"

Sam walked in and closed the office door behind her.

"Saturday, at the game, Zach gave me this to give to you." Sam held out a piece of paper.

Jessie frowned. "What is it?"

Sam rolled her eyes. "Open it."

Carefully, she unfolded the piece of paper. Inside was scrawled a phone number.   Next to the number, it read, "I'm not a playboy but I really want to play with you."

"You've got to be kidding me."

Sam walked around her so she could read the note. "Yeah, he needs to work on his game. I'm guessing with his looks, he's not used to being the pursuer."

"It doesn't matter. I'm not calling him."

"There's more."

Sam now avoided her eyes.

"What did you do?"

Sam winced. "Not me. But Kaila might have given him a copy of the softball schedule."

"She what?!?"

Jessie fell back into her chair. Twice she'd hidden the effect that man had on her, but she wasn't sure if she could do it again.

Chapter Five

By the time Jessie made it home Friday evening, she was exhausted. All week, she'd spent most of her time in her car—first watching the warehouse, and then today following trucks, looking for evidence and coming up short.

After tossing her takeout onto her kitchen table, she took off her boots and poured herself a large glass of red wine. After a few sips, her mind drifted back to Zach. It had been drifting there all week. Part of her itched to text him to see what would happen. The other part of her knew he would probably infuriate her again so why bother?

God, why did she have to be so attracted to a man she couldn't really stand? He was so damn cocky. He probably thought she would have given in and contacted him already.

The fact he went out of his way to attend her softball game threw her. He was clearly a player who was looking for something short and fun, so why put in so much effort? He likely got hit on nightly at his pub. She'd bet those women didn't tell him they'd rather clean their carpet.

But maybe the fact she didn't like him was perfect. Her friends told her all the time she needed to get laid, and one look at Zach told her he could get the job done.

Dillon was probably having sex. A lot of sex. So why shouldn't she? Perhaps she could convince Zach to come over for one night. Only one night. Then she wouldn't have to deal with all the trust issues of a relationship.

She groaned. *Do people my age do that?*

While she ate her teriyaki takeout, she texted Sam and Kaila that very question.

Sam: *Yes! Now call Zach and invite him over!*

Well, damn. She wasn't fooling anyone.

Kaila: *Yes, people do. I highly recommend it.*

By the time she finished her dinner and glass of wine, she was ready to text Zach.

Jessie: *Hi, it's Jessie. The one that tackled you.*

She hit send and the reread her message then cringed. God, she was so bad at this.

Zach: *Hi, Jessie. I was starting to think you wouldn't text me.*

She almost didn't.

Jessie: *I wanted to apologize for being rude at the*

game.

Zach: *No worries. I knew you were just trying to hide that you liked me. ;)*

Jessie rolled her eyes. Well, here it goes.

Jessie: *I'd like to see you. Can you come over tomorrow night?*

Her phone rang in her hands. He was calling her.

"Hello?"

"Are you asking me out on a date?" Zach asked.

His voice was even sexier through the phone. All low and gravelly.

"Sort of. Well, no." She took a deep breath and figured she'd better get to it. "I wanted to ask if you'd consider coming over for one night."

No response.

"Zach, are you there?"

"Yeah, I'm here."

She'd overstepped. He'd probably moved on. Hell, he could get sex in Fisher Springs without the long drive to see her. Now she felt like a fool. This is why it was easier to play it tough all the time. She didn't like feeling vulnerable.

"Sorry, I should go," she said.

"Not a chance," Zach said. "Sorry, I'm just a little thrown off by your request. You turned me down twice, and then I haven't heard from you all week. Now you call to say you want one night? What changed?"

My nightly fantasies of you finally won me over.

She might as well be honest. "I can't stop thinking about you, and I've never really had great sex. Something tells me you could deliver," she admitted.

"Fuck," he said under his breath.

"I'm sorry. I don't mean to put you on the spot."

He laughed. "Believe me, I have no problem with that. The problem is I'm working at the bar tomorrow night—"

"So that's a no? I get it. You probably have hordes of women lined up."

"You interrupted me. I was going to say, 'let me see if I can get my manager to close up.'"

Jessie poured herself another glass of wine and took a healthy sip. "Okay."

"Let me ask you this. How do I know you aren't going to put me off again because you have to wash your hair?"

She laughed. "I won't. The moment I see you, I'm going to do what I've been fantasizing about."

"Just a moment."

Jessie heard some rustling noises and low voices. "Hi, I'm back. I decided I might need some privacy for this conversation."

"Privacy?"

"Yeah, because I'm going to need you to explain exactly what you've been fantasizing about. I need specifics. You know, so I'll be prepared tomorrow."

Holy shit, was she really going to share her fantasies?

"Let me ask you this. If I came over to your place right now, what would you do?" Zach asked.

"Um."

Shit. She had no experience talking so openly. He was much more forward than the men she had dated. He had her at a loss for words.

"You still there?" Zach asked.

"Yeah, you're a lot to take, you know that?"

He chuckled. "You have no idea."

She rolled her eyes at his innuendo. Deciding it was better to get back to the prior topic, she asked, "Are we in the hallway or inside?"

Now he barked out a laugh. "You can't give a straight answer to anything can you?"

"Sorry, comes with the job."

"All right. I want you to think about this and answer me tomorrow. Let's say I come over to your place, you let me inside. We sit on your couch and start talking. But then you look at me with those hungry eyes—"

"I don't have hungry eyes!"

"Don't interrupt me. And yes, you do. I saw them at the game every time you looked at me. *And* the day we met, but we can skip that for now."

Jessie rolled her eyes again, even though he couldn't see it. This guy was so full of himself.

He might be right, though.

"As I was saying, I'm at your place, and we're

together on the couch. I put my hand on your thigh as we talk. Slowly, I inch it up."

He spoke low, his voice doing all kinds of things to her. He continued.

"You stare into my eyes and then lean in to kiss me. I haul you onto my lap so you're straddling me. Now you're kissing me senseless while grinding against me. Tell me, sweetheart, what happens next?"

Fuck. He was good, she'd give him that. In a few sentences, he had her more turned on than she could remember ever being. Her friends kept insisting this is what she needed, and she was starting to agree with them.

"You'll," she growled out before clearing her throat. "You'll have to come over tomorrow if you're up for finding out." She wished she could see his face right now.

"Why do I get the feeling you might get me all the way over there just to throw me out?"

Now she laughed. "You think I would do that?"

"Wouldn't put it past you."

"Zach," she said in what she hoped was a sultry voice. "I'll see you at eight tomorrow."

Then she ended the call and texted her address before she chickened out.

That was when the nerves hit. While she was confident when it came to her job, she was a bundle of nerves around men. Especially a man like Zach who clearly knew what he was doing.

She needed advice. Grabbing her phone, she texted her friends.

Jessie: *I invited Zach over tomorrow night for a booty call. Help.*

Kaila: *You asking for a threesome?*

Sam: *I'd be up for that. Zach is hot.*

Jessie: *No! Seriously, I'm nervous.*

Kaila: *You're nervous? I didn't think you knew what that was.*

Sam: *Relax. Just pretend you are on assignment and get into the character of a sexually confident woman.*

Actually, that was great advice. She could do that, right?

Kaila: *You might want to schedule a wax tomorrow. Based on how long you've been out of business, I'm guessing you need taming down there.*

Jessie: *Seriously? You don't need to worry about my bush.*

Kaila: *Oh my god, I'm dying. You called it a bush! I'd say if it's a bush, it needs taming!*

Sam: *Do you have sexy underwear?*

Jessie: *Shit. Maybe?*

Sam: *If it's maybe, then it's a no.*

Kaila: *What time is he coming over?*

Jessie: *Eight.*

Sam: *We are going shopping tomorrow.*

Jessie: *Can't. I have to work all morning, and then I have a late afternoon softball game. It's alright. I'll be ready when he gets here.*

At least she hoped she would be.

Sam: *Based on the way he looked at you at the game,*

I'd say you could wear a grocery bag and he'd be happy. Have fun. And afterward, tell us all the details!

Kaila: *Yes, ALL the details!*

Jessie: *Maybe. I have to go. I have to work early in the morning.*

Jessie laughed and tossed her phone on the couch. Tomorrow, she would be following another truck around to see where it went. Based on her prior surveillance, she knew those trucks left the distribution center early.

After getting ready for bed, she checked her phone for messages, and found a text from Zach.

Zach: *Can you send me a photo of you?*

Jessie: *Why would I do that?*

Zach: *It's only fair.*

A notification that he'd sent a photo flashed on her screen. Nothing could have prepared her for what she saw. It was a photo of Zach, lying in bed.

Holy shit.

She knew he felt muscular, but damn, he had a six-pack and that V, that drool-worthy V that men have. The sheet was so low, she could see his happy trail.

It was hot. Holy hell, it was hot.

Now he wanted a photo of her? There was no way she could give him anything that hot and sexy. She thought about what she could do.

A photo of me…

She couldn't help herself. She grabbed her license out of her wallet and snapped a close-in shot.

Zach: *Is this your driver's license photo?*
Jessie: *You're welcome.*
Zach: *Really not what I had in mind.*

She knew exactly what he had in mind. *As long as my face isn't visible, there's no harm. What the hell.*

With one hand, she pulled her shirt down, exposing her cleavage, and with the other, she snapped a photo. Then she sent it before she could change her mind.

Zach: *Mm. That will work just fine. Thank you.*
Work? Was he...? Would he tell her?
Jessie: *What are you doing?*

A second photo came through, with the sheet still barely covering his lower half. It was clear he was gripping himself. But it was the look on his face that got her: pure desire.

Yep, she'd made the right decision. This photo alone could get her though a long winter, so memories of tomorrow night would probably get her through *years.*

Reaching into her nightstand, she grabbed her vibrator. Then she laid on her bed, pulled her shirt up to expose her flat stomach, and placed the vibrator next to her panty line. She took a selfie, making sure her face was cut off, and then sent it.

Chapter Six

Zach finally found a spot in the garage to park. It was a good thing he really wanted to see Jessie; he'd just spent the last thirty minutes driving two miles and parking.

Seattle was not his favorite place, though it did remind him why he loved small towns. The distraction had been welcome. He had not been able to get that image of Jessie with her vibrator out of his mind.

He wondered if she would take charge in the bedroom the way she'd taken charge of him when she thought he was Carl. *Down, boy.*

He needed to cool down.

As he rode the elevator to her place, he calmed his libido, but his nerves took over. Why the hell was he so nervous? He'd never been this nervous around a woman before.

Well, no, that wasn't right. When he was sixteen, the girl he'd been dating for a few months agreed to go all the way. He'd been really unsure of himself and what he was doing. But now, standing in the elevator with a small present in his pocket for the woman that was in his thoughts every waking hour, he was breaking out in a small sweat.

He reached up to rub his beard but hit skin, forgetting he had shaved it off. It was time. He'd had that beard since he was eighteen.

He replayed their phone conversation from the night before. Jessie had said things that normally sent him running. She only wanted him because she thought he'd be good in bed? Well, he would show her a night she wouldn't forget. But what had him hooked during that call was her humor. The woman sent her driver's license photo. He chuckled to himself remembering it. No woman had ever made him work so hard before. His goal was to leave her wanting more because he was certain he wanted more than one night with this woman. He wanted to get to know her.

The elevator arrived on her floor, and as he walked down the hall, he noted the building was nice, newer. Not his taste, as he preferred things that were a bit more worn so he could fix them up.

The door to her condo opened before he could even knock. Jessie stood in the doorway wearing a flowing dress that ended about mid-thigh. Her legs were tanned and muscular. If he had to guess, she was a runner. Her eyes looked bigger and brighter than he remembered, and she wore some kind of pink gloss on her lips.

It took all his self-control not to step forward

and kiss her.

Jessie had turned him down flat twice. Then called him to come over and have sex. She was a puzzle he couldn't wait to figure out.

"Hi." She stood in the doorway, wringing her hands.

Aw shit, she's regretting inviting me over. Zach leaned on the wall next to the door, hoping like hell she'd still invite him in. "Hey, we don't have to do anythin' you don't want to. We could just sit and talk, if you'd like. I'm just happy you gave me the right address."

Her eyes widened while she stared at him. "Why are you talking like that?"

"Shit," he muttered. "When I get nervous, a bit of an Irish accent comes out."

Her eyebrows shot up. "You're nervous?"

He nodded.

She smiled. "Me too."

Then her gaze moved up his body. Her eyes widened when it hit his face. "You shaved?"

"After the way you just checked me out, that's what you're focused on?"

She grinned. "Yeah, what else would I notice?"

Damn, this woman made him work... and damn if he didn't love it.

"Seriously, why did you shave?" she pressed.

"A beautiful woman told me I shouldn't hide behind it."

She gave him a small nod. "Come in. Sorry I'm

sending mixed messages. I've never done this kind of thing."

"And what kind of thing are you referrin' to exactly?"

Time to verify they were on the same page.

"Let's sit down." She led him to her kitchen table, where he sat down. "Want a beer?" she asked.

"Sure."

She returned with two beers, and Zach had to keep himself from cringing.

He could admit he was a beer snob. Which is why he had to hide his cringe at the idea of drinking a commercially mass-produced beer.

Jessie laughed.

"What?" he asked, defensively.

"You should see the look you just gave. I should have figured a guy who owns a pub would be particular about his beer. Sorry, but this is all I have."

"It's fine."

He cracked open his can, took a sip, and tried to not make a face. Based on Jessie's laugh, he failed.

"Sorry." He couldn't help but laugh himself.

"You're from Ireland then?" she asked.

He shook his head. "No. My mom is. Her accent is thick. It rubbed off. It's not usually a problem unless I get nervous."

"It's gone. You're not nervous anymore?"

He held her gaze. "I'm focused on other things at the moment. Tell me, Jessie, what did you mean when you said you've never done this kind of thing?"

Her cheeks turned a light shade of pink, and he couldn't help but be a little happy he'd flustered the tough agent.

"I've never asked someone to come over just to have sex. I'm nervous."

"No need to be nervous. We can just talk if you like."

She nodded but didn't seem to relax.

"I have an idea." He pulled up a playlist on his phone. As the music started to play, he stood up and held out his hand. "Dance with me."

For a moment, she hesitated, then she took his hand.

The moment he had her in his arms, his body tingled with desire; he was wildly attracted to this woman. And based on the way she was looking at him, it was mutual. But it was more than just physical. He couldn't put his finger on it but he felt a connection he'd never felt before.

They danced around her kitchen, and during the second song, her hands moved to his chest and then up and around his neck while she stared into his eyes. When she licked her lips, his cock twitched. Then he felt her lightly tug on his neck.

He bent until their lips almost touched — she needed to be certain and make the final move. He saw the hitch in her breath and the way her pupils darkened. Then she pressed her lips against his.

What he felt next, he'd only heard of in movies, and he was sure she felt it too, because her legs seemed to give way. He caught her as a zing moved throughout his body just from the touch of her lips. Her arms tightened around his neck as her lips parted. Then he took full control of the kiss. He nipped at her lower lip, and she let out a small moan. That was when she seemed to lose all sense of control.

He was vaguely aware that his hands were inching down her back, and hers were on his chest, bunching the fabric of his T-shirt.

The next few moments gave way to their clothes flying off as they made their way toward her couch. Hell, he knew her bed would be more comfortable, but he wanted her now. Their bodies came together in a frenzy of kisses and touches and he couldn't get enough.

She pushed him back until he fell onto the couch and then she straddled him. While earlier, she'd been shy, there was nothing shy about her now.

He had the wherewithal to reach for his pants and grab a condom, putting it on in record speed. Then his hands moved down her legs as he stared at her. God she was beautiful. Her body was both muscular and curvy.

"What's wrong?" She frowned.

"You're beautiful."

The faint blush was back in her cheeks.

"You're not so bad yourself." She ran her hands down his chest and across each ridge on his stomach, then up his arms. "You have a lot of tattoos."

He did. He had two sleeves, and a few more

pieces on his chest and back.

"Do you like tattoos?" he asked.

Her eyes said yes as they roamed up and down his body.

"Eh." She grinned.

"Think you're funny?" he asked.

She nodded. "I know I am."

He moved his hand, cupping it between her legs, and groaned when he discovered she was wet and ready for him. He slid his fingers across her wetness, and she drew in a breath. Craving her, he pushed a finger inside, then two.

Damn she was tight. He wasn't sure how long he'd be able to last.

Her smile had given way to a moan.

"Fuck, Jessie. You're so wet. You ready for me?"

"Yes. Stop stalling already." She ground against him, her wetness coating him.

He moaned, he had to be inside her. Seeming to know his thoughts, she took control and guided him to her entrance. Slowly, she lowered.

He grit his teeth. "God damn, you are so fucking tight."

She grinned and then slid down, taking him all the way in. They both stilled, her adjusting to him, and him trying to make sure he'd last longer than two minutes.

Once she slowly started moving, he reached down and found her clit, circling it as she began to ride him. Any hesitation she'd had earlier was gone as she rode him harder and harder, pressing into his finger.

"Faster, rub faster," she demanded.

"God, you're so sexy. I can't wait until I can get my mouth on your clit. You're gonna love my tongue all over you, aren't you?"

He felt her body tighten around him as her orgasm hit her.

"Oh Zach!" She threw her head back and a throaty moan escaped her lips as her body quivered above his.

He was done. He sped up the pace, racing for his own release, then he stilled as it hit.

"Jesus, Jessie," he ground out. "You love the dirty talk, don't you?"

She collapsed on his chest while they panted, out of breath.

"Yes. Very much."

He pulled her tight against him, taking a moment. That was hands down the best sex he'd ever had.

"Hey, I need to take care of the condom. I'll be right back," he whispered in her ear.

She nodded and moved off of him.

When he returned, she was curled up with a blanket, but opened it up for him to share. He pulled her into his arms, amazed at what had just happened.

He'd known before, but he was certain now — one time with Jessie was not enough. He just hoped she felt the same way.

"I brought you something, Macushla." He leaned forward and grabbed his jeans, pulling the item from his pocket.

"*Macushla*?"

He smiled. "'My darling'. It's Irish. Now open your hands," he said.

"It's not a frog, is it?"

He frowned. "A frog? Why would I give you that?"

"I don't know. But I have brothers, and I know when they say 'open your hands,' I need to proceed with caution."

Zach laughed. "It's not slimy, I promise."

That earned him a smile as she did as he asked.

He set the charm in her palm. It was a tiny, silver revolver.

"You didn't seem like a flowers kind of woman, and when I saw this in a shop in Fisher Springs, I thought of you."

Jessie studied the charm in her hand. "I love it. Thank you."

"Now you need to keep seeing me."

He felt her tense in his arms. Her head jerked up and she was frowning.

"What? Why? We agreed, one night."

Not the response he was hoping for. He took a deep breath to calm the nerves before his accent came out again. Right now, he wanted to keep Jessie focused on the issue at hand, and not on his issues.

"I never agreed to that, and obviously, you

need a bracelet to hang that charm on. Then you'll need more charms."

She lifted her chin, looking him in the eyes. "Is that so? What if I don't wear jewelry?"

He leaned down and kissed her. "Then I guess you'll have to keep seeing me for the great orgasms I offer." He moved his mouth down to her breast.

Her body tensed. "I'm not sure that's a great idea," she said, slowly.

"I think it's a great idea." He kept kissing lower. "I do believe I said I wanted to taste you."

When he reached her sweet spot, she wove her hand through his hair and held on tight.

"Oh god, Zach. Why am I so on fire around you? I don't understand."

"Don't think. Just feel." He flattened his tongue against her clit and she moaned.

He made sure she spent the rest of the evening *feeling*.

Chapter Seven

Zach grinned to himself, remembering the fire in Jessie's eyes Saturday night. God, he wanted to put that fire there again and again. He'd spent more time thinking about her than he would admit.

When he left Sunday morning, they hadn't discussed seeing each other again. He didn't want to risk her shutting him down. No, he decided he'd message her this week, and remind her how good they were together.

That started right now.

Zach: *Can't stop thinking about Saturday night… and Sunday morning.*

After a short walk through downtown Fisher Springs, he arrived at Harrow Accounting. Lauren was staring out the window, waiting for him. Pushing through the door, he saw her worried expression and knew she didn't have good news.

"Tell it to me straight. How bad is it?" he asked.

"You shaved? Wow, you look good."

Zach laughed. "As opposed to normal, when I

look like shit?"

"Shut up. You know you're hot, so you can stop with the pity party. Seriously, though, why did you shave it off?"

He rubbed his chin. It still felt odd to him. "It was time for a change."

Lauren grinned. "Time for a change, huh?"

Shit, he forgot how much Nick and Chase talked. Of course, it would have gotten back to Nick's fiancée.

"You going to give me crap, too?" Zach asked.

She shook her head. "Nope. I'm happy. It's the first time I've seen you show interest in any woman."

"Is that so?"

"It is. I see you flirting at the bar, but your eyes don't smile. I know you aren't really taking all those women home."

Huh. Imagine that. Lauren may have been in Fisher Springs a short time, but she seemed to have him pegged.

"How do you know so much when Nick and Chase are clueless?"

She waved her hands. "They're guys. They aren't really paying attention. Now, let's discuss your finances." Lauren led him to her desk, and she turned her laptop so they could both see it.

Lauren had gone through a hellish situation with her family. One that had involved the police department and his friend Detective Nick. It was great they were together now, but when they'd first met, they mixed like oil and water. Now she was settled and had recently opened up her own accounting business. Zach was proud to say he'd been her first client.

After he sat down, she clasped her hands and stared at him.

Jesus, this wasn't good.

"As you know, business has slowed down. That combined with the increases in business expenses, and you are not making enough to pay all your current employees."

"Increases in business expenses? What increases?" He wracked his brain. Lately, he'd been cutting his orders due to less demand. This didn't make sense.

"Between the raise you gave Adam and the increase in fees from the distribution company, it has eaten all your profits."

He didn't hear anything after her first few words. "Raise? What raise?"

She clicked on a spreadsheet and then pointed. "Right here. Three months ago, Adam was given a twenty percent raise. Looks like there's a copy of the note to payroll service in the file."

The screen slowly loaded with a note scrawled in Zach's handwriting.

'*Add twenty percent To Adam salary.*'

"I didn't write that."

Lauren cocked her head. "Isn't that your handwriting?"

He stared at the screen. "It is, but I never

authorized that. Besides, I would have said *Adam's* not Adam."

Lauren magnified the note.

"See that right there?" Zach pointed.

Between 'Add twenty percent' and 'To Adam,' he could make out a faint line.

"I do. It looks like two notes taped together."

Zach dropped his head into his hands. "A few months ago, I wrote Adam a note to add twenty percent more of a particular craft beer to our order. I can't believe he did this. I trusted him."

"I'm sorry."

Why would Adam do this? Why wouldn't he ask for a raise if he needed one? Zach would never have agreed to twenty percent, but asking would have been better than this. What else had Adam taken?

If that kid is the reason my business goes under, I'll —

Yeah, what would he do? Nothing. Not unless he wanted to end up like his father.

Dammit. These past few months, he'd been so focused on finding the next big craft beer to have in his bar that he'd missed what was going on under his nose. Adam had been helping Zach manage the bar for six months, and the plan was for him to take over most of the managing so Zach could have a life. That was his goal. But he'd put his trust in the wrong guy.

"Thank you for alerting me to this. It looks like I have an employee to fire."

Zach stood up, still in a daze.

"Hey," Lauren was next to him with her hand on his arm. "You look a bit shell-shocked. Why don't you take the day to figure out how to handle Adam?"

He nodded. She was right. If he confronted Adam now, he'd probably land himself in jail. "I'll go see if Kate is working at the diner. Thanks again for your help."

"Anytime."

Zach left Lauren's office and walked up to Main Street then down a few blocks. He checked his phone and saw Jessie had replied.

Jessie: *Me too. I guess that's the magic of a one-night stand.*

One night. She was back to that? Fuck that. He never agreed to it, and he knew he could convince her what they had was worth pursuing.

He shook his head. He'd never imagine he'd be chasing a woman like this, but damn if it didn't feel right.

Lucky's Diner came into view. He hoped Kate was working. She had been one of his first friends when he came to Fisher Springs several years ago; it helped that she reminded him of his younger sister Gina in a lot of ways. Kate was tough and didn't really care what anyone thought of her. She lived her life by her rules.

Entering the diner, Zach spotted Kate right away. He nodded to her and made his way to the counter. That was usually where he ate—at the counter, alone. Normally that suited him just fine, but today, thoughts of Jessie floated through his mind. Hell, he couldn't stop thinking about her.

Before meeting with Lauren, his biggest issue had been trying to figure out his next move with a mesmerizing woman. Now he had to fire an employee, which would essentially leave him tied to the bar. He didn't have a lot of help. Ariel was a great employee, but she was a part-time bartender, and had only been there for a few short months.

That was the thing about this town. Everyone was looking to get out, so those few employees he did get never stuck around. Well, except his kitchen staff, but they were better kept in the back.

"Wow. You shaved? I almost didn't recognize you. It looks good," Kate said.

"Thanks. I needed a change, I've had a beard since I was eighteen."

Kate let out a whistle. "Wow, that's a long time. You look younger. Hey, is that a scar?"

She was staring at the mark on his cheek.

"Yeah," he grunted.

"How'd you get it?"

He sighed. That was not something he cared to share. Ever. "It doesn't matter," he said, hoping she'd drop it.

"Got it. Where's your usual smile? What's wrong?" Kate asked as she placed a cup of coffee in front of him.

"Thanks."

He was grateful to have a place like the diner

and a friend like Kate.

"Employee problems," he said.

"Want to talk about it?" she asked.

He shrugged.

Before Kate could get another word in, someone plopped down in the stool next to him.

"Hey, Harvey," Kate said. She poured him a cup of coffee. "I'll let Harmony know you're here."

Officer Chase Harvey was one of Zach's best friends, but the moment Chase turned to Zach wearing a shit-eating grin, he knew what was coming, and he wasn't in the mood.

But then Chase's smile fell. "You shaved your beard? Did you lose a bet?"

"No, smartass."

He took a drink of his coffee, wishing Chase's memory wasn't that great, but he knew it was only a matter of time before—

"Oh shit! You shaved it for the FBI agent!" Chase was laughing. "Wait, does this mean you saw her again?"

Zach shrugged.

Chase snorted. "You shaved, so you clearly either saw her again, or thought you had a chance."

"I saw her, but she said it was only a one-time thing."

"You're not smiling."

Zach turned to his friend. "I want more. I just have to convince her."

Chase took a sip of coffee, watching Zach the

entire time. "You really like her."

"I do."

"What's your plan, then?"

Zach smiled. "I'm going to use all of *this* to win her over." He waved his hand up and down, indicating his body.

Chase barked out a laugh. "Damn, you are more of an arrogant ass than Nick."

"Who's more arrogant than Nick?" Harmony asked. She was suddenly behind the counter.

"Zach here."

Harmony's lips curved up. "True, but at least has reason to be." She winked at Zach, and he knew that meant *game on.*

Chase's head jerked up. "What? What do you mean?" He jerked his head back and forth between his friend and his girlfriend.

Zach bit back a smile. Harmony was a riot. She'd do anything to get a rise out of Chase, and today he was eager to play along.

"Thanks for the support, baby," he said, giving Harmony's arm a squeeze.

Chase jumped up. "You two had a thing?"

Now Zach felt bad. The guy looked like he was either going to throw up or punch something.

Chase had been crushing on his best friend Harmony for years, then had to watch as she dated a suspect in a case he was investigating. Fortunately, they finally figured out they should be together, and had been sickeningly sweet since. It was cute, actually.

"Never," Zach said, then grinned.

Chase punched him in the arm. "What the fuck, then? That's not cool."

"No, but it's fun," Harmony said sweetly. "You know, if you're angry, I get off in an hour. We could work that out..." she offered.

Chase's frown turned into a big grin. "An hour? Yeah, I think I need to teach you a lesson, Ms. Brose."

Zach shook his head. "Stop. That's a visual I don't need."

Harmony and Chase both laughed.

"Zach, you look good without the beard. It brings out your eyes," Harmony said.

The bell over the door rang as a couple of customers walked in.

"I'd better help them. Behave now," she said to Chase.

Chase turned on his stool to face Zach. "How are you going to use your body to woo the agent? Do you plan to go shirtless and stalk her?"

Zach let out a sigh. "I'm sending her texts reminding her of Saturday, but so far, it's not working."

"Maybe you can go to another one of her softball games," Chase offered.

"Will you be playing?" Zach asked.

Right now, Chase was his only legitimate tie to those games. Showing up on his own was borderline stalking, especially if she kept turning him down.

"I don't think we play her team again for a

while. But I can see if anyone needs a sub in her games that don't overlap mine."

"You'd do that?"

Chase grinned. "I've never seen you like this, so yeah, I'll help you out. I have to go finish up at work, though. It looks like I have something to do in an hour that I don't wanna miss." He winked.

"Dammit. Don't tell me about shit like that," Zach said.

After Chase left, Zach pulled out his phone.

Zach: *I never agreed to just one night, Macushla. In fact, I think I'll need many more to memorize the look on your face when you come on my tongue and my cock.*

Zach finished his lunch and made his way back to his pub, slipping into the back office where he worked through his inbox. He'd been in contact with numerous new brewers hoping to find the next big craft beer before any of the other bars did. If he could do that, he could possibly save his business.

He was happy he was the one closing tonight and not Adam. There would be no way he could keep his cool around that guy right now. Since business had slowed, he spent most of his time stewing about Adam and thinking through the last few months.

Had there been any signs?

No, there really hadn't.

By nine o'clock, Jessie still hadn't responded to his texts. Damn, had he scared her off?

Zach: *Tell me this, when can I see you again?*

Her response came right away.

Jessie: *I'm afraid I can't.*

Zach: *Let me guess, you need to clean your carpets again?*

Jessie: *No, I have to clean my makeup brushes.*

He let out a big sigh. One step forward and two back.

Zach: *Do I really scare you that much?*

He was calling her out.

Jessie: *It's not that.*

Zach: *You strike me as someone who isn't afraid of anything.*

Jessie: *I'm not. Saturday was great. Let's not ruin it by trying to have a do over that we both know wouldn't be as good.*

He ran his hand over his face, still unused to his missing beard. Rereading her message, he shook his head.

Zach: *We know it won't be as good? Underestimating me, are you?*

Jessie: *Not underestimating. Just being realistic.*

Zach: *You're wrong Macushla. Next time will be even better.*

Chapter Eight

Lauren had been right about Zach taking a day before talking to Adam. He needed to cool down. The fact Adam also had the next several days off helped as well. It gave Zach a chance to go through his desk.

He wasn't normally one to invade someone's privacy, but this was his business, and Adam had already proved to be a liar.

Despite a thorough search, Zach didn't find anything incriminating. That was good news. Hopefully, Adam hadn't caused any other damage.

Checking his phone, he saw Jessie still hadn't responded to his last text. Since she admitted he scared her, he thought it was possible he'd come on too strong, so he backed off the rest of the week. He would convince her that they should see each other again, but for a real date.

God, he had to laugh at himself. Ten years ago, he would have loved the one-time thing. Now here he was, wanting more.

By mid-week, his patience was wearing thin. He sent her a text asking if she wanted to get together the next morning. As much as he wanted to see her that night, he would have to close up since he'd fired Adam. Sunday, she'd mentioned she'd be on the road most of the week, so he figured he probably wouldn't get a response until later.

There was no way she could deny what they had. Not after the night they'd shared. He relived it again and again. He'd been with his share of women, but he could say without a doubt, that had been the best night of his life. He'd never connected with a woman the way he did with Jessie. Between her barbed comments and the smiles she tried to suppress, she saw him for more than his bad boy looks. And damn he loved her smart mouth. Hell, it was refreshing. And he wanted more.

Now he was debating if showing up to another one of her softball games would put him firmly in the creeper category. Chase had confirmed he would be subbing on Saturday on the team playing hers.

Shit, of course he couldn't do that. That would still be coming on too strong. Fuck, he needed to focus on something else. This was going to drive him nuts.

"Delivery's here," Ariel called from the bar.

Zach walked out, but instead of the usual driver, he was met with someone new.

"Hey, where's Tom?"

"Who's Tom?" the man asked.

"Our usual delivery guy," Zach said.

The man stared at him. Then he stepped forward, extending his hand. "I'm Roger. I've been doing the deliveries for the past few months."

Months? Zach shook his hand. "I guess it has been longer than I realized since I was here on delivery day."

Roger laughed. "Yeah, I usually work with the manager, Adam."

Zach nodded. "I'm afraid Adam no longer works here."

Roger's smile fell. "I'm sorry to hear that. Did he quit?"

The man's disappointment was a surprise. Although it shouldn't have been... Adam could charm anyone. That's what made him so great at working with the vendors.

"No, unfortunately I had to let him go. Business hasn't been good lately."

Roger nodded.

"Go ahead and unload around back. I'll open the door for you," Zach said.

The man didn't move.

"I'm sorry to hear about your situation," he said. "You know, if you're in a tight spot, my boss may have some additional business he could offer you. I've seen how much we deliver to the new bar in Davenport, Bucky's. You should think about it."

"I'm sorry, your boss could have business for me?" Zach furrowed his brows. "What do you mean? Like a company get-together or something?"

Roger tilted his head and then laughed. "No, but that's a great idea. I meant a different kind of business. One that pays cash."

Zach stiffened. He knew the kind of jobs that would pay cash wouldn't likely be legal.

"No thank you. I'm not interested in that sort of thing."

The man shrugged. "It's fine. If you change your mind, let me know. We'll get your inventory unloaded and then be on our way. We have a pretty big delivery to Bucky's anyway."

Was that some kind of dig?

Roger smiled then left.

No, Zach was just sensitive about his business situation. Roger had no reason to insult him.

He opened the back door and watched Roger and his partner unload the truck.

On his way out, Roger waved. "Have a good one."

Zach walked over to shut the door and caught sight of the man stepping into a truck that said *Hawthorne Distribution*.

What the hell? That's not the company we use.

He made his way back to his office and looked up the number for his distributor, then made the call.

"Zach?" a familiar voice greeted. "Didn't think I'd hear from you again."

"Larry, what's going on? I just had a different distributor unload our shipment. I didn't realize until I saw their truck."

"What's going on? Are you forgetting you let us go three months ago?" Larry sounded annoyed.

"Let you go? No, I never authorized that."

"Well, Adam said you did, and he even sent us a signed letter stating you wanted to move on. It was right after we notified you that we'd be increasing our rates. I was sad to see you go, but I understood."

Shit. What the hell else did Adam do, and how had Zach not known about it?

If it had only been this, he could have justified it with the excuse that Adam was trying to save money. But he knew the truth; his manager was saving money to pay himself more. And it was Zach's fault for not knowing what was going on—he hadn't been around the bar as much the last few months. He'd been too focused on craft beers and how to draw customers back to the pub.

"Can you email me a copy of that letter?" he asked.

"Sure. I'll do it when we hang up. I was sorry to see you go. You've been a good customer all these years."

"Thanks. I'm not sure what Adam was up to, but I'll figure it out. Larry, you should know… I had to let Adam go."

"Hopefully, you can sort it all out. I'm guessing he hired Hawthorne Distribution? They seem to be stealing our business from us. Not sure what they are offering that's so much better. I'd be curious to find out, though."

"I'll keep that in mind. Thanks, Larry."

A few minutes later, an email popped up on his laptop. Sure enough, it was a letter typed out to Larry stating Brannigan's would no longer be using their services, complete with Zach's signature.

Now Zach was concerned. What else had Adam touched? Lauren hadn't mentioned finding anything else, but he had a bad feeling there was more than just an increase in salary. Maybe this was it. But why would Adam care about what company they used to order liquor? He had to benefit in some way.

He researched Hawthorne Distribution, figuring it would somehow tie back to Adam or some relative of his, but he didn't get far before his phone buzzed. Jessie texted him back.

He couldn't help his grin… until he read her text.

Jessie: *Sorry, busy working tomorrow.*

That was it. Nothing more. No offer for the next morning. No flirting. Maybe she really was busy, but something in his gut told him otherwise. She'd been skittish from the moment she met him, always keeping him at a distance. Saturday had been intense… Perhaps the thought of seeing him again was too much.

He laughed. She was right. He was one cocky motherfucker if he thought her lack of response was because he was too much man for her. But he had to know if something was going on.

Zach: *Sunday morning? I'll even cook you breakfast. (Eggplant emoji)*

He shoved his phone in his pocket and went back out to help Ariel. They were due to open soon, and he was hoping things would turn around this weekend, and business would pick up. Plus, he wanted to see if Ariel had any idea what Adam was up to. He hoped she didn't... he couldn't handle losing two employees.

"Ariel, did you know we have a new distribution company?"

"No, was I supposed to?" She continued restocking the bottled beers. "I'm not usually here on delivery days. Adam always covered those." When she looked at Zach, the concern in her eyes was genuine.

Normally Ariel opened the bar, but Adam had been swapping hours with her. Zach thought it had been due to Ariel's social life, but maybe it had more to do with Adam than he realized.

"Did you request those mornings off?" he asked.

She cocked her head. "No, Adam said it was easier to restock with less people here."

Well, that was bullshit. He and Ariel had restocked the bar together many times before he hired Adam.

Shit, Adam, what were you up to?

Chapter Nine

Jessie had envisioned something far more glamorous when she joined the FBI. While she understood the need to follow the distribution trucks and learn who their customers were, she had to wonder why the informant couldn't have provided a list. At least she was able to listen to several books on tape as she tailed the truck around the state.

Her first truck fortunately appeared to have a short route. They'd exited the highway several miles back and were headed to a small town at the base of the mountains. The area reminded her of Fisher Springs; of course, that could be because she'd passed the turnoff for it.

Great. Now she was thinking of Zach again—like she'd stopped. Jessie was pretty sure the reason was nothing more than her lack of sex life, and Zach being the sexiest man she knew.

Memories of Saturday flooded her mind. While her first impression of him as a cocky playboy still seemed to be accurate, he hadn't been quite what she expected. He could be tender and romantic and...

No, she needed to stop obsessing over him. Yes, that's what she was doing, obsessing. He took up every moment she wasn't thinking about the Hawthorne case. A man like that could ruin her.

She'd never been this obsessed with Dillon and look what he had done to her. Meanwhile, Zach likely had a different woman for each day of the week. And here she was checking her phone nearly hourly, hoping he'd send her another text? That's why she had to say she was busy. What other choice did she have?

She forced herself to pull her mind back to the truck. She had yet to figure out how they were transferring the money. Was it in a bag? Or were some of the boxes filled with cash instead of liquor?

It would help if she knew how many of their customers were dirty. She'd worked a similar case in Virginia before transferring to Seattle. In that case, a distribution company had a mix of clean and dirty customers, which had made it harder to follow the money.

Her current quarry drove through the small town and kept going.

Huh, there's nothing really out here.

The truck then turned down a narrow road that looked more like a driveway. She fell back a little more. They were the only two vehicles on the road...
Hopefully, the trucker was unaware of her.

As she wound down the road, it became more

and more forested, and tapered to one lane. If anyone came from the other direction, there was nowhere to go to let them pass.

She shivered as she realized how hard it would be to turn around. Was this a trap? She reached for her phone in case she needed to call for help. No service.

Shit.

Of course there was no service, they were in the middle of nowhere.

She'd realized she'd lost sight of the truck when the road opened up and forked.

Now which way?

To the right, she saw a large warehouse and dust whirling in the air near it. The truck had likely driven around to the other side.

She took the left fork and parked behind some bushes. Then she eased her car door open, not sure how close the trucker might be. She breathed a sigh of relief when the only sounds that met her ears were birds chirping at each other.

She peeked through the trees; the front of the warehouse appeared deserted. Making her way past a few bushes, she came onto a small dirt path. It led around the warehouse parking lot, and after she rounded a corner, the back of the warehouse came into view.

A large garage door was open, and the truck she'd followed was now parked just outside of it. Standing beside it, in addition to the delivery driver, was another man. Using her binoculars, she tried to get a better look at his face.

"No, it can't be," she said to herself.

She looked again. The telltale tattoo peeked out of his tank top, the serpent weaving up his collarbone and wrapping around to his back.

Marcus Beyers.

Marcus had been on her department's radar for quite some time. He was a known criminal, but always managed to escape any investigation. Not this time.

She moved closer without detection then whipped out her phone and took several photos. The odds of them being more than a blur were low, but she had to try.

After ten minutes, a third guy came out, and he and the delivery driver unloaded what appeared to be box after box of liquor into the warehouse.

If only she could get a warrant and find out what was really in those boxes. But not today. She didn't have a shred of evidence that it was anything but liquor. Just a hunch.

Creeping back onto the trail, careful not to make noise, she made it back to her car. Hopefully, the men wouldn't hear her start it, but just to be safe, she did it and then turned around as fast as she could.

After staring into her rearview mirror for twenty minutes, she was convinced no one was following her. She had to report in what she saw. Her boss would be very interested to know Marcus Beyers might be involved. But then a sign for Fisher Springs and Davenport came into view.

Without thinking, she exited.

There was something about Fisher Springs that drew her in. Sam and Kaila would say it was Zach, but no, it was that it was so different from Seattle. She loved the city, but Fisher Springs reminded her of the small town she'd grown up in, north of where she lived now.

The day she was here investigating the Carl Marucam case, she'd had a chance to walk around the town a little bit. She swore she'd come back, but never did. Well, here was her chance.

She drove through town, admiring the small shops and all of the flower baskets hanging on the light posts. It really looked like a postcard. As she approached the diner, she remembered Zach's pub was near. She'd never been inside, and part of her was curious.

Zach wouldn't make anything of this, would he? She hadn't driven out of her way by much. This was sort of on her way home.

Peering through the windshield to find the pub, her eyes caught on a big truck parked outside. And on the logo she knew well. Hawthorne Distribution.

Dread consumed her. *No, not Zach.*

She parked a block off Main Street, then walked until the truck came into view. She snapped a photo then turned to stare into the window of the shop behind her. An antique sewing machine and brightly printed fabric were on display. She pretended to study it while she kept an eye on the reflection of the pub, but her impatience won, and she quickly crossed the street.

The pub door opened as she stepped up onto the curb, so she walked up the sidewalk to the next store. In the window was a cat. She glanced up to the name. *Mandy's Gallery.*

An art store. With a cat.

She stared at the cat as the man who had exited the pub walked to the delivery truck. Another man came around from the back of it.

"What's going on? You were in there talking for a while before I came in," she heard the tall guy ask.

"I overheard the owner fired his manager. I was offering him some business, if you know what I mean," the other guy said.

"Cool. Think you'll get a finder's fee?" the tall guy asked.

"No finder's fee, but it's always good to be useful." The short guy grinned.

The men got into the truck and drove away.

Jessie remained crouched down, playing with the cat, until the sound of the truck faded.

Shit, Zach. Really?

How the hell could she have misjudged him? Well, she hadn't *misjudged* him. The truth was, she didn't really know him. She'd let her hormones lead, and look where it had gotten her... Her one-night stand was right in the middle of her investigation.

Pulling out her phone, she thought about texting Zach and asking him to come outside so she could confront him. But what if he just denied everything? No, if they propositioned him, she had to hope he wouldn't take them up on their offer.

He wouldn't. Would he?

She grabbed her phone and declined his invite for the next morning. As predicted, he texted back. She rolled her eyes when she saw the eggplant emoji. His mind was clearly on last Saturday, and why wouldn't it be? That night had been amazing. But she had to shift the conversation. She needed to figure out how to question him without him realizing that's what she was doing.

In the meantime, she didn't want to act differently until she had a plan.

Jessie: *I'll think about it.*

Chapter Ten

She'll think about it?

At this point, Zach didn't know if she was toying with him or if she really was skittish. The attraction was there, no doubt about it. But why did she seem to run cold then hot then cold again?

If patience is what she needed, he could give it to her. She wanted him, he was sure of it. From the way she'd curled into him all Saturday night as they slept, to the way she checked him out every time they saw each other. But why not admit she wanted to see him?

Maybe asking her for breakfast was too much like a date? Could that be what scared her? Should he have just asked if she wanted to come to his place and fuck?

God, she was driving him crazy. No, he was driving himself crazy.

Unfortunately, he had more time to think now that he was basically living at the bar since firing

Adam. Adam had filled in several bartending shifts throughout the week that Zach now had to take over. He'd also offered to open the pub and give Ariel the day off. She worked hard, and he needed to keep her happy until he could find someone to replace the employee he'd let go, which he couldn't really afford to do.

Firing Adam had been a shit show. The entire time, Adam looked like he was about to cry. He kept apologizing instead of answering Zach's questions but eventually he explained he was in a great deal of debt. It didn't excuse what he did, but Zach sort of felt bad for the guy. Adam said he never meant to hurt Zach, but he feared for his own life if he didn't pay back the debt.

Now Zach felt bad for himself. With no new messages from Jessie, he was starting to wonder if there would be any more. Chase had asked him the day before if he wanted to go to the softball game, but Zach said no. If she wanted to see him, she would respond.

Besides, he was beginning to feel used. He thought they had a great connection, but maybe he had just been a bucket-list fuck for her, just like the others.

Zach sighed in disappointment and brought himself back to the moment. It was going on early evening, and the pub was actually empty. This never would have happened last year. He knew it was because everyone was going to the new bar in Davenport.

"Dammit," he muttered.

He needed to come up with some creative ideas before he lost the place altogether.

The creak of the door alerted him a customer had come in.

He tossed a coaster on the counter. "What can I get you?" he asked before looking up.

When he did glance at the visitor, he had to grab the counter for support. Before him was one of the few people he hoped he'd never see again.

Marcus Beyers walked up to the counter, leaned on it, and stared at Zach for a moment. "Brother. It really is you." Marcus, his brother-in-law, sat down at the bar and stared at him. "I thought you were dead."

It was an accusation. Zach knew that. There was a reason he'd changed his name and moved out of Idaho all those years ago.

"I'm alive," he said, keeping it simple.

Hell, last he knew, Marcus still lived in Idaho. He had no business here. Not any good business anyway.

Marcus smiled. "Brother, you don't look happy to see me."

"I'm not your brother."

The man leaned back on the stool grinning. "You can't even imagine my surprise when my employee ran a background check on Zach Brannigan, and it turned out he was using the same social security number as my brother."

"Again, I'm not your brother. And why the hell would you be runnin' a background check on me?"

Marcus waved his hand. "Brother-in-law, close enough. I had to come in here and find out what this *Zach* knew about my brother. I figured he'd stolen your identity. I never thought I'd see you again. How many years has it been? Oh right. Thirteen."

"Fourteen."

Marcus smirked. "You know, if it weren't for that scar on your face, I might not have realized it was you."

Dammit. There was a reason he'd worn that beard and had his tats: to live a new life and escape the one he'd left.

"Oh wait, yes I would have. That accent always was your tell, wasn't it?"

Fuck.

"I have a proposition for you, brother."

"You haven't answered my question. Why was someone runnin' a check on me?"

Marcus laughed. "That's funny. You still think you have a choice, don't you?"

Zach's stomach churned. Memories of the night he left Idaho came to him faster than he could digest them.

His father hadn't been dead a week before his oldest sister Bethany and her husband Marcus made their demands on him clear.

"Dad is dead, and you're his only son," Bethany had reminded him. *"They all expect you to take over.*

What's the problem, anyway? Who wouldn't want to be in charge? I'd do it in a heartbeat if they'd let me."

"Just do it. If you don't like it, I'll take over," Marcus had said.

"Why don't you just take over now?" Zach had asked.

Bethany had shaken her head. "That won't work. Dad's associates made it clear it has to be his son."

"Give me the night to think it over," he had told them.

They had agreed.

After they fell asleep, Zach threw some clothes in a duffel bag and took off. He'd hoped to never see either of them again.

"I'm not a kid anymore," Zach told Marcus firmly. "I have a choice now. You should leave."

"Actually, you don't. The guy who's been running this place got himself into quite a bit of debt."

"If you mean Adam, he doesn't work here anymore."

Marcus watched him. Zach knew he was trying to assess if he was lying.

"Well, then you can pay off Adam's debt," the other man decided. "If you don't, I'll tell the Bannon brothers you stole their heroin."

The Bannon brothers?

Tony Bannon had been one of Zach's only friends in Idaho. His older brothers had sold drugs, but he didn't have anything to do with it.

"What are you talkin' about?"

"Oh yeah, you wouldn't know because you *left*." Marcus helped himself to the dish of peanuts on the counter as he explained. "Someone stole about a hundred grand worth of heroin from the older Bannon brothers the night we last talked. I went to your room the next morning to tell you about it, but you were gone. Anyway, they blamed this guy who lived down the street, but he denied it till the end."

The end? Yeah, he knew what Marcus meant. The Bannon brothers were known for their brutal punishments.

Zach held back his shudder. Marcus wanted him to react. He'd forgotten how dramatic his brother-in-law could be.

Growing impatient, Marcus offered him an ultimatum. "You don't do me this favor, I'll tell them it was you. Tell them that's why you left town. They'll believe it too—it's more believable than the rumor that went around."

Okay, he'd bite.

"What was the rumor?"

Marcus grinned. "I killed you so I could take over."

"Jesus, that's grim... even for that town."

Marcus shrugged. "They like gossip. You know how it is."

Yes, he did. And that was why he'd gotten the hell out of there at his first opportunity.

"The rumor helped me with business." Marcus grinned. "No one fucked with me after that. So, thank you." He continued grinning like a fool, figuring he had Zach cornered.

His brother-in-law was always pleased with himself. Zach had never understood what his sister saw in him, but then, marrying him likely wasn't so much his sister's choice as what his dad had wanted.

Marcus laughed. "God, you always were stubborn. Not even going to ask what I want you to do? Alright, I'll tell you. Hawthorne Distribution will continue to bring your deliveries. Next time, you'll find money in the bottom of the liquor boxes. Run it through your till and give us new money the next week. Easy peasy."

Shit, money laundering. "What happened to strippin' cars?" Zach asked.

"Not as lucrative."

"I don't get enough business these days to accommodate you."

"No worries. We'll make sure you get some additional customers. Consider it free advertising."

Nothing with Marcus was ever free, and he wasn't someone Zach wanted to owe.

"No."

Marcus finished off the bowl of peanuts. "I'll let you think about it. But I know the universe didn't bring you back to me if not to help me out."

What a pompous, self-centered asshole. That hadn't changed. He had another thing coming if he thought for a minute Zach would help him.

"And before you say no, think long and hard

about what the Bannon brothers would do if they thought you owed them that kind of money." Marcus stood to leave, then looked around. "You know, Bucky's is way better. They have pool tables. You should get some pool tables."

Zach swallowed, not buying Marcus's sudden casual act. *Shit.* "If they think I stole from them, they'll kill me," he ground out.

"Yeah, they probably will. I guess we'd better never let them find out." Marcus grinned again.

The sick fuck.

Zach's jaw clenched. How the hell was he going to get out of this?

"A delivery will be dropped off in a few days, in the morning before you open," Marcus continued nonchalantly. "They'll bring it in the front. They'll show you where the money is and where it goes when you're done. I trust you'll do as your told."

Marcus walked to the door then turned back. "Good seeing you again."

Once his brother-in-law walked out the door, Zach picked up the nearest thing—a pint glass—and threw it at the door. The sound of it shattering echoed through the empty pub.

He had to find a way to get out of this. He didn't leave in the middle of the night, change his name, and live the last fourteen years as a law-abiding citizen to get pulled back into his family's crap.

After cleaning up the broken glass and turning on the closed sign, he called Nick.

"Zach, hey! I was about to come to the pub."

"How about you come to my place instead? I closed the pub fer the night."

"What? Why? Something wrong?"

"Yeah, somethin' is very wrong. I need your help."

"I'll be right over."

Zach stepped outside and was locking the door when Chase called out to him.

"Hey! Wait up."

Zach turned to see his friend jogging toward him.

"Why did you close the pub?" Chase asked. "I was coming in to say hi."

As much as Zach wanted to tell as few people as possible, the fact was, if he involved Nick, he would have to share the information with Chase, the other officer in town. Hell, they might have to tell Chief Dunin, too.

"Some personal business came up. I'm headin' to my place. Can you meet me there? Nick's on his way."

The furrow in Chase's brow signaled he wasn't going to let Zach go until he knew more.

"Look, I'll tell you what's goin' on when we get to my place. I don't want to talk about it here."

Chase nodded. "Understood. See you in five."

Now Zach had to tell his two best friends who he really was. He hoped like hell they wouldn't hate him in the end.

Chapter Eleven

Nick paced back and forth in Zach's kitchen while Zach leaned against the counter and took another pull on his beer, watching the guys process everything he had just told them. Chase sat at the kitchen table, shoveling chips into his mouth.

Zach hoped that was a sign they weren't about to walk out. He enjoyed the nights they came by to shoot the shit over chips and beer. Truth be told, they were his testers for new craft beers he was considering serving at the pub. They didn't mind.

After a minute of silence, he couldn't take it anymore.

"Say somethin'!" he finally pleaded.

Nick stared at him, and then shook his head. "I'm stunned. You had a whole other life, and I never once suspected."

"Nor should you have. I'm not that stupid kid anymore."

Zach had finally told them his whole sordid

past. Not that he'd wanted to. He'd never planned on telling anyone.

But that was before Marcus showed up tonight.

"You kind of glossed over your life of crime. When did it start? How bad was it?" Chase asked.

This was the first time he was telling anyone his history. He had gotten lucky with the friends he made when he was younger; they understood he didn't want to talk about it. Then he made new memories he could share.

Now, having the life he'd built collide with the life he ran from, he was pissed, frustrated, and nervous. These were his best friends, and he was telling them he wasn't who they thought he was.

His dad used to tell him that people would only see him as a thief. No one would ever trust him again.

He stared up at the ceiling, hoping it would provide answers on how to skim over this. There was no way. His friends were cops, they needed to know the truth.

"Look, the statute of limitations would be up on everything except murder. As long as you didn't kill anyone, you can tell us," Nick said.

Zach locked gazes with the detective. He was serious. Zach pushed off the counter. "Do I feckin' look like murderer to you?"

Nick folded his arms across his chest. "Don't get all self-righteous on us now. You just threw a bomb. You can't blame me for asking."

He let out a sigh. "You're right. Sorry. I'm just

worked up."

"We can tell by your accent," Chase said.

That damn accent. Whenever he was excited or nervous, the bit of Irish brogue he'd picked up from his mom came out. He couldn't control it. He didn't used to mind it, until it got him in trouble with his dad.

"Speaking of which, you told us you grew up with your Irish mother in Seattle. But now you are saying you lived in Idaho?" Nick asked.

In preparation for digging in and telling them the details of his past crimes, he grabbed another round of beers from the fridge. After opening them and handing them around, he sat at the table across from Chase and took a long pull to calm his nerves.

Just telling them he was part of the Murphy family, which they unfortunately knew all about, had been enough to stun them; he wasn't sure how they'd take the details. But they hadn't left, and that's what was important. That thought calmed him.

"I lived with my mom until I was fourteen. Then my dad came around and insisted I live with him fer the summer. My mom objected, but I was a teenage asshole and said I wanted to go. I didn't really know my dad, but I figured he wouldn't be as strict as my mom."

"How did that go?" Chase asked.

"Not good. I was only there a week before he asked me to help his friend drive a car from one location to the next. I was so naive. I didn't realize the guy had hotwired it until we pulled into a garage where guys were scrapping cars."

Zach grabbed the bag of chips from Chase and started eating. His dad never loved him, he knew that now. He'd just wanted another worker.

"What happened after that summer?" Nick asked.

"My dad threatened to turn me in if I didn't stay. He said he would tell my mother what I'd done, and she wouldn't want me. He really fecked with my head. I was dumb enough to believe him."

Zach took a pull from his beer before continuing.

"I'd been there fer four years when my dad died. My older sister and her husband told me I had to step up and take over. I had the family name, and I looked like him, so they said I didn't have a choice. But I had just turned eighteen and I knew if I was caught again, I'd be doin' time in a real prison."

Nick sat down. "Caught again?"

Zach nodded. "Spent a few months in juvie."

They drank their beers in silence until Zach broke it.

"So I left."

He explained that after he ran away, he stayed with an old friend in southern Idaho—just long enough to get his name legally changed. Then he drove west, intending to be near his mother. But a flat tire changed his plans.

"Why did you change your name?" Nick asked.

After taking another pull on his beer, Zach sat

in a chair at the kitchen table. "I didn't know if they would come after me. It was one way I thought I could guarantee they'd never find me."

"What about your mom?" Nick asked.

"I call her from time to time and let her know I'm safe. And I talk to my other sister, Gina. I swore them to secrecy about my calls."

Nick fell into a chair across from him. "So you ran and your brother-in-law took over?"

"He was married to my sister, so he was technically family."

"And how did he find you?" Nick asked.

"Unfortunate luck. My manager, Adam, was the one who got mixed up with Marcus and his money-launderin' scheme. Apparently, when they learned Adam was no longer workin' at the pub, they ran a background check on me."

Chase shook his head. "But how did they connect the dots?"

"Same social security number. When I left, they were scrappin' cars. I never thought they would be runnin' background checks on people."

"Zach, you said they are laundering money, and it sounds like this crosses state lines. I'm afraid this is out of the Fisher Springs Police Department's jurisdiction. You need the FBI. Why don't we call Agent Doyle?" Nick suggested. "It would give you a great excuse to spend time with her."

Zach groaned. "No, I don't want the FBI. You mentioned once that some guy you knew in the Army was now working security… I thought you might have a contact there."

Popping a chip in his mouth, Nick nodded. "I can call him. Is that what you want? Personal security?"

"I want more. What Marcus is holdin' over my head is the threat of tellin' our old rivals I've taken something of theirs. I need to make sure they know it wasn't me."

"You need a plan." Chase aimed a chip at him for emphasis.

"I'll call my friend and see if he can help. But you have to know I'm obligated to alert the FBI as well."

Zach closed his eyes. He should have known Nick would play by the rules. That was the kind of guy he was. And once the FBI was involved, he could kiss his chance with Jessie goodbye.

Of all the women he had to choose from, why the hell did he have to want to pursue an FBI agent?

The idea of not talking to her or seeing her again bothered him a lot more than he wanted to admit. But that was something he would have to deal with later. Right now, he needed a plan, like Chase said.

"When is the money supposed to be delivered?" Nick asked.

Zach shrugged. "Marcus said some mornin' in a few days. That could mean tomorrow or next week. The good news is I'm not runnin' low on supplies, but that's largely due to the fact all my customers are over at Bucky's now."

Nick sat down at the kitchen table. "I was wondering why everyone is going to that bar. I thought it was because they are new, I figured the excitement would wear off, but that doesn't seem to be the case."

"I'm pretty sure they are launderin' money for Marcus and getting some kind of perk fer it," Zach said.

Chase smiled. "Really? Well, I think that might be your play, then. Get the FBI to focus on Bucky's, they can take out Marcus and his crew there, then you can ride off into the sunset with your agent."

Zach liked that idea. "Sounds good, except that doesn't keep me safe. One word from Marcus, and I'll have people comin' after me. Also, after Jessie learns all about my history, she's not going to want to be with me."

"Hey," Chase said. "You are talking about something you did as a teenager. We all did stupid shit as teenagers. I've seen the chemistry between you two. Don't get in your head and ruin it."

Nick laughed. "Damn, you freelancing as a couple's therapist on the side? Because that was some deep shit."

Zach laughed too.

"Shut up. Both of you. I know what I'm talking about," Chase said defensively.

Nick and Zach laughed harder.

Chapter Twelve

After a Monday morning briefing to fill Carter in on all she'd learned, Jessie was finally getting a chance to do the one thing she'd been wanting to do since she saw the delivery truck outside Brannigan's Pub the day before.

Once the search engine loaded on her computer, she typed in *Zach Brannigan*. Her stomach lurched at the idea she was invading his privacy, but she had to know. If he was involved, she had to cut all ties.

It felt wrong, but what choice would she have?

"Doyle?" Carter walked into her office unexpectedly.

She minimized the search window as he tossed the folder he was carrying onto her desk.

"This is what we have on Marcus Beyers," he continued. "Study it. We may have to send you in undercover."

"Wait, undercover? But I already went to the

warehouse posing as a customer. They know my face, and have a name attached to it."

The last thing she wanted was to go undercover and risk Zach outing her.

Carter smiled. "If Agent Blaese gets a contract with the distributor, it's a possibility you both will have to go undercover. He's going in as your business partner you forgot to mention. We've given him a bit of a problematic past, so he should be a shoo-in."

"My business partner? Doesn't that sound suspicious?"

Carter sat down in the chair across from her desk. "Not at all. He has an appointment later this afternoon, and he's going to ask them to please not turn him away based on his history. That should pique their curiosity. They will think they are getting a customer with a problematic past they can manipulate. There really is no way they could deny him."

Carter was too confident. He underestimated the fact that guys like Marcus, and probably the guys he worked with, could identify an officer or agent. And Blaese was going in claiming he had a questionable past? The man couldn't look more like an upstanding citizen than if he were Clark Kent himself.

She stared at her boss. "You really think that will work?"

"Worth a try. Let me know if you have any questions on Beyers, or if you find anything that could help." Carter shot her a smile, then stood and left.

Alone again, she reopened the search window.

Then she heard it. Dillon was whistling again, and the sound came closer until he stood in her doorway, smiling.

"Are you settling in all right?" he asked.

"Yes."

Maybe he'd get a clue if she kept it short. With her door open, she didn't dare ask him why he'd lied about her to Carter. Hell, it was probably best to just avoid him and let it go.

"Good. If you need anything, let me know."

He turned to leave, but then turned back. "Hey, are you dating that bearded guy you were talking to at the softball game?"

What the fuck?

None of your damn business, she wanted to scream. "No."

It was true. But again, none of his business.

Dillon's face lit up. "Good. I'll see you around." He walked away, continuing his whistling.

What the hell? *Good?* If he thought she'd consider him again, he had another thing coming.

After an hour of searching all the databases, search engines, and anything else she could think of, she had very little on Zach. He was as clean as they came. Not even a speeding ticket.

That made her smile. He wasn't involved. He couldn't be.

Part of her may have judged him because, when she first met him, he did resemble another man guilty of many things. But he had no record and a great

102

credit score. Zach was a good man.

Between that and what the delivery men had said yesterday, she felt certain Zach wasn't involved in any of this mess. His employee likely had been, though. She'd need to get his information and track him down.

"All right, Mr. Brannigan. Maybe you aren't such a bad guy after all."

Her attention turned to the folder on her desk. Time to dig into someone who wasn't so good.

Marcus Beyers, what sent you on your path into crime?

For the next hour, she read through notes and his arrest record. Marcus had first been arrested at age fourteen, but his crimes were minor until he became connected with the Murphy family.

The Murphy family was based in Idaho, and for many years, their crimes consisted of stealing cars and selling off the parts. They'd also been suspected of dealing marijuana, but it had never been proven... any time the agency tried to get an informant, the candidate had run scared. Everyone who knew that family was scared of them.

"Marcus, why did you become involved with them?"

When she turned the page, she had her answer. Marcus Beyers had married Bethany Murphy, the oldest child in the family. If Marcus was involved in the money-laundering scheme, the Murphys likely were too.

A knock on her door pulled her attention from the file. She glanced up to see Sam.

"Want to go to lunch?" Sam asked.

Sam was someone she could actually discuss all of this with, and she needed a sounding board right now... and a break from the file.

"I'd love to."

They ended up in one of their favorite delis. After ordering and sitting at an outdoor table, Sam grinned at her.

"What?" Jessie asked suspiciously.

"Tell me, did you see Zach again? I want details!"

She closed her eyes.

The last time she'd talked to Sam, Jessie had said she didn't think she should see him again. Her friend had then told her she was crazy to not repeat, as Jessie put it, *'the best sex she'd ever had.'* But before she had made a decision, she'd discovered the distribution truck at his pub. It was only today she'd discovered he had a clean record.

"I haven't seen him. I'm not sure what to do," she admitted.

Sam frowned. "Why not?"

Jessie relayed the sequence of events over the weekend, up to the search she had conducted earlier.

Sam stared at her for a moment. "You ran a background check on him?"

"I had to. What if I found out he was caught up in my case, and I'd been flirting with him? That would jeopardize everything."

Sam leaned back and bit the inside of her cheek. Jessie had learned early on that was her tell when she disagreed with something. "Flirting? Is that what you're calling it?"

Jessie glanced around to make sure no one could hear them. "You know what I meant."

Sam continued to watch her.

"What?" Jessie asked.

"Just because he has a clean record doesn't mean *you've* cleared him. You know that. So let's get to the real reason you ran that check."

Jessie shifted uncomfortably under her friend's gaze.

"You're wrong. The perp in my case only works with those who have a shady background, therefore searching Zach's history was necessary."

Sam took a bite of her sandwich but kept staring.

"Besides, I'm not dating him, so it's not like I looked up the man I'm seeing."

Sam choked on her sandwich. She put it down while she coughed.

"You all right?" Jessie asked.

Sam nodded and drank some of the coffee she'd ordered with the sandwich. "Sweetie, you might not call it *dating,* but you still did a background check on the man you slept with. I know you have a hard time trusting. I get that. But don't lie to yourself. You are interested in this man, but scared to pursue anything beyond sex."

"I'm not scared," Jessie said defensively. "And you were the one that said I should use him for sex. And while he is a bit intense at times, I'm not *scared* because I'm not planning on having a relationship with him."

Across the table, her friend laughed.

"What is so funny?"

"You are completely in denial."

An image of Zach naked flashed in her mind. She tried to shake it away. "No, I'm not."

"Oh girl, you have it bad. He has a clean background, and based on what you said, he's not involved with your case. Maybe you could subtly suggest he find a new distribution company. Then there would be no issue."

That was actually really smart. Instead of grilling him like a suspect, she could just say she'd heard bad things about that company without going into detail. Brilliant.

"That's a great idea. Thank you."

"You're welcome."

Now that the Zach issue was solved, she wanted to talk about anything else. "Enough about me. Let's talk about you. How's it going with that guy you've been seeing?"

Sam smiled. "I was about to call it off, but then he became all attentive. I think I'll keep him around a bit longer."

"Attentive?"

Sam leaned forward and whispered, "Oral. Every time I see him, he goes down, and I don't think I've ever had so many orgasms in a night. The man has skills."

Jessie laughed.

Sam talked openly about sex and thought everyone else should too. Hell, maybe she had a point. At least her friend was getting what she wanted.

Sam had complained about the last couple of guys she'd dated because the first one refused to go down on her, and the second one was the equivalent of a Hoover—he sucked on everything but used no tongue. A visual she really wished her friend had never given her.

"Sounds like you met your Prince Charming, then," Jessie said.

Sam wiggled her eyebrows. "My prince for now."

On the walk back to the office, Jessie checked her phone. Sure enough, she had a text from Zach.

Zach: *Still thinking it over?*

She couldn't help but smile. She'd missed their

texts.

Jessie: *No.*

Zach: *When am I taking you out, then? Let's do lunch? I told you I had to fire an employee, which means I'm needed here more in the evenings.*

The man was persistent, and she found she liked that. She really liked that.

Jessie: *Wednesday.*

Zach: *Sounds great. Pick a place close to you.*

Jessie: *I will do that.*

Zach: *See you then, Macushla.*

Normally, she didn't like being called anything other than Jessie, but when Zach called her his darling, it warmed her all over.

By the time she returned to her office, she was smiling and saying hi to everyone. She normally wasn't the cheery type, so she received a few odd looks. But that was alright, she wanted to enjoy this moment.

She knew he wasn't involved. She had a plan to make sure he wouldn't be involved, and damn, he was a sexy man. She had a right to enjoy that for now.

Taking one more big breath as she resumed her seat at her desk, she reopened the file on Marcus Beyers. The manila envelope was full of surveillance photos, which she poured out on her desk.

Based on the notes, the Murphy family was suspected of moving heavier drugs, and an agent had hoped to get some incriminating photos. Since there had been no news of any big busts in that family, she knew she wouldn't find anything. The ones she looked at now had been taken nearly fifteen years before, and Marcus looked like a kid in them. He had been so young when he got caught up in all this.

One image was of an older man. He wore a scowl and appeared to be yelling at Marcus. She flipped the photo over. Cole Murphy, the father of the Murphy family.

Carter's words came back to her. Undercover. She hoped it wouldn't come to that. Maybe if it was needed, Carter would send in Agent Blaese instead.

There were a few more photographs, and in two she found another kid — about the same age as Marcus, based on his build. Both photos only showed the back of his head, and his shaggy, brown hair. There was no name on the back of the photos, and there was nothing in the file about Marcus having a friend.

Who are you?

Chapter Thirteen

Jessie couldn't wipe the smile off her face. Since she'd finally decided to stop letting her trust issues interfere, she was looking forward to her lunch with Zach.

While it felt like a date… she still had to ensure he wasn't wrapped up in her case before she could really call it one.

Yeah, keep telling yourself that, like that will make it feel less like a date.

She'd texted him the night before with an address to one of her favorite takeout places. It wasn't in Seattle, so she'd need to drive to it. Zach had grumbled, since his hope had been to drive to her and take her out, but once she pointed out this gave them more time together, he had gotten on board.

Sam knocked on her office door. "Want to check out the new Italian place for lunch?"

Standing, Jessie shrugged on her jacket. "I can't, I've got a working lunch."

Technically, it *was* a working lunch. She had to convince Zach to change distribution companies.

Shit. What she was going to ask him was a really big deal. What if he wouldn't do it? She couldn't tell him why he should.

Her friend frowned. "Are you following more trucks? I'm sorry, but that doesn't sound fun at all."

"No trucks today. I'm meeting with Zach to maybe find out his ex-employee's name."

"Oh shit. You're going to interrogate your one-night stand?"

"Shh!" Jessie said, waving Sam into her office.

"I thought you figured out he likely wasn't involved, and could go back to fantastic sex?"

"Actually, I'm taking your advice. I may subtly suggest he find a different company."

"Oh. Well, good luck. I hope it goes well."

Jessie quirked a brow. "This was your idea. Now you sound skeptical."

Sam shrugged. "I mean, how are you going to bring up something that's a business decision for him without giving away any classified information?"

Her friend had a point.

"I'll figure it out." Jessie was almost running late, so she grabbed her keys and headed for the door. "I've got to go. Wish me luck."

"Good luck," Sam called after her.

Yep. She needed a lot of luck today.

When she arrived at the taco truck, the clouds had parted, and the sun was blazing warmer than usual. That could be the only explanation for Zach leaning up against a pole in a very fitted, short-sleeve T-shirt.

His arms were crossed, of course, which seemed to make everything flex. He wore a baseball hat backward, which drew her attention straight to his eyes. Cornflower blue eyes that she could stare into for days. He was still clean-shaven, and she itched to reach out and touch him.

"Hi," she said as she approached.

"Hi," he grinned. "Do you like tattoos now? Or are they still 'eh'?"

She touched his arm and traced his ink up his forearm to his bicep. She wanted to know the story behind each one.

"I was a bit distracted that night, but yes, I do like it."

When her gaze met his, he reached out and pulled her into his arms. She buried her nose in his chest, and *damn* he smelled so good. Melting into him hadn't been a choice, it was just something she did.

He leaned back, staring into her eyes.

"Did I ever tell you that mole of yours is sexy as hell?"

She shook her head.

He leaned down and kissed it sending tingles throughout her body.

"It is." He grinned. "We should order our food.

Where do you want to eat it?"

"There's a park five minutes from here. We can take my car."

After they had their order in hand, she drove them to their destination, and they found an isolated picnic table.

"Tell me about Fisher Springs," Jessie said as she sat down.

Zach sat down across from her. "It's your typical small town as far as everyone being in your business. But that's also what's so great about it. Everyone is friendly for the most part."

"Did you grow up there?" she asked before taking a bite of her taco.

"No. I grew up outside of Seattle."

She waited for him to elaborate but he didn't.

"Where did you grow up?" he asked.

"Buckley. It's a small town south of here."

"I know it. When I get a day off from the pub, if it's not raining, I often go riding out that way."

She unwrapped her first taco. "Riding?"

"Yep. I have a motorcycle. You ever ride?"

Zach finished off his taco while she imagined his muscular frame straddling a motorcycle.

"Jessie?"

"Huh?"

He grinned. "Did you hear my question?"

Shit. What did he ask? Oh yeah.

"I have. One of my brothers has a bike. He let me take it out a time or two."

Zach tilted his head. "Wait, you rode by yourself?"

Leaning back, she quirked a brow. "Yes, not used to a woman riding a motorcycle?"

He threw his head back and laughed. "No, it's not that. It's just that you don't seem so—"

His smile fell.

"So what?" she crossed her arms waiting for his answer.

He scratched his scruff. "The women I've known that have ridden motorcycles were a bit rougher around the edges than you. That's all."

"You don't think I'm rough around the edges?"

He smiled. "No, not at all. I think you put on a bad ass exterior but underneath you're a softie."

She averted her gaze. Not wanting him to delve any deeper, she changed the topic. She needed to learn more about that truck she saw outside his place.

"How's business at the pub?" she asked while watching his reaction.

He groaned. "Not great. As I mentioned in the text, I'm there most evenings now."

"Because you fired someone?" she asked as she finished off her first taco.

"Yep."

She watched as Zach continued eating. She was nervous to ask the next question. While squeezing lime on her second taco, she decided to just go for it.

"Tell me about the manager you fired," she started.

114

Zach took a bit of his taco and she could feel his stare while he chewed. Then he set it down. "Why?" He eyed her skeptically.

Shit. He was suspicious. So much for being subtle.

She shrugged. "I'm just curious." She risked glancing up but regretted it. His arms were crossed, and he was watching her closely.

"Look," he said sternly, "I've made my intentions with you clear. But you've got to give me something. Is this a date for you? Or is this something else?"

An uncomfortable silence stretched out between them.

"Jessie, you've been squeezing lime on that taco for a solid minute. What's going on?"

Fuck. Forget subtlety, she had to be straight with him. Tossing the lime aside, she met his gaze. "I want it to be a date, but I'm not sure if it can be."

He furrowed his brow. "Do I still scare you?"

She shook her head. "No. Well, yes. But that's not the problem." Letting out a sigh, she was more nervous than she should be. His intense stare wasn't helping.

"I'm working on a case, and you might be in the middle of it. That means I can't date you."

What the fuck? Why did she just run her mouth off like that? Now that she'd told him he's in the middle of a case, she couldn't bring up the distribution company. What if he is involved and says something?

They couldn't know they were being investigated.

Using his napkin, he wiped his mouth as he chewed the last bite of his taco. "You think I might be in the middle of an FBI case? Why?"

"I can't say." She took another bite of food to buy time.

"You can't or you won't?" Zach shook his head, stood up, and tossed his wrapper in the nearby garbage. "Jessie, I like you a lot. I can honestly say that night we had was the best sex of my life. I've never felt the chemistry we have with anyone else. But if this isn't something you want, I'm not going to keep pushing. Ball's in your court, Macushla."

He turned and walked away.

Best sex of his life? How could that be?

It had been pretty amazing, but a guy like him had to have had plenty of amazing sex.

"Where are you going?" she yelled.

"Back to the taco truck."

What? He was leaving her there? All because he thought she wouldn't date him?

"The taco truck? That might take an hour," she shouted to him.

"Don't care."

Jumping up, she jogged after him. When she reached him, she grabbed his arm. She couldn't let it end like this. "Hey, it's that I *can't*. I can't say more without revealing too much. But I also can't let you walk away thinking I don't want you. Because I do. The way I feel with you does scare me Zach. I don't have a great track record with men and something tells me you could hurt me more than anyone else. And the sex was unbelievable, but all I can think is was it a fluke? Or is that how we are together? Because I want—"

Her words were cut off when his mouth came crashing down on hers. Her mind told her she shouldn't surrender to him like this, but everything about this man felt right.

His tongue demanded entry, and she gave it.

"Hey! This is a family park!" someone behind them shouted.

Zach pulled away, paying their interrupter no mind, and he and Jessie stared at each other for a moment in a daze. Then she glanced around and realized some kids had just arrived at the park.

"At least now you know," he said.

Confused, she asked, "Know what?"

"The chemistry between us isn't a fluke. And I want to do it again. But maybe not in such a public place." He grinned, and his scar gave way to a dimple.

"You have a dimple." She reached up and touched it.

"Manmade, as I call it." He took her hand in his but kept it on his face.

"What do you mean by 'manmade'?"

The happiness disappeared from his eyes. "That's a story for another time. There's something else we need to discuss now. But first, you might want to save your taco." He nodded over to her half-eaten lunch.

A crow had landed on the picnic table and was eyeing her food.

"Oh no you don't!" she yelled as she ran toward the table. "Shoo!"

The crow flew off. Fortunately, her taco looked fine.

She sat down and motioned for Zach to join her. Before taking a bite, she asked, "What do you want to discuss?"

"Before we get to that, we should get back to what you were askin' me about. Shit."

She grinned. His accent had come out. "Something has you wound up."

"Yeah. Your hot body pressed up against mine a minute ago."

Damn. His forwardness was such a turn-on.

"You probably don't play much poker with a mouth like that, huh?" She was still grinning.

Zach was a large man. Most would find him intimidating, especially when he had his beard; he looked like a mountain man. But the more she got to know him, the more she realized he was a sweet teddy bear.

"I learned about poker the hard way. My older sister insisted I say, 'I'm uppin' the ante,' so she could always tell when I was excited about my hand. She won every time."

"I'm sorry. That sucks. I've got four brothers, so I know how sibling teasing goes."

"Four? Ha, I thought I had a big family. Of course, that's on my dad. Any of your brothers bigger than me?" he asked, grinning.

"First of all, I'm the one you've got to worry about. Don't forget, I took you down once. I'll do it again if I have to."

His gaze darkened. "Can we make that a sex thing?"

She nearly choked on her taco. She eyed him. "You got a fetish for being tackled? Or handcuffed?"

"Maybe both." He winked. "Back to your brothers, tell me about them."

Standing to toss her wrapper in the garbage, she thought about the best way to tell him. "Well, they are all younger. The oldest is a professional hockey player. The two in the middle are in college and also play hockey. The youngest is in high school and, this will shock you, he wants to go pro too."

"A hockey family? Shit, they might all be bigger than me then."

She grinned. He could learn that on his own. *Wait, that would mean I have to introduce him to my family.*

The thought didn't scare her like it had with Dillon.

"Well, now we are a hockey family, but my father pitched in the minor leagues and envisioned his kids would follow."

Zach leaned in close. "So that's why you're so good at softball."

"Yep. But to my dad's dismay, his sons weren't

interested. And being a woman, I can't play baseball professionally. And I really didn't want to pursue softball professionally."

Zach nodded. "So naturally you joined the FBI. I see the connection."

For some reason, that made her laugh. Then he laughed. God, he was sexy when he truly smiled.

"Do you have any other siblings? Besides the older sister?" she asked.

"I do. I have five sisters."

Her mouth fell open. "Wow, I couldn't imagine growing up with so many."

His smile dropped and he looked out to the park. "I lived with only two sisters and my mom and stepdad. My oldest sister lived with my dad. The youngest is in high school, and I don't really know her. She lives with her mom. Then there's Gina. She's the one I'm closest too. She grew up with her mom, but they lived down the road from us. Dad didn't look far. You'd like Gina. She's a bounty hunter," he informed her, turning his gaze back to her.

"A bounty hunter? You're right, I like her already." Jessie reached out and touched his chin as she'd been itching to do. "I'm sorry. That must have been rough, being all split up like that."

He shrugged. "It's what we knew. It was fine."

But the way his jaw ticked, she wondered if that was the truth.

"What did you want to discuss?" she asked, hoping to bring back his smile.

No luck. He stared out at the park again.

"The employee I let go hired a new vendor. I didn't know about it until a couple of days ago. A man came in and told me that Adam, the manager, had worked out a deal with him. Basically, he said Adam owed him a lot of money, and now that debt falls to me."

"Fuck. I'm sorry, Zach. What do they want you to do?"

"Take a delivery. He said it will arrive some morning in a few days. I have no idea."

She knew he was talking about Hawthorne, but she couldn't insert herself without more information.

"Did you tell anyone about it?" she asked instead.

Zach nodded. "I told Nick and Chase. Nick knows a security guy."

Jessie bit her lip. Zach had no idea what he was involved in, if he thought some security guard could help him. "Do you mean Nick and Chase from the Fisher Springs Police Department?"

"That's them. Nick was going to call you a couple of days ago. The only reason he didn't is because I promised him I'd tell you today."

Well, at least she had a lead and possibly an ally. She'd worked with them on another case earlier in the year. It looked like she would be working with them again.

"Please listen to Nick and Chase on this, all right?"

He leaned forward and kissed her lightly. "I will."

"I need to get back," Jessie said.

They cleaned up the rest of their lunch, and he followed her to her car. Her mind was spinning as they drove back to the taco truck.

Before he got out, he leaned over and kissed her again. "Maybe next time, we'll have more than an hour together."

She frowned then tried to cover with a nod.

"What's wrong?" he asked.

"I'm worried for you. I've been worried since I saw that delivery truck outside your bar."

The moment his smile fell away, she realized what she'd said.

Shit.

"You were in Fisher Springs? When?" His eyes had turned cold. "Jessie?"

She had to be honest with him. That was the only chance they had.

"Last weekend. I was driving back from... I can't say, but I was on my way back, and I was going to say hi, but then I saw the truck parked in front of your pub."

"Are you investigating Hawthorne Distribution?"

He was direct.

She wanted to tell him.

"I am. I didn't realize you used them, Zach."

"And you didn't come in to say hi. So... what?

You saw the truck and assumed I was doing what exactly?" His fists were clenched.

Jessie knew this looked bad, but at the moment, she needed to focus on keeping him safe.

"Can you hire a new delivery company?" she asked. "Maybe we can get them to be less interested in you."

She knew it was a long shot but damn, she had to try.

He shook his head. "You don't think I haven't looked into that? I can't afford to sign a new contract, and I'm sure as shit not getting any more loans. Besides, they won't back off me. It's personal." He flinched.

"What do you mean it's personal?"

He stared out the window. "I told you. Adam owed them money. It's my debt now."

"But if the vendor's threatening you, the FBI is already involved. We need someone working from the inside. I'll tell my boss, we can get you a wire, and we can take these guys down."

"No," Zach said.

She couldn't have heard him right.

"What?"

He turned his stare to the taco truck. "I can't work for or with the FBI."

She reached for his hand. "Zach, listen to me. I'm working to bring this company down. You have to be on my side when that happens."

His eyes moved to their hands right before he

pulled his away. "I'm sorry but I can't. You don't know these guys... they can sense FBI agents a mile away. "

She leaned back. "How would you know that?"

He pinned her with his gaze. His eyes were sad. He almost looked defeated. "I had a few relatives who were into some shady stuff. I learned more as a teenager than I would have liked." He rubbed the spot where his beard once was.

She'd seen him do that a few times and was pretty sure it meant he was uncomfortable.

"What aren't you telling me?" she asked.

"Nothin'."

His tell.

"I'll talk to my boss. Instead of sending an FBI agent in, I can tell him a pub owner is willing to help. He'll likely want you to wear a wire," Jessie said.

Zach shook his head. "Me wear a wire? Did you already know I was being squeezed? Did Nick tell you?"

"What? No, I didn't know."

"No? You start by asking me about Adam, you were watching my pub and already knew about the distribution company, and now you want me to wear a wire? It looks like you had your own agenda all along. I need to go."

Zach pushed out of the car and was in his truck before Jessie could follow.

Chapter Fourteen

Zach slammed the pub door open, still pissed at himself. What the hell had he been thinking? With his history, there was no way he could date an FBI agent. Once she knew who his family was, she'd be salivating to use him to make a bust. It seemed like that point was going to come sooner than he thought.

"Hey, boss," Ariel said from behind the counter, where she was restocking clean glasses.

He'd made it back to the bar in time for opening, but he knew Ariel had it under control. Openings were easy; it was the closings that could be tricky, when some customers became unruly and didn't want to leave.

"Any deliveries arrive today?" he asked.

He had been certain they wouldn't come this soon, but the realization hit him that if they had, Ariel would have had to face them alone.

"No, boss. Not today."

Ariel was only twenty-two, but before his

brother-in-law had shown up, Zach had often thought she would make a great manager if only she was open to full-time work. But she was going back to school in September for her last year of college, then she'd probably move out of Fisher Springs. Most of the kids did. But they usually came back to settle down.

That was why he loved this small town—it had a great sense of community. Something he hadn't had growing up.

But now that he knew Marcus was sniffing around, he didn't want to leave Ariel alone.

Checking his phone, he found no message from Nick. The detective had said he'd be in touch today, once he knew if someone from his friend's security team could help him out.

"Something wrong?" Ariel asked. "You threw open the door and now you're stomping around."

Shit, he was. He never lost his cool. Always professional in the pub. Well, except when he'd flirt with some of the patrons. But he never took them home like they wanted, that would be bad for business. Although, hell, with the lack of customers now, maybe those were missed opportunities.

Letting out a sigh, he couldn't really believe that. Those women had wanted what they thought he was, not who he really was. And while he shouldn't care, he did.

"Zach? You okay for real?" Ariel was standing in front of him on the other side of the bar.

Alright, he needed to be alone now.

"I'm fine," he ground out. "I've got some paperwork to do. I'll be in the office."

"Okay. But if you ever want to talk, I'm here."

Zach shot her a smile. "Thanks for the offer. You're a great bartender, you know that?"

She smiled. "I've been told."

He snorted and shook his head as he left, this time making sure not to stomp.

Once inside his office, he leaned against the closed door, cursing to himself. Then his mind drifted back to his conversation with Jessie.

She wanted him to wear a wire and help the FBI. She'd already known about the distribution truck. Hell, she probably even knew what they wanted from him.

Wait a minute.

He pulled up his calendar on his computer. Adam had gotten involved with the new distribution company three months before—or at least, that was when he'd involved the pub. Jessie had been working in Fisher Springs on another case until shortly after they met. She had turned him down flat after she tackled him, and again at her softball game. But then not long after, *she'd* contacted *him.* At the time, he thought it was odd, but then she admitting to having fantasized about him. And hell, he'd been fantasizing about her so there was no reason to suspect she was lying.

Shit, was her sudden interest in him because of this case? Maybe she'd seen the truck at his pub before and decided to get close to him. And on what he'd hoped was their first official date, she asked him to wear a wire.

Shit. She wasn't interested in him so much as using him. Calling him over for a one-night stand had been a risky move, but it worked. It got him hooked.

Goddammit! He picked up a stapler from his desk and threw it at the wall.

He'd let his desire for her cloud his judgment. Although, he never would have predicted he'd be in the middle of this shitstorm.

"Fuck!" He ran his hands through his hair and then down to his beard — no, his face.

Fuck. He'd shaved for her.

God, I'm an idiot.

The buzzing of his phone pulled him out of his pity party. There was a text from Nick. Finally.

Nick: *Cody will be there tomorrow morning at 8am. Good luck.*

Luck. Yeah, he needed more than that. Hopefully, Cody was good enough to handle both Marcus and the FBI, because something told him Jessie didn't take no for an answer.

Later that evening, Nick walked into the pub and plopped down on a barstool.

"Hey, I wasn't expecting to see you tonight,"

Zach said. "Everything alright with Lauren?"

He'd never seen two people more made for each other than Nick and his fiancée. They loved to poke each other with barbs, but everyone knew it was their form of foreplay.

"Everything is fine," Nick assured him. "I didn't plan on stopping by, but as I was driving past on my way home, I noticed a car out front."

"There are a lot of cars out front. People park on the street all the time."

Nick glanced around. "No, you don't understand. The car has someone in it, watching this place."

The hair on Zach's arms stood up. Had Marcus sent someone to watch him? Had they followed him to see Jessie earlier?

"I'm pretty sure it's the FBI," his friend continued. "The guy sitting in the driver's seat looks like one of the agents that worked with us on the Rodney case."

Zach let out a sigh. On one hand, he was relieved it wasn't his brother-in-law, but on the other, it meant Jessie had gone forward with her plans of getting agents involved. And as he'd told her, those guys could smell the FBI a mile away. Hell, Nick had picked them out while driving by in the dark.

The more he thought about it, the more it confirmed his earlier thoughts.

"Thanks for letting me know."

"Did you tell Jessie what's going on?"

Zach pulled out two shot glasses and poured them. He pushed one to Nick. Then he downed his own.

Nick lifted his eyebrows. "Shit, that bad? I don't think I've ever seen you drink while working."

"It turns out Jessie already knew what was going on. She asked me to wear a wire."

"What do you mean she knew?"

"After I was honest and told her someone came to me demanding I pay the money Adam owed, she let it slip that she had been concerned since she saw the delivery truck outside my place." Zach poured another shot and drank it.

"So? Why wouldn't she be concerned?" Nick stared at his shot but didn't take it.

"I never told her about the delivery company. And she never told me she was watching my place." Zach raised a brow.

"Oh. Shit." Nick drank his shot, then Zach watched as the realization hit. "Oh *shit*. Do you think she used you for her case?"

He shrugged. "I can't say for sure, but she did turn me down twice before enthusiastically asking me to come over for the night."

"That's fucked up. I'm sorry, man."

It was fucked up. And it was really fucked up how much he still cared about her.

But how could he? It was clear he didn't really know her.

It must just be the idea of her. Shit, that would make

him no better than the women that hit on him, or the idea of him.

"Are you going to wear a wire?" Nick asked.

"No."

"Why not? If they hear your brother-in-law's threats, they can take him in."

"Marcus would know what was happening. Hell, if that car is out front when the guys bring the delivery, I don't know if they will frisk me or kill me."

"Neither. Your brother-in-law said Adam owed him money, right?"

"Yeah."

"Well, my bet is you're safe until they get it."

Zach poured them each another shot, then drank his down. "Newsflash. They aren't going to get it. I have no idea how much he owes them or what he did with it, but I can guarantee you it's not fucking here. I've looked everywhere."

Nick nodded.

"There's more. Jessie's wire request was *after* questioning me about Adam. Oh, and did I mention I thought we were on a date?" Zach grumbled.

"Shit. How did she know to ask about Adam?"

Zach poured another shot. "She wouldn't give me the time of day, you know. After she tackled me and at the softball game, she blew me off. Then out of the blue, she wanted to get together. I'm such a dumbass for falling for it."

"I thought you said you two had crazy chemistry."

"I thought we did, but apparently I'm just a means to an end. It's all about the case for her."

Chapter Fifteen

Jessie couldn't sleep after what happened with Zach. She'd called him the night before but got his voicemail. He hadn't returned her call.

She needed him to know she was not using him for this case. Yes, she'd asked about the case at lunch, but that's not why she was there. She'd been so excited to see him again. How could he not see that?

Equally infuriating was the fact that he was clearly in danger but refused to wear a wire. Why the hell would he think the FBI would be so obvious and stupid as to risk his life?

Lucky for her, they didn't *need* a wire. While the listening devices the agency had weren't as good as having something inside, they would have to do.

At least she'd called Nick and found out that the security guy Zach mentioned to her had been a Navy SEAL. She felt a little better after hearing that. But even if the guy could protect Zach, he wasn't in the business of collecting evidence, and *that* was what would be needed to take down Marcus Beyers and the Bannons.

God, if Zach only knew the kind of people running this, he might cooperate.

She tried to tamp down her anger as she walked from the elevator to her office.

"Jessie, that file you wanted came in. I put it on your desk," said Trina, their assistant.

"Thank you."

The file on Cole Murphy had finally come in. It had been in Idaho, but Carter made sure it was rushed over as soon as Jessie asked for it. Hopefully, it would provide some answers as to how Marcus Beyers had gone from small time car thief to possibly working for the Bannons and laundering money.

Once in her office, she closed the door.

In the front of the file, a printout of all of his charges, both state and federal were listed. Cole Murphy was your typical criminal, except he had never done time. From what she read, he had people working for him and *they* were the ones who got caught and did time. The notes depicted a career criminal who used his children and other relatives in his schemes.

Why did everyone fall in line for you?

An hour later, she had her answer. A police report for domestic violence filed against Cole Murphy by Celeste Murphy.

Wait, there aren't any domestic violence charges in his criminal history.

Digging further into the file, she discovered why. The charges had later been dropped.

Asshole probably threatened her or her kids.

Someone had drawn a family tree into the notes. Cole Murphy had six children by five women. As she stared at the names, she saw that Cole only had one son. The rest were daughters. Based on the family tree, that son would be thirty-two today.

Why isn't the son running the family now instead of Marcus Beyers?

By the time she finished reading the file, all she'd learned about Cole's sole male heir was that he had lived with his mom until he was fourteen. Then he was sent to live with his dad and stayed until he was eighteen. An agent had written about him.

"Informant Tiffany stated Jazz Murphy disappeared shortly after turning eighteen. A large group looked for him, but it was like he just vanished. Informant believed Jazz was killed for a crime gone wrong, but there is no evidence to support this theory."

Jessie sat back in her chair. *Would Cole have had his only son murdered?*

She made a note it was a possibility. Maybe her boss would know more.

She made her way to his office, where the door was open.

"Carter? Do you have a minute?"

He glanced up from his computer. "Sure, come in."

Jessie walked to his desk. "I read Cole Murphy's file, and I have some questions."

135

He laughed. "Don't we all. Sit. Let's chat."

She sat on the edge of the chair. "Cole Murphy had one son. What happened to him?"

"We don't know officially, but there were rumors that his son crossed him and Cole had him killed. No evidence was ever found. Honestly, we didn't really look because the son wasn't our concern. It was Cole we wanted to take down."

"Then it's possible he's still alive?"

Carter frowned. "Well, technically it's possible, but I'd say it's unlikely. The kid was eighteen when he disappeared, and according to one of his sisters, he didn't have any money nor a vehicle."

But if he was smart, he would have had a plan, she knew. "Which sister?"

"I don't remember her name, but she was the oldest. She's the one that married Marcus Beyers."

Jessie smiled. "For a moment there, I thought you had this file memorized."

Carter laughed. "I'm pretty familiar with it. We had a case several years ago where we thought the Bannons were bringing their meth into Seattle, so I reviewed all the files relating to them and the Murphys."

"How are those two families connected?"

"I don't know how it started, but they are from the same area of Idaho. I think the kids all grew up in the same town."

Two crime families in the same small town. Maybe they were more intertwined than she realized.

"Thank you. I need to get back to reviewing that file." She stood to go.

"Jessie, wait a moment. I wanted to talk to you about the Hawthorne case."

She lowered herself back into the chair.

"Have you been able to gather any more information?"

Her mind raced. The distribution company. She now knew that Zach was in the middle of everything, but he wouldn't help her out. Why wouldn't he help her? Zach would have to understand. This was her job and she couldn't take risks. Besides, what if he was more involved than he let on? And then it came out she knew him?

That would explain why he wouldn't even entertain the idea of the FBI helping him. He didn't want her colleagues there.

"I discovered a pub that was part of the money laundering scheme."

"Which one?"

"Brannigan's Pub in Fisher Springs."

"Fisher Springs? Wasn't that the town you were just in on the Carl Marucam case?"

She nodded.

"How do you know this pub is accepting the money?" Carter asked.

"It is. I overheard the driver talking to another worker, and they plan to use the pub for their distribution."

There, that was close enough to the truth.

"I'm glad you mentioned it. Agent Blaese heard the same thing from the informant. I've assigned him to surveillance detail for the time being."

The informant knew? They likely know all of the customers that are laundering money. Why the hell aren't they giving us that information?

"Did the informant name other places as well?" she snapped.

Carter cocked his head.

"Sorry, it just seems the informant is spoon feeding us information when we need to know all the facts."

Carter shook his head. "No, Blaese said he asked for more customers and the informant said that pub was the only one they knew about. Since you discovered it too, it must be true."

She pursed her lips.

Only knows of one pub. Uh-huh.

"You mentioned surveillance?"

"Do you have a better idea? We can't send someone in because, as your research indicated, they do these deliveries before the bars open. Although..." Carter trailed off, and she could see the wheels turning in his head.

"Blaese is already watching the place?"

"Yes, started yesterday."

Shit. If Zach saw, he'd think she turned him in, although she kind of just did.

Why the hell did she have to have feelings for a guy who could be a suspect? This is why she knew better than to date. Her job came first, and the last thing she needed were complications.

"You knowing people there might actually be a good thing," Carter decided. "I need you to spend some time in the bar and figure out who knows what's going on and who doesn't. Also figure out which employees would be willing to help us out. Run background checks, find out what you can about any of them. We can use that as leverage."

Leverage. Carter was a hard-ass and not always the nicest guy. If he had any idea of the leverage she had on Zach, he'd figure out a way to use it. But even though she was worried Zach was in on this after all, something told her not to mention him yet.

But how the hell was she going to explain hanging out in his pub?

"You want me to be in the bar during the day or until closing?" she asked.

Carter nodded. "Mix it up but that will make for late nights, you'll need to stay in that town. I assume they have a hotel. Start tonight."

Tonight? No, she needed time to figure out what she was going to say to Zach. But she couldn't exactly ask for that. Although, she did have plans tomorrow...

"All right but I can't go in tomorrow night. I promised my dad I'd be at family dinner. I haven't been in weeks."

Well, it was true there was a family dinner, but she wasn't sure if she really wanted to go. She should.

Her family kept her grounded, and right now, she needed something to get her mind off Zach.

"All right. Go tonight and maybe tomorrow afternoon, then take tomorrow night off."

"Okay." She stood and was at the door when Carter called her back.

"Hey, does your dad still make that lasagna for your dinners?"

"He does."

"Seriously, I haven't stopped thinking about it since that time you brought in a whole pan to the office. It was so good."

That made her smile. She had done that. After missing several family dinners, her dad had made a lasagna just for her, to entice her to start coming to them again. As much as she'd loved the meal, she knew if she kept it at home, she'd eat it all in a couple of days. Instead, she'd brought it in to share.

"Ask your dad if I can have his recipe," Carter suggested.

She chuckled. "Sure. I'd better get going so I can pack. How many days do you think I'll need to be in Fisher Springs?"

He shrugged. "Pack for a week. We'll know more in a few days."

Chapter Sixteen

Zach slammed his phone down on the counter. After checking it for the hundredth time, there was still no response from Jessie to his texts about the agent outside his pub.

When he'd woken up that morning, he was angrier than he had been the night before. He'd sent her several texts, basically asking why the fuck the FBI had been watching his pub after he had made it clear that would be bad for him. It was true he hadn't responded to the texts she'd sent after their lunch, but dammit, he had every right to be mad.

Her lack of response was more proof that she'd only seen him as another step on her way up the food chain at the FBI. Fuck, how could he have been so wrong about her? After the night they'd shared, he thought she could actually be the one. But no, she'd been using him all along. And his misjudgment might get him killed.

He'd also spent another morning on pins and

needles, wondering if Marcus was going to show — or send one of his minions. But again, no one came.

He knew what Marcus was doing. If they waited until Zach was out of inventory, he'd have no choice but to work with them. Maybe if it was business as usual, that would be true. But thanks to the damn bar in Davenport, he still had enough stock to get him through for a bit. That was the only thing that damn bar was good for — buying him time.

At least he felt a little safer. The security guy, Cody, had shown up. He wasn't sure what he expected but the guy was much more capable than he'd imagined. After Zach explained what was going on, the guy went into full defense mode and was now sitting at a table where he could watch all exits. Well, maybe not the back exit, but he could see down the hallway if anyone came from there. He'd also advised Zach what to say when the delivery was made, especially if they commented on the agent parked out front.

Yep, the observer was back and still reeked of FBI.

Zach's gut told him that the delivery would happen the next day. People seemed to like to deliver bad news on Fridays.

Damn, he was so hyped up about this meeting, he wished he could go home and relax tonight. But that wasn't an option. He had to close. Fortunately, he only had a few more hours.

Maybe Cody's presence had Zach letting his

guard down, but he didn't even realize someone new had entered the bar.

"Can I get a beer? Whatever you have on tap."

The voice behind him was familiar, and he was suddenly both angry and curious.

He turned. Jessie sat on a stool, staring at him without a smile.

"You have got to be kidding me," he scoffed. "I told you that those guys would smell you a mile away, and you'd be putting me in danger, but you couldn't resist, could you? Parking an obvious-as-fuck agent outside for two days. For what? You think that is going to help you close this case and get some sort of promotion? Well, think again, sweetheart."

She flinched at his endearment, and he immediately regretted using it. But only because any endearment was only meant for the Jessie he thought she was—the warm, tough as nails woman who'd let down her walls just a little for him to see. It was not meant for this cold, work-comes-first person sitting before him.

"I had nothing to do with the car out front," she said.

He poured her beer and set it on the bar. "No?"

She closed her eyes. "Well, not directly."

He leaned back against the counter, crossing his arms, waiting for her to say more.

"My boss was told about this place from someone else," she explained.

He choked out a laugh while shaking his head.

"You expect me to believe that? It looks like you served me up on a platter. I told you what would happen if they sense the FBI is involved."

She stood up and leaned over the counter, lowering her voice. "I did not serve you up. Someone else did."

He rubbed his beard—no, his damn scruff.

Fuck that. The first thing he was doing was growing his damn beard back.

"Someone else?" he asked.

Who else knew? He thought about that. Only Nick and Chase. But they wouldn't, would they? He needed to talk to them, but first he had to deal with the woman in front of him who had done nothing but break his heart.

His heart? Why the fuck was he thinking that? He hadn't known her that long. But what he had known, he'd really liked.

"Why are you here? To apologize for possibly signing my death sentence?"

"No! I mean yes, I'm sorry, but they won't harm you, I'll make sure of it."

"Oh yeah? How are you going to do that?"

Before she had a chance to answer, someone sat in the stool next to her.

"Anyone ever tell you that you have gorgeous eyes?" the dickweed said to her.

Zach's gaze moved to the dickweed only to discover it was Marcus. He ground his teeth together to keep from saying anything.

"I see you are still smooth with the ladies. If looks could kill, you'd be a dead man, brother." Marcus grinned at him.

Fuck.

He wanted to wipe that grin off his face. Hopefully, Jessie didn't pick up on the literal meaning of that 'brother' comment.

"What do you want?" Zach barked out.

"Nice to see you, too."

Zach watched Cody move closer and take a stool at the bar down from Jessie.

"I want to finish our discussion from the other day," Marcus continued. "I have something for you." Marcus tossed a manila envelope onto the bar.

"Where's my delivery?" Zach asked.

He noticed Jessie sit up straighter. Yeah, he might as well make sure they all knew what this is about.

Marcus shook his head. "I'm not dumb. I know there is an FBI agent out there monitoring everything that comes in and out of here. I also know he's likely looking for a delivery truck. That's why you're going to take this." He motioned to the counter. "It's not much but it's a start for now. I recommend you go swap it with what's in your safe."

A start?

What was he expecting? The packet on the counter looked thick. He didn't have enough stashed in the back even if he had agreed to what Marcus was offering.

"Sorry, can't leave the bar," he said, hoping Marcus would drop it.

"That's no problem. I'll cover for you, I'm sure it won't be too hard." Marcus grinned, enjoying the dig.

"No." Zach stood his ground and hoped like hell Marcus would back off.

As a kid, Marcus had a short fuse and wouldn't hesitate to throw a punch. But after all these years? Zach had no idea what the man was capable of.

The door opened, drawing all their attention. A man in a suit walked in, looking very much like an FBI agent.

He must have sensed the tension his presence causes because he walked straight to the back toward the bathroom.

Marcus grabbed the envelope and stuffed it back in his jacket eyeing Zach the entire time.

"Can I get a beer please?" Suit man must have changed his mind about the restroom because he suddenly appeared at the bar.

Jessie noticeably stiffened as the man chose a stool on the other side of her. When she turned to him, the man gave her a nod. A nod that Zach noticed and based on the scowl now spread on his brother-in-law's face, Marcus noticed too.

Up to this point, Marcus hadn't realized Jessie was FBI. Probably because she actually dressed like she was going to the pub instead of donning a suit. But now Zach could practically hear Marcus putting the pieces together.

"Wait a minute," his brother-in-law said, looking back and forth from Jessie to Agent Dumbfuck. "You're FBI."

And because Agent Dumbfuck had to screw this up as much as possible, instead of claiming to be Jessie's boyfriend or some such bullshit, he pulled out his badge and introduced himself.

A wide smile grew on Marcus's face as he turned to Jessie. "I didn't realize they had agents as beautiful as you. Makes me think maybe I picked the wrong line of work."

Then he turned his gaze to Zach. "An agent watching the front wasn't enough? Now you got two inside? Do you really think this was your best choice?"

"It wasn't my choice," Zach bit out.

Agent Dumbfuck kept staring at Zach. "You look really familiar."

His brother-in-law's grin grew even bigger. "Oh, this is about to get real fun."

"Do I know you from somewhere?" the agent asked as he continued to stare.

How the hell could the agent have put together who he was? It had been fourteen years since he'd left town. His dad certainly didn't have any photos of him—he wasn't the sentimental type. Unless Jessie took a photo he was unaware of, and had put it in the file.

Before the agent could think too hard, Zach extended his hand. "Zach Brannigan. This is my pub."

The man shook his head. "You must look like someone else I know. Huh."

Agent Dumbfuck then had the good sense to walk to the bathrooms.

Marcus waved his hand toward the end of the bar summoning Zach to follow. Since this was already a clusterfuck, he walked the few steps and met Marcus. His brother-in-law leaned across the counter, whispering so Jessie couldn't hear. "I'll be back for that money tomorrow."

"I still won't have it."

Marcus shook his head. "Listen to me. You will give me my money and you will get rid of these two agents. If I so much as *suspect* the FBI is involved, I'll take my anger out on your girlfriend here."

Zach followed Marcus' eyes to Jessie.

Marcus wasn't the smartest man, but he knew how to motivate people.

His brother-in-law didn't wait for an answer. He figured Zach would fall in line, just like he had as a teenager.

"Get your hands off me." Jessie suddenly had a man bent over the counter, his face smashed in someone's spilled beer as she secured his hands behind his back.

"I'm sorry. I didn't realize you were so sensitive," the man said.

"Sensitive?" she hissed. "You think I'm sensitive because I don't want you to touch me?"

Zach looked on, incredulous. *What the hell did I*

miss?

He was about to jump the bar when he caught Cody's eye, and the man shook his head. Zach's gaze fell back to Jessie. Cody was right. She could handle it. Shit, she could likely handle anything. But could she take Marcus? He couldn't put her in that danger.

When Jessie released the man, he pulled his jacket down and tried to straighten it out.

"She's a livewire. I'm going to enjoy this." Marcus smiled and then walked to the door.

Zach turned back to Jessie, eyeing her as she calmed herself down. She was using him for a case, so why had he been ready to jump the bar in her defense? And why was it that, as soon as Marcus threatened her, all he could see was white, seething anger?

Shit. Because like it or not, he had feelings for her.

Well, he needed to put those out of his head so he could get through this and keep her safe from his crazy family. Then they'd go their separate ways. She'd have solved this case, like she seemed to want, and he would hopefully rest better, with Marcus behind bars.

"How do you know Marcus Beyers?" she asked.

"I don't. I told you, he threatened me because of Adam." He hated lying, but he couldn't tell her the truth.

"He's kind of a dick," Jessie said.

"So's your coworker." Zach glanced up and locked eyes with Agent Dumbfuck, who was now talking to Cody by the first booth.

"Yes, he is."

"Jessie, you should know Marcus threatened you," Zach said.

Cody stepped up. "Threatened her how?"

Zach told them word for word what Marcus had said and what he knew it really meant. "I don't have any money for him, even if I wanted to try to pay him off."

"Can you give me the name and last known address of your ex-manager?" Cody asked. "I need to chat with him."

Zach wasn't sure what he meant by *chat*, but if the ex-military, six foot four man who looked like he could kill someone with his pinkie showed up at Adam's door, maybe he could get some answers.

"Sure. I need to go to the back and grab it. I'll be right back."

He got out from behind the bar and walked down the hall to his office. When he returned, Cody and Jessie stood very close together, talking.

"Here's the information." Zach handed Cody the paper he'd written it down on.

"Thank you. Agent Doyle has agreed to stay in her motel room until tomorrow night."

"Motel? You're staying in Fisher Springs?" Zach asked.

She nodded. "For a little while."

"And text me before you leave tomorrow," Cody told her. Then to Zach, "I'll be back before you close."

The security guy wanted Jessie to check in with him? Zach's gaze moved between the two as Cody headed for the exit.

Had he just witnessed some sort of match? While he may not be able to trust Jessie after all this, the idea of her moving on so easily made him angry. But Cody didn't know their history. As much as he wanted to, he couldn't take this out on him.

Cody was almost to the door, but walked back over to Zach and Jessie. "Zach, Jessie and I talked. I know you don't want to wear a wire, but we can place a couple of listening devices around the bar. That way, if they frisk you, they won't find anything. But you should try to get Marcus to threaten her again."

He didn't reply.

"Zach, he threatened her. You've got to do this for her."

Damn, Cody was right.

He scratched the back of his neck. "All right." He let out a sigh. "I'll do it."

The other man nodded and left.

Jessie stood. "I should go too."

"Dating Cody now?" he spit out.

Shit, he just couldn't hold it back.

Her eyebrows shot up and she laughed. "No. I have no interest in him. Unfortunately, I'm drawn to stubborn, cocky men with tattoos." She reached out and put her hand on his. "Zach, I know you're a good man. And I know you don't believe this, but I never used you for this case. I would never do that."

"And why should I believe that?"

She pulled her hand away as if burned. "Alright, when I first discovered the distribution truck out front, I wondered. But after talking to you about your ex-manager and getting to know you, I knew you couldn't be involved."

While she was saying the right thing, he couldn't get past the feeling he'd been betrayed.

"Yeah, too bad you didn't realize that in the first place." He walked away but was fully aware of her watching him.

"Zach, we should talk. I'm sorry I didn't trust you before."

He turned. "There's no need to talk. I'm sure you'll wrap this case up soon and move on to the next."

The hurt in her eyes gutted him.

He hadn't meant to sound so cold, but he couldn't help it. He was really falling for her, and the idea that she'd thought the worst of him was too much.

Without another word, she left the pub.

Chapter Seventeen

By mid-morning, Zach had nearly worn a hole in the floor from pacing. Between worry over Marcus and the regret he felt watching Jessie leave the pub the night before, he was a mess.

"I think you have your ten thousand steps in for the day," Cody said. He was leaning back in one of the booths, looking about as relaxed as a cat in the sun.

"Why don't you look nervous?"

Cody raised a brow. "I've been in worse situations."

Shit, of course he has. "Sorry, I don't know how I could have forgotten you were a SEAL. Nick mentioned it. I didn't mean any disrespect."

"Look, you're all worked up. Sit down and take a few deep breaths to calm down. Okay?"

Zach nodded and sat across from Cody. "Are you sure Blaese is nowhere in sight? I don't want him fucking this up."

"I'm sure. Now breathe."

After a few breaths, he did feel calmer.

"Thank you for arranging it so I wouldn't have to wear a wire," he said. "You're sure your guy can hear everything?"

Cody laughed. "Yes, and he said to tell you to calm the fuck down."

"Easy for him to say, he's sitting safe in a truck."

"Van. But that doesn't matter. Let's focus. You know Marcus wants the money. He probably owes someone higher up, so he's not going to hurt you if that hurts his chances of getting the money. He'd prefer to hurt the person who's actually holding the money."

"You mean Adam? What's the plan, tell Marcus where he lives?"

Cody shook his head, then nodded to the door.

At that moment, Adam walked into the bar.

Zach's mouth fell open. "You convinced him to be here when—"

"No," Cody cut him off. "Adam is here to collect some backpay he believes you owe him."

"What the f—"

"I told him to meet you here at this time. Now, I recommend you offer him a beer… anything to stall and keep him here."

This guy was good. Instead of going to his home and demanding answers, he'd put him right in the line of fire instead of Zach.

"How the hell did you convince him of that?"

he demanded on a whisper. "I fired him for taking too much."

"Greed knows no bounds," Cody responded quietly.

"Hey, boss. Er, I mean Zach." Adam stared at the ground, avoiding eye contact.

"Adam," Zach replied.

"Your new manager came by last night and mentioned he found there was some backpay I was owed," he mumbled.

Damn, this guy had guts coming in here. Had he really thought Zach wouldn't find out about the distribution company? Although, the fact the guy stole from some sort of money-laundering cartel and stayed in town probably told him all he needed to know.

He wondered if Adam had any idea who Marcus was working for.

"Can I get it in cash?" his ex-employee asked.

Nevermind, he highly doubted this guy knew much of anything.

"I can't do that, but how about a beer while you wait?" Zach gritted out.

Adam glanced up for the first time, and a smile spread across his face. "Sure. I'd like that. Thanks."

Zach took his time getting up and moving toward the bar. Once he was stationed, he decided to give Adam a rundown of all their beers, even though as a former bartender, Adam was well versed himself.

By the time he'd finished and a choice had been made, at least ten minutes had ticked by.

"Alright, I need to go in the back. You know, Cody's new... If there are any tips you want to give him, I'm sure he'd appreciate it."

Adam turned on the barstool, and Cody gave him a wave.

"Yeah, sure," Adam said as he slid off the stool.

Zach bit back a laugh as he watched him make his way to Cody's table. The big guy didn't seem like much of a talker, but hopefully he could keep Adam distracted.

Once he was back in his office, he checked the time. This was about when the delivery truck had arrived last time. His phone buzzed.

Jessie: *Good luck.*

Despite what he'd said, she was still thinking of him. One text, and he felt like smiling.

Dammit, she still got to him.

Zach: *You still at the motel?*

Jessie: *Not exactly.*

He dialed her immediately, and she picked up.

"What's going on?" he asked.

"I'm down the road from your pub. The diner is quite popular."

"Dammit, Jessie! You were supposed to stay in the motel," he snapped.

His outburst was met with silence.

"Hello?" he asked.

"I'm here. I'm trying to decide whether to be pissed that you think an FBI agent can't take care of herself or flattered that you care."

Fuck. He did care.

"The latter. How's it going out there? See anything?"

She laughed, and he could imagine her eyes lighting up. "I did. A man went in the door a few minutes ago. Who is he?"

"That's Adam, the ex-employee. Cody didn't just go see him last night, he convinced the guy to show up so that he's here when Marcus arrives."

"Shit. That might set Marcus off."

"No. He won't do anything until he gets his money."

"Oh, Marcus is crossing the street. I'd better let you go. Remember to stay calm and keep him talking."

"Got it."

"Good luck."

Yeah, he needed plenty of that.

He walked back out to the main space of the bar just in time to see Marcus walking in. He wasn't alone—Zach's sister was right behind him. The sister he hadn't seen in fourteen years. The sister that told him he needed to man up and take over the family.

Yeah, she'd never been his favorite.

"Bethany," Zach said.

Her eyes grew wide, and she walked up to him. "Jazz," she whispered.

He didn't correct her. He'd prefer not to hear his new name come from her mouth. It would taint it. Thank god Jessie wasn't in the van listening in, though he knew he'd have to come clean about his past to her sooner rather than later. Or hell, maybe she already knew. Maybe that was why she'd showed interest all of a sudden.

No, stop.

He had to stop going in circles. Focus on the here and now.

"Why are you here?" he asked.

Bethany rolled her eyes. "You think I trust this guy to deal with you? No. I know my little brother. Smart enough to stay away for years. If it weren't for your fuck-up over there" — she nodded to Adam — "we'd have probably gone on assuming you were dead."

She stepped right up to Zach and looked him up and down. "You aren't that scrawny kid anymore, are you? Come here." She pulled him in for a big hug.

He patted her on the back, then stepped back, wanting distance between them. This wasn't some warm family reunion. Marcus had threatened Jessie.

"Did Marcus tell you what he said he would do if I don't give you the money?"

Bethany frowned. "No, he didn't." But instead of asking Marcus, she continued to stare at Zach. "Why don't you tell me, brother?"

Shit. Bethany was smart, unlike Marcus. Though Marcus hadn't said a word since he came in, most likely following Bethany's orders.

Memories of her bossing Marcus around came to him. How could he have forgotten that?

Well, it looks like not much has changed.

But he needed to get Marcus to talk.

Zach turned to him. "I thought you were the leader of the family. Guess I should have figured Bethany would take charge. She always had more balls than any of the guys she dated."

Adam stared from Zach to Bethany to Marcus like they were in a tennis match. Cody crossed his arms, closely observing.

"I am in charge," Marcus scoffed.

Finally, he speaks. "No, it looks to me like Bethany is. You were sure talkative last night, but now that she's here, you've fallen in line. That's what you do in the Murphy family. You fall in line."

Marcus slammed his hand down on the bar. "Yes, and *you* will fall in line and give me my damned money."

Bethany watched Marcus, wearing a smirk. Yeah, Zach knew who was really in control.

"I told you, no," he replied calmly.

"And I told you what would happen if you didn't pay."

Zach stepped into Marcus's space. "And what was that?"

Marcus lowered his voice so that Cody and Adam couldn't hear. "Your little girlfriend, the FBI agent at your bar last night, will pay your price."

"I'm not sure how. She doesn't have the money either," Zach growled out.

"She won't need money. She will pay with her life," Marcus said.

Got him. Now time to turn the tables.

"Why don't you get the money from the man who has it." Zach pointed to Adam, who grabbed onto the booth he was standing next to.

For a moment, Zach almost felt sorry for the guy. He was turning green and looked like he might vomit at any moment.

"What? I don't have it," Adam said.

"What did you do with it?" Zach asked.

"Nothing. I was moving it through the till as I had been, and then you fired me. I didn't have time to gather it up." Adam stood taller, fully committing to his defense.

"Well, it must be in the till and safe, then. Let's look." Marcus charged back behind the bar.

"No," Cody said. He was now standing behind the bar with Marcus. How he'd gotten there so fast, Zach had no idea.

"Who the fuck are you?"

"He's the new manager," Adam offered.

Cody didn't correct him.

Marcus pulled his jacket back to flash the gun he had in his waistband. "Open the till," he ordered.

Cody smiled. "If you really want to find out which one of us is faster, then by all means, pull your gun. But I advise that you don't."

Marcus's faced flushed red as he looked Cody up and down. "Fuck! New manager my ass."

"Marcus, the money is not here. If there had been extra money, do you think I would have been so surprised when your driver showed up? The only discrepancy I discovered in my books was that Adam had given himself a twenty-percent raise. That's why I fired him."

Marcus moved quickly, coming to a stop in front of Adam. "I don't know what your plan is, but I know when my brother is lying, and he isn't lying. Where's my goddamn money?"

Adam must have realized he had no out. "I have some at my house."

"Let's go." Marcus grabbed the other man's arm and led him to the door. When Bethany stayed put, Marcus turned back. "Bethany, let's go."

"No, I think I'll stay here in case this is a ruse."

Zach could see Marcus fighting to stay calm. That man didn't like was when his orders weren't followed, and knowing his sister, she rarely followed his rules.

"Alright. I'll call you once I have the money." He left with Adam.

Bethany spent the rest of the time holed up in one of the booths playing on her phone.

After thirty minutes, Zach was getting nervous. *Adam lives five minutes from here. What is taking so long?*

Bethany broke the silence, "Tell me, what are the odds my husband will call and say he has the money?"

Cody stood up. After Bethany left him alone, he'd sat at the bar with Zach.

"About fifty-fifty. There's no doubt Adam took

the money, but that was a week ago. Do you think a guy like that sat on all that money for a week?" Cody asked.

"Who the fuck are you?" Bethany's voice was angry, but her eyes slowly took in every inch of the man.

"I told you. The manager," he said.

That brought a smile to her face. "I don't buy that for a minute. You have military or police written all over you."

"Sorry to disappoint," Cody said.

Bethany rose out of the booth and walked over to him. "Well, in that case, we should get to know each other, since we'll be working together." She put her arm on his bicep. "You're very muscular for a bar manager."

Cody pulled his arm away. "We won't be working together."

Bethany's phone rang.

"Did you get it?" she answered. Her smile turned to a frown. "Are you injured?"

Well shit, that doesn't sound good.

After ending the call, she put the phone in her purse.

"Apparently, Adam took Marcus to some abandoned house and then hit him in the head with a baseball bat. Marcus said Adam took off in a car before he could get to him." Her gaze met Zach's. "Next week, we'll resume our arrangement. The shipment will arrive Tuesday. Be ready."

She left before Zach or Cody could respond.

"Shit!" Zach yelled. "How the hell do I get rid of them?"

"I have an idea," Cody said. "But you aren't going to like it."

His phone rang. Jessie.

"It looks like you're alone now. You okay?"

"Yeah. But Adam didn't pay. Marcus expects me to take the money on Tuesday." He let out a breath.

"Hey, we'll get him."

Zach sat on a bar stool. "I'm sorry about last night. I snapped. I was angry."

He could hear Jessie breathing through the phone. Was she pissed? Upset?

"Let's forget about it. It was a tense situation," she said.

"After you arrest Marcus and wrap up this case, we should talk."

Jessie cleared her throat. "Arrest Marcus?"

"Yeah, we got him. He threatened your life again."

"Zach, no."

Zach began to pace. "No what?"

"We won't be arresting Marcus."

Zach jumped up. "Why the fuck not?" he yelled. Wasn't that why he'd agreed to the listening devices? If they didn't care about the confession, then what the hell?

"Listen, my boss is after the Bannons. If we arrest Marcus, not only will they know the FBI is investigating them, they'll just find someone to take his place. We will lose our advantage."

"Advantage? Are you fucking kidding me? I only agreed to those listening devices because he threatened you."

"Thank you for that. But there is a bigger picture here we can't forget," she said.

Bigger picture. It was becoming pretty clear that bigger picture didn't include him. Damn, he had to stop letting his feeling cloud his judgment. But right now, he was too angry to trust what he might say to her.

"I have to go." He ended the call and tossed his phone on the bar.

"She used me, again!" he shouted.

Chapter Eighteen

Jessie was parked outside her dad's house. All she wanted to do was go home and sleep, but she'd promised she would be here for the weekly Doyle dinner.

God, she was spending her life in her car, driving from one place to the next. She was tired of it.

Right now, her dad was likely putting the finishing touches on his signature lasagna. Just thinking about it made her mouth water. It had been so long since she'd had any. When she'd first transferred to Seattle, she'd religiously made it to her dad's for the weekly dinner. But then around the new year, she realized she had to work harder if she wanted to move up and driving out to her old home had been one of the first things to go.

She hoped she wouldn't have to lose something else too. She couldn't stop going over everything that had happened earlier in the day. After their lunch in the park earlier in the week, Zach had been so angry.

But she'd felt him softening during their phone call this morning. Then he'd returned to his pissed-off state when she told him she wasn't going to arrest Marcus.

She'd confirmed with Cody that Marcus had threatened her life on tape, but Marcus alone wasn't the goal of the case. She'd use it as potential leverage, but not for one arrest. She would bring down Hawthorne Distribution and prove they laundered money for the Bannons.

Despite spending most of the afternoon in Fisher Springs, she and Zach never had a chance to talk again, focused as they were on the situation at hand. The tension rolling off Zach was intense. She hoped to talk to him to resolve everything tomorrow.

The friction between her and Zach made it hard for her to concentrate so instead of listening to the tape, she got the brief version from Cody and Zach: Marcus still wanted to use Zach's pub for money-laundering.

She wasn't sure what Marcus was after. He had already seen two FBI agents at the pub, and that alone usually caused bad guys to look for other targets.

That's when it hit her.

Marcus knew the FBI was watching Zach, and Zach had said the situation was personal. Although, his manager owing money hardly made it personal, by her standards, but she knew men like Marcus twisted words to scare people. But was it possible that Marcus was really trying to set Zach up? If so, what motive would he have?

She'd promised Zach they would talk the next

morning; Marcus's motives would be at the top on her list of topics.

Her cell phone rang, which made her jump. The screen flashed with a familiar number.

"Hello?" she answered.

"Are you going to sit on the street all night, or are you going to get your ass in here? We're starving, and Dad insists on waiting on you."

Silas, the oldest of her younger brothers, was always hungry. Actually, she was surprised he was here. It was midseason.

"Silas? Why aren't you playing hockey?"

He laughed. "It's good to see you too."

"Silas," she warned.

He let out a breath. "Coach thought I should take a few days off. I'm fine."

"What happened?"

She heard him swallow hard. It was one of his tells she knew well. Something was wrong. "Nothing I want to talk about. Now get in here, or we'll eat without you."

"Well, I'll get in there sooner if you stop yapping at me on the phone."

She ended the call, grinning to herself. With only one year between them, they'd always picked on each other. But something was wrong, and she made a mental note to talk to him about it later, privately.

When she got to the door, she pushed it open but remained on the front porch.

Another thing about growing up with four

brothers is she learned quickly to protect herself.

Voices drifted to her from the dining room, and she realized food had won out over pranks. Feeling safe, she walked in.

Something cold and wet hit her in the chest.

She looked down to find remnants of a broken water balloon sticking to her shirt. Glancing up, she saw her youngest brother, Ryder, laughing so hard, he had to lean against a wall. "A water balloon inside the house? Dad will kill you!"

She took off toward the kitchen, where she knew her dad was.

Ryder jumped in front of her. "No, you can't. I'm already on thin ice." The pleading look in his eyes said he was telling the truth, but then she saw his lip curve for just a split second.

Ryder was still in high school, but already over six feet tall. Despite his size, she grabbed him and spun around, switching their positions.

She was just in time. Four water balloons pelted him in the back.

"Stop! You got the wrong person!" he yelled back over his shoulder.

"What's going on in here?" Her dad came out of the kitchen and surveyed the mess then shook his head. "Hunter, get a towel and clean up the water. Seb, you clean up all the pieces of balloon. Ryder, you're grounded. Jessie, come in here. I've missed you."

He barked orders, and despite everyone except Ryder being adults, they listened.

"Hey! Why doesn't Silas have to help?" Ryder complained.

"He didn't make this mess," her dad said.

Ryder's eyes widened. "Whose idea do you think this all was?"

But his words fell on deaf ears because their dad was leading Jessie away.

"Hi, Daddy," she said. "I missed you."

"I missed you too, Buttercup. Why do you stay away?" he asked.

"I don't, I just get busy with my cases and can't get away."

"Hmm. Well, we can discuss that later. It's time to eat." He led her to the dining room where her brothers had already set the table.

Silas was already seated and staring at his phone. He had a black eye, which wasn't unusual, but she knew him well enough to know something was up.

"What's wrong?" Jessie asked him.

Silas shook his head.

"If you change your mind and want to talk, I'm here okay?"

He gave a quick nod as the others poured into the room.

As usual, dinner was a chaotic affair. It wasn't uncommon for two or three conversations to be going at one time. She just did the best she could to keep up.

"The reporters are saying Silas is having the best year of his career," Hunter said to Jessie.

"I know. I still catch all his games."

"You do?" Silas asked. "I thought you were too busy with your job."

She shrugged. "I often catch the recording later, but I watch them. You're looking really good out there."

He smiled for the first time. "Thanks. That means a lot."

After losing their mom, she and her brothers had become each other's support. It was important to all of them that they were all there for each other. But Silas's comment made her realize maybe she hadn't been as good at that as she'd thought.

"I'm sorry about work. I'll try to make it to more dinners. All right?"

"Sounds great," Seb said. "Now tell us, are you dating anyone? Because if so, he will need to pass the Doyle test." He was grinning ear to ear.

Now she was thinking about Zach again. Something told her they'd love him.

"It's complicated, but if things work out, I'll bring him by," she promised.

Hunter cracked his knuckles. "Just let us know. We'll be ready."

Jessie laughed. "He won't be intimidated by you guys, so you can save your energy."

"Based on the photos we saw of the last guy, I'm not so sure your type can handle us," Silas smirked.

She'd forgotten about those. She'd taken a few photos of Dillon and shared them with her brothers.

Dillon had a much thinner build than her brothers, and Zach, so Silas's comment made sense. But there was no need to tell them more about Zach right now.

Deep down, she hoped she would be able to bring him to a dinner soon.

She closed her eyes. He was only supposed to have been a one-night stand, and now she wanted to bring him to family dinner? Somehow, that man had managed to make his way into her heart.

The next morning, Jessie couldn't focus on anything other than what was going on with Zach. When was Marcus going to send the money? Would Zach still refuse to pay, and if so, what would happen to him?

Zach had texted her the night before, asking if they could talk this morning. And after realizing she cared more for him than she'd been willing to admit, getting a *'We need to talk'* text scared her.

Now she stared at her phone, trying to conjure up the nerve to call him. When her phone rang, she assumed Zach was reading her mind again.

It was Carter.

"How was the lasagna?" he asked.

She laughed. "It was really good."

"Anything new on the case?"

"Mr. Brannigan got Marcus threatening me on

tape. Now we have to get Marcus talking about the Bannons."

"That's good. I'll send Blaese out to that second warehouse and see what he can get."

"I thought Blaese was doing surveillance during the days," she asked cautiously.

"No, I have Agent Harris covering that today."

Dillon? In Fisher Springs? Thank god she was sitting on the bed, or she would have fallen over. "Agent Harris is on this case now?"

Carter chuckled. "Crazy thing, he was between cases, and I was going to tell him to take a day off, but instead, he volunteered."

I bet he did. She held back a groan. "There's more with the case, sir. Apparently, Marcus is moving forward and insisting that Brannigan launder his money, but something isn't right."

"What do you mean?" Carter asked.

"Blaese walked into the pub when Marcus was there the other night, and Beyers made Blaese in a second. Then Blaese asked if I was doing all right, essentially outing me."

"Why would Blaese do that?"

The magical question.

"I have no idea. But Marcus knows two agents are sniffing around, so why is he pushing Brannigan to do this?"

"You think Brannigan is being set up?"

"I do."

Chapter Nineteen

The moment Jessie responded to Zach's text stating she was awake and willing to talk, he was out the door and on his way to her motel.

Marcus had returned to the pub the night before and confirmed that Zach still owed the money. He also suggested working out a deal with Bucky's to faster launder the new money coming in.

Zach had told Marcus, again, that he wasn't accepting any new money, and Marcus had only laughed.

There was something more going on, but he couldn't put his finger on it.

Marcus was not the most patient man; he would not have waited this long for his money unless he had some other plan. And Zach knew for damn sure that his brother-in-law wouldn't normally keep pressing his luck when he knew the FBI was listening. But he couldn't figure out the guy's end game.

Would Marcus really hurt Jessie just to get to

him? Did he hate Zach that much? Hell, it was possible. Marcus had pretty much been forced to take over in Zach's absence. But that was what he'd wanted, wasn't it?

Forget Marcus. Right now, he needed to focus on protecting Jessie. This was proving especially difficult, as she wasn't having any of it.

God, she was a stubborn woman. One he shouldn't still want, but he did.

When she'd texted this morning, she'd said she was sorry for making him feel like the case was her priority. That was all he needed — hope that she felt what he did. After he had a chance to cool down, he realized he wouldn't be so worked up about it if he didn't care for her. He cared more than he wanted to admit.

Ten minutes later, he was knocking on her room door, holding two coffees from the diner. "It's Zach," he announced.

She opened the door wearing a fitted T-shirt and jeans. His traitorous body immediately reacted. Glancing into the room, he tried to focus on something that wouldn't send all his blood south. They needed to talk.

"You got here faster than I expected," she greeted.

Trying to focus on anything other than her body, he stepped past her to set the coffee down. "I was worried about you."

She smiled. "Zach, I've already explained I can

take care of myself. Do I need to tackle you again?"

He stepped into her space. "Already wanting to use the handcuffs on me, huh?"

Her eyes darkened.

Oh yeah, she still wanted him too. All he wanted to do was kiss her, but...

"We need to talk," he said.

Was it even possible to get past the mistrust they'd already had? He sure as hell hoped so because every time he saw her, it was another reminder that what he felt for her was different, stronger.

"After you said you weren't arresting Marcus, I felt used. I've felt you used me a couple of times now," he spat out.

The look of shock on her face answered his question. He sighed in relief that she hadn't been faking her feelings.

"Used you? Never. I can't believe you'd think that. I thought I was clear with you that I don't call men over for a night. I thought you knew I was letting down a wall with you. I'm sorry about Marcus but trust me, I didn't use you. I would never use you."

Zach grabbed his coffee and took a drink. "I want to believe that, but after our night together, you didn't respond to my texts. It was like you ghosted me. But then once you realized I might be involved in your case, you showed interest again. What else was I supposed to think?"

She stepped into his space. "You were supposed to think that I liked you. I intended for it to only be one night, but you got under my skin, Zach. I don't open up to men. Not after what happened with my ex."

"What happened with your ex?"

She shook her head. "That's a story for another time. The point is, I don't trust easily, as I'm sure you can tell. But I trusted you. Then, when I was driving back from… well, part of my job, I drove through Fisher Springs, and a Hawthorne Distribution truck was parked outside your pub. I was confused, and wondered if you were you involved in their crimes?"

"So you thought the worst of me."

"For a moment, yes. But you have to understand, Zach, that's on me and my past. I know in my heart that you're a good man. That's what I was trying to tell you the other night at your pub. A good man who, despite my fighting it, has won my heart."

Stepping back into her space, he stroked her cheek and then ran his thumb across her bottom lip. Every time he touched her, it ignited something in him, a desire so strong that he knew had had to be with this woman again. It had never been like this with anyone else. The way she was melting into him under such a light touch, he had to wonder if she felt it too.

"Jessie?"

"Hmm?" Her hands moved to his chest.

He reached behind her neck and pulled her forward one inch. She looked up and licked her lips.

Aw hell, he couldn't wait.

He leaned in and crushed his lips to hers. She

immediately returned the kiss, and her hands grasped at his shirt as if to hold on.

The kiss went from tentative to molten in seconds.

"God I've missed this," Zach said as he pulled back.

He lifted her up, and she wrapped her legs around his waist. Then he carried her to the bed while kissing her neck.

"I missed you too," she said on a moan.

As he laid her down, she pulled up his T-shirt. He quickly pulled it up and over his head, then tugged the hem of her T-shirt. When she sat up to pull it off, he snaked his hand around her back and undid her bra. She tossed both articles of clothing on the floor.

He stared, taking her in. "Mm." Her nipples were rosy and begged for his mouth.

Then his mouth was on her, and something in him lost control. He sucked hard, and her hands flew to his belt, undoing his pants in record time.

He stepped back to pull them off. "You too," he nodded toward her lower half.

She complied, removing her jeans.

Then he was above her, kissing her neck down to her nipples, but before he got too far, she flipped him over onto his back.

He chuckled. "I see that actually comes in handy."

She was straddling him wearing a pink thong, and she ground against him. "Handy, yes."

He groaned. "I need to be inside you now."

He knew he was probably taking this too fast, but his need for her was too strong. Next time, he'd take things slower.

Jessie leaned down and kissed him while her hands pushed down his boxer briefs.

"Condom," Zach panted.

Jessie moved to the side so he could get up. When he returned, he crawled over top of her.

"You can't stand not being in control, can you?" She grinned.

"No, it's you who needs control. But today, I'm in charge."

Jessie glared at him, and he recognized the signs she was getting all riled up to argue with him. But he had a plan.

"You think you're in charge?" she asked dangerously.

Before she said another word, he was between her legs, and he licked her wetness through the skimpy fabric of her thong.

"Oh god," she cried.

"Yes, I do." He removed her panties and tossed them to the ground then licked again. "Is that going to be a problem?"

"No," she whimpered.

He loved to see this side of her. He knew giving up control was hard for her, so he was going to make sure she didn't regret it.

"Zach, I'm so close."

She was. He felt her body quivering, and didn't let up until she was over the edge.

While she caught her breath, he rolled on the condom and positioned himself at her entrance. Then he swiped her hair from her face and kissed her, more tender than urgent.

She wrapped her legs around him, urging him on.

As he entered her, it was different than that night at her condo. Then, it had been a frenzy to kiss and touch and fuck. Now, as he moved with her body, this felt more like making love. He kept his eyes on hers, not breaking their connection. With each movement, it was as if the lock on his heart was chipping away and she demanded entrance.

He couldn't keep her out any longer.

"Jessie."

He leaned down and kissed her and, feeling his own orgasm building, pulled her hips up, changing her angle so her clit was rubbing against him with every push.

"Zach…" She closed her eyes as her orgasm swept over her.

The pulsing of her orgasm was too much, and he thrust in harder, chasing his own release. He exploded and his vision went dark. He'd never come that hard.

"Jesus, Jessie. I'm pretty sure I saw stars."

"Me too," she panted out.

He couldn't suppress the grin or the fact he was

deliriously happy. Leaning down, he kissed her.

"I'll be right back."

After he took care of the condom and returned, she curled up in his arms.

"That was beyond amazing," she said. Her eyes were glassy, and he knew she felt as emotional as he did.

"You know, the moment I first saw you, I wanted to grab you and kiss you. But you had literally just tackled me and cuffed me, plus you carry a gun, so I decided not to."

Out of nowhere, a pillow hit him in the face.

He chuckled. "Seriously. When I found out Chase was playing a game against a team from the FBI, I'd hoped to see you again, but what were the odds? Then there you were, their star player."

"I was shocked to see you there."

"I know. I remember. But you liked it."

She propped up on an elbow to look at him. "I thought you were an arrogant playboy who only wanted another notch on his belt. You wouldn't give up, and I took that to mean you thought you were God's gift to women."

"Is that why you were so hard on me?"

She nodded. "But then the night you came over, you were different. You had to go and be romantic. For fuck's sake, you *shaved.*"

"You said I should. Did you know I'd had that beard since I was eighteen?"

Running her hand along his chin, she moved

up to his cheek and found his scar. She bent down and kissed it. "You can grow it back if you like. I'm not going to walk away because you have a beard." She settled down into his arms.

"Wait a minute." He pulled back to stare at her again. She was grinning. "You liked the beard, didn't you?"

"Maybe," she said.

"Then why the hell did you tell me to shave it?"

"I didn't, I just said you shouldn't hide behind it. How was I supposed to know you'd actually shave it off for me?"

Before she tried to squirm away, he flipped her on her back and loomed over her.

"You were just trying to irk me?"

She laughed. "Irk?"

"Or flirt?"

"I was not flirting," she said.

"You were. Admit it."

"Never!"

He tickled her, and she was laughing hard, trying to tell him to stop.

He stopped. "Ready to admit it yet?"

"No!"

He tickled her more.

"Okay! I admit it."

He stopped tickling her and sat up.

"Where are you going?"

"Just turning on some music."

As music started to play through his phone, he

dropped it into one of the room's empty water glasses to amplify the sound. He knew it might look corny, but he also knew he'd never felt like this before.

He held out his hand. "Dance with me."

A familiar Ed Sheeran song played, and she laughed as she stood up.

"You're asking me to dance again?"

"Why not?"

"You are crazy, Zach Brannigan."

"Crazy for you."

She was smiling as he twirled her around the room.

"This is our song now," he said.

As it ended, she lifted up onto her toes until their lips met.

"I'm sorry I didn't trust you."

He shrugged. "You had a crazy ex. That can mess with your head."

She smiled. "It has, yes. I'm happy I ran that background check on you and—"

Zach stepped back. "You what?" He grabbed his phone and turned off the next song that was starting to play.

His heart was racing. He'd been careful to cut all ties, there's no way she could have found out. If she had, she certainly wouldn't be here with him now. Would she? Shit, but if she didn't know, he had to tell her.

"I'm sorry, but I had to be sure," she said sheepishly. "And after the check, I felt better. There were no ties to the Murphy or Bannon families."

Zach swallowed. If he didn't say anything now, he was essentially lying to her. But he couldn't. Once she knew, she'd never look at him the same. He really would become just a piece in her case.

"I'm sorry," he said. "I have to leave."

She watched him get dressed. "What's going on, Zach? Are you upset about the background check?"

Slipping his legs into his pants, he glanced up.

Her eyes welled with tears.

"Yes. No. I'm not sure," he admitted. "I'm sorry, but I need to leave. I have to open the pub."

He shoved his feet into his shoes, grabbed his shirt, and was out of the room before he'd even finished dressing. He pulled his T-shirt over his head and slid his arms through the holes while he took the stairs to his truck.

What the hell was he going to do? There was no way he could have a future with Jessie without telling her who he was—honestly, it was a miracle she hadn't figured it out yet. He *had* to tell her. It was better than waiting for the other shoe to drop. He would tell her soon.

He just wasn't sure how.

Chapter Twenty

Even though she knew Zach was giving a bullshit excuse, saying he was leaving to open his pub, she let him go. The truth was she knew when she did the background search that she was crossing a line. All she could do now was hope he would see why she had to do it and forgive her for invading his privacy.

In the meantime, she was supposed to meet Agent Blaese to discuss the case. For that, she needed more coffee.

Every time Jessie walked into the diner, the waitresses gave her a knowing smile. When she had asked Zach about it, he explained it was a small town and they all knew the story about how she'd tackled him. But today, Detective Moore and Officer Harvey turned to smile as well. She was pretty sure they knew more than just the tackle.

"Morning, officer, detective," she said as she walked to the counter.

"Good morning, Agent Doyle. You look happy

this morning," Harvey said with a grin. "Any chance our boy Zach is responsible?"

Nick punched him in the shoulder. "Why you asking her that? Don't be rude."

Harvey's hands flew to the air. "How's that rude? I'm just asking if Zach is making her happy."

Nick shook his head.

A redheaded woman came out from the back. "We all know damn well what you meant, Chase. I apologize for him," the woman said to Jessie.

Harvey laughed. "How the hell did you hear that? You were in the back!"

The woman walked around the counter and up to the man and laid a kiss on his lips. "I can always hear you. Don't forget that."

Jessie laughed. "It's fine. Yes, Zach makes me happy. I'm afraid he might be mad at me right now, but I hope to fix that."

"Hi, I don't think we've formally met. I'm Harmony." The redhead was now standing next to Jessie with her hand extended.

"Jessie."

"I know. I've heard so much about you. And Zach's accent has come out quite a bit recently." She smiled at her then walked behind the counter. "What can I get you?"

"Just a couple of coffees would be great. I'm meeting someone."

Moore's eyebrow arched.

"A co-worker," she said.

Nick nodded, as if giving his approval.

"Should I expect this kind of questioning from everyone?" she asked.

After pouring coffee into two to-go cups, Harmony placed them on the counter. "It's a small town, and everyone loves Zach. We're all just looking out for him."

Jessie wasn't sure how to respond; thankfully, she didn't have to.

"Two-fifty please," Harmony finished with a smile.

Jessie's eyes widened. "Total?"

Hell, you couldn't get one coffee for that price in Seattle.

Harmony laughed. "Yes, total."

After Jessie paid, she left the diner, heading toward the park where Blaese had agreed to meet. Walking down Main Street, she was struck by the beauty of the town. All the store fronts were decorated, and several red benches brought even more color to the downtown area. Everything about this place screamed *storybook small town*, and she couldn't help but be drawn to it.

After a couple of blocks, she turned. The park came into view, and so did Blaese's car. But he wasn't alone. The sight of the woman next to him made her stutter to a stop.

Quickly, she moved up next to the building, hoping he hadn't seen her. Checking the time, she realized she was ten minutes early.

Jessie squinted and almost dropped her coffee when she realized Bethany was in his car.

Why the hell would he be talking to her?

He was waving his hands around. He appeared upset. Bethany glared at him and then she grabbed his face.

What the hell was going on? Was she about to witness some kind of attack?

Blaese stilled, and Bethany leaned in and kissed him.

Jessie had to blink to make sure she was really seeing what she thought. Bethany was kissing Blaese. Was he kissing her back?

She continued to watch for signs that Blaese didn't want this.

Blaese pushed her away, shaking his head. Bethany wore a smirk.

What the hell did I just see? Is Bethany the informant? Or is Blaese a dirty agent? Or both?

Bethany exited the vehicle and got into another car parked next to it.

Shit, she'll likely drive right past me to get out of town.

Jessie jogged back to Main Street as best she could while holding two hot coffees. When she heard the sound of an engine approaching, she had just rounded the corner. Swiveling, she turned the corner but pretended to be focused on the coffee. Hopefully, Bethany hadn't seen her.

Bethany freaking Murphy was a known

criminal. One who was very much involved in their case. Even if she was the informant, kissing her would be unethical. But it did appear that he had tried to stop it. But why the hell was she in his car trying to kiss him in the first place?

Blaese had been acting shady, outing her to Marcus at the pub. If he was working for the other side, what did he have to gain? A payday? It was true FBI agents didn't make very much money, especially new ones. But would Blaese really sell her out for a few bucks?

Why wouldn't he? He didn't really know her. And by outing her at the bar, he had stopped Marcus from saying anything else. Hell, it made her a weapon against Zach to get him to continue the money-laundering.

Shit. Why hadn't she pieced this together before?

Instead of trying to solve the puzzle in the moment, she walked to Blaese's car. As long as she acted normal, he'd be none the wiser as to what she just witnessed.

Putting on her game face, she took several deep breaths as she approached. She could do this. She'd trained for this. *Remain calm and don't give anything away.* Maybe a few questions would clue her in as to what he was up to.

Jessie plastered a smile on her face and approached the car. His driver's side window was down. "Good morning," she said.

"Hey, is one of those for me?"

"It is." She handed him the coffee.

"Thanks."

"Do you want to sit on a bench?" She indicated the park bench a few feet from them.

"No, get in. I want to talk in private."

Jessie glanced around the empty park. There was no one around to overhear them.

"Are you sure? It's such a nice morning," she tried.

"I'm sure. Get in."

She swallowed hard. *Act normal.* Maybe she'd find a clue in his car.

Had she not known Bethany had been in the car, she still would have known a woman had been there. The reek of cheap perfume hung in the air.

Pretending not to notice, she took a big gulp of her coffee. But it tasted like the perfume, and she struggled not to make a face.

"As you know, we have Marcus on tape, threatening my life," she began.

"Yes, and as you know, that's not enough," Blaese snapped.

She let out a sigh. "Is everything all right? You seem tense," Jessie said.

Blaese turned away and stared out the driver's window. "Yeah, sorry. I didn't mean to snap. I've got some personal issues I'm working through."

I bet you do. "Want to talk about it?"

His head swiveled to hers. "What? Like

friends?"

She shrugged.

He scoffed. "Unlike *some* agents, I find it's better to keep personal and professional separate."

She knew it was a dig. He'd given her enough looks to know he'd picked up on the sexual tension between her and Zach. At least, she thought he had. Maybe all his odd looks had been related to his own issues.

"Speaking of, how's our favorite bartender?" he continued.

Okay, he knows. Is that why he outed me?

She studied him. His jaw ticked, and he was glaring at her.

What the fuck? "Why did you blow my cover in front of Marcus?" she snapped.

Regardless of his opinion of her and Zach, the way he handled himself in that bar was unprofessional.

He leaned back in his seat and blew out a breath. "I saw how Marcus was looking at you, and I had a feeling he was going to threaten you to get to Zach. I thought if he knew you were an agent, he'd back off."

Her mouth fell open. Was Blaese actually trying to protect her? Or was he trying to get rid of her?

He continued to glare at her.

"Blaese, if you have something more to say, say it."

"I'll keep my opinions to myself, but I need to

know if your *boyfriend* is ready to wear a wire yet. Because I got some new information."

Jessie bit her cheek to keep from commenting on the 'boyfriend' remark. "Where did you get this new information?"

"Our informant."

"Who's our informant?"

Blaese smiled. "I believe Carter explained that to you. Only he and I are to know their identity."

Convenient. "What's the new information?"

"I was told Marcus is going to Bucky's Bar later today, and he's bringing the Bannon brothers with him."

"What? Why would they show up at the bar? I thought they wanted to keep distance between them and the operation."

Jessie thought through all the scenarios, and in no way did it make any sense for the Bannons to show up together in Davenport.

"I can't tell you why," he said. "I can only tell you what I heard. But you'll need to do the surveillance, I have to go to Seattle."

Blaese spoke as if giving an order, but he was a junior agent. No way in hell was she taking an order from him. Especially not when she suspected he might be dirty. No, she needed to stick around town and figure out what the hell was going on.

"I can't. Carter wants me here, inside the pub."

"Call Carter. He told me to relay the message to you when he asked me to go back to Seattle."

Well, shit. She would call Carter to confirm, but it was unlikely Blaese would lie this blatantly.

"Why do you have to go back to Seattle?" she asked.

"Carter wants a full report on all the surveillance I've done. Photos, field notes, everything."

And you can't send them to him in an email?

Now she had no doubt something was going on.

"Thanks for the coffee," he interrupted her thoughts. "If there's nothing else, I should get going. Beat the lunch traffic." He started the car as if dismissing her.

It took all her control to hide the fact she was pissed as hell. She glanced around the car for more clues. Her gut told her to stall him.

"Do you know Agent Dillon Harris?" she asked casually.

He frowned. "I do. We worked together on my last case. Why do you ask?"

"What do you think of him?"

He laughed. "I thought you were hung up on the bartender. Harris is all right, I guess."

Well, shit. Now he thinks I want Dillon too.

No point in correcting him. Maybe she'd find out more this way.

"What do you mean, you guess?"

Blaese shrugged. "He's nice enough, and he did his job in the field, but something seems off about him. I can't put my finger on it."

Jessie nodded. She knew exactly what he meant. Unfortunately, she'd learned the hard way. "Has he mentioned where he's from?"

"Yeah. One time in the car, we got to talking. He mentioned he had been an instructor at Quantico when his girlfriend kept talking about moving back to Seattle. He said that was why he put the transfer in. Apparently, it only took five months for an opening. How lucky is that? I've been trying to get transferred to Los Angeles since I came here."

"When did he start?"

She knew Blaese would know. He had been sent to the Seattle office right out of training two years ago.

"Right after Labor Day. Wait, didn't you transfer from Richmond? That's near Quantico. Did you two know each other?" he asked suspiciously.

"Thanks for the information," she said quickly. "I'll let you go. I know how traffic can be." She hopped out of the car without answering his question.

She knew he'd bring it up again, but right now, she needed time to process what he just said.

Five months prior to September was April. Dillon had planned their move all that time and never mentioned it to her? And why the hell did he go through with the transfer after she broke things off in August? And more importantly, why would he pull for *her* to get transferred after their relationship was over?

She couldn't understand why he would give up all those women he had wrapped around his pinkie.

Although, he likely had the same set up here. He was a smooth talker.

After Blaese left, she called Carter to confirm he had asked Blaese to return to Seattle. And yes, he did indeed want her in Davenport, but not until the afternoon.

Dammit.

Chapter Twenty-One

A few hours after leaving Jessie's motel room, Zach was still wound up. He'd had his chance to 'fess up to her and he didn't take it. Now, he was lying. Hell, he had already been withholding that he was part of the case, just not the way Jessie would think.

She wouldn't look at him the same when she heard the truth. He knew that. He'd been living in denial thinking they could go on and she'd never know.

Could she look past it? That was the real question. Because dammit, he wanted a future with her. Hell, after this morning, he'd realized he wanted everything with her. He had no idea how that would work, but he was willing to try.

Jessie walked into the pub, and the way she averted her gaze, he knew he needed to set her straight right away. He hadn't meant to leave her feeling guilty over the background check. Yeah, he wasn't happy she'd run one, but he could understand why she'd done it.

"Jessie."

"Zach. Hi, Cody." She waved to the other man, who was sitting on a stool at the bar.

"About this morning," Zach started.

Jessie raised her hand. "No, you don't need to say anything. I'm sorry. It was an invasion of your privacy to run that background check. I get it. I just didn't know what else to do at the time. I'm not sure how I can make it up to you, but I'd like to try."

Zach smiled. "I'm not mad."

She looked up. "You're not?"

"No."

She smiled back. "Good, because we have work to do."

Her smile vanished as she changed into work mode.

"Everything has been taken care of," Cody said. "I double-checked the listening devices, and Vince can hear everything we're saying."

"Good." Jessie sat on the barstool next to Cody.

Zach returned to wiping down the bar.

"You're nervous." Cody wasn't asking. He knew. "Remember, Zach, I'm here to keep things from going bad."

"Well, get ready, then. I still don't have his money, and I'm still saying no to laundering it for him."

Cody chuckled.

"What?"

"You are one of the most stubborn men I've met. Doesn't the FBI want you to take a delivery if offered, and the money, so they can catch that company in the act?"

"That's the second option," Jessie said.

Cody leaned forward. "What's the first?"

"A confession," she said.

Cody turned to Zach. "You think you can get one?"

"I'm going to try." He dropped the rag and turned to Jessie. "I really need to talk to you about something."

"Okay, let me run to the bathroom, then we can chat. But we have to keep it short. I want to get out of here before Marcus shows up."

Zach laughed. "It's too early for Marcus. He won't get here for another hour or so."

"Okay but better safe than sorry." She pushed up on her toes to lean across the bar, gave him a kiss, then walked down the hall to the bathrooms.

"Looks like you two are cozy. Isn't that some sort of conflict?" Cody asked.

He hadn't thought about it, but Cody was probably right. He wondered if she was risking her job. And if so, why. She struck him as a by-the-book kind of woman.

His musings were interrupted by Marcus pushing through the door of the pub.

"He's early," Cody said under his breath.

And Zach's brother-in-law wasn't alone; two

men walked in behind him. The sun blazed through the open door, making it hard to make out the new faces. Then the door closed, and Zach stood frozen.

"Hey, you remember our old friends the Bannons, right?" Marcus asked.

Yeah, he remembered the Bannons. He remembered befriending Tony Bannon when they were both fourteen. He remembered Tony pressuring him every day for the last year he was with his dad to take on some of their business. Sure, they'd made more money, but he had no interest in dealing drugs. Hell, he didn't even want to steal and scrap cars. He still wore the scar from the one time he made a mistake and the cops caught him.

"You're a long way from home, aren't you?" Zach asked Tony.

All of them were, actually. Unless Marcus and Bethany had moved from Idaho to Washington.

"Once we heard our old friend was back, we had to come over right away," Tony said.

Zach winced, but knew better than to tell Tony they weren't friends.

"As I live and breathe, Jazz Murphy is alive! Better pay up, brother," Jonny Bannon said.

Jonny was Tony's little brother, but he wasn't so little anymore.

"Why 'Jazz'?" Cody asked.

Zach shook his head. He didn't want to get into any of this right now.

"You know, Marcus had to convince us to

detour to this shit town. But the prospect that it really was you had us intrigued." Jonny stared at Zach. "So, tell me, why is your dipshit brother-in-law running the Murphy business now and not you? You were the rightful heir."

Zach closed his eyes. Not only was the FBI hearing all of his history and where he had come from, he was sure Jessie was in the hallway listening in. He kicked himself for not telling her sooner.

"I have no interest in the Murphy business," he said.

"Well, that's too bad, because you really don't have a choice," Tony said.

Zach crossed his arms. "And why is that?"

Tony sat on a stool and stared at Cody. "Who are you?"

"The manager," Cody said, not taking his eyes off Tony.

The visitor nodded, then turned back to Zach. "We heard about that FBI agent that was giving you sweet eyes. Sounds like she's crushing on you."

"What does that matter?" Zach asked.

"Well, if you don't help us out, things won't end well for her," Tony said. "But I have good news. Marcus explained your situation with the missing cash. Because you are an old friend, we are going to let you pay us back over time—with interest, of course. In the meantime, we have a delivery coming in tonight that we need you to accept."

"And if I don't?" He knew, but he wanted them

to say it again.

"Are you hard of hearing, Jazz? I just said your FBI friend will pay the price. I know you don't want that to happen."

"Yeah, Marcus already beat you to that threat," Zach said.

Tony smiled. "Guess it's a double threat, then."

"Be ready when the truck arrives," Marcus said.

Tony stood from his barstool, staring hard at Zach. "That scar healed up real good. I looked up to you that day. Never saw a teardrop, but I know that shit must have hurt." He shook his head. "Alright, we need to go to some shithole in Davenport."

"A bar that has been much more willing to help than you, Zach. If you cooperated, we'd get you back that lost business," Marcus said. "Think about it."

Zach watched the three of them walk out the door. As soon as they were gone, the panic set in. "Shit!"

"So, you were the heir to the Murphy family crime business?" Cody asked.

"You're familiar with the Murphy family?"

Cody nodded. "It's come up in my work."

Zach closed his eyes. "Shit. You make it sound like it was something. No, I was a prisoner as long as I had that name. People looked down on all of us. Rightfully so. But fuck, Cody." He snapped his eyes open to look at the man. "What if the FBI can't stop them?"

"Then I will."

The man looked serious, but Zach wasn't about to question him now, he had a lot more on his mind.

"Jessie!"

He ran from behind the bar to the bathrooms. She wasn't there. Then he ran down to the hall to his office. She wasn't there either. Then he checked the storage area. She wasn't there, but the back door had been left ajar.

She must have snuck out the back.

Was that before or after Bannon called him Jazz?

He reached into his pocket, pulled out his phone, and called her. It went to voicemail. He'd have to text her.

Zach: *Marcus came and brought two Bannons with him.*

He waited a few minutes, though there was no reply.

He pocketed his phone and walked back out to the bar. They were close to opening, and Ariel wasn't due in for another couple of hours.

An hour later, Jessie still hadn't answered his text.

"Cody, Jessie isn't responding. After Bannon's latest threat, I want to make sure she's all right. You have the other FBI agent's number, right?"

Cody nodded. "I'll call him right now."

When the first customer of the day walked in, Cody took his call to the back office.

"Hey, Zach."

"Hey, Kate, what can I do for you?"

"Just a beer would be great."

"Afternoon beer? You want to talk about it?"

"No. I have a day off from the diner and decided to day drink." She grinned.

"Really?"

"No." She winked at him. "I'm meeting someone here."

"Ah, a man?"

"As a matter of fact, yes. A guy I've been seeing on and off."

"Anyone I know?"

Kate smiled. "Maybe."

Cody walked back into the main bar, shaking his head.

"What's wrong?" Zach asked.

"According to Blaese, Jessie is supposed to be in Davenport by now. He was supposed to go, but he got called back to Seattle."

"Oh shit, not that bar."

"Yes, Bucky's."

"Wait, did you say Blaese is in Seattle?" Kate asked. "I have to go."

"Kate, wait!"

Why did she care about Blaese?

Kate was out the door before he could get another word in.

Zach frowned, hoping he was wrong. Kate had better taste than that dickweed, didn't she?

"Something wrong?" Cody asked.

"Yeah, my other bartender won't be here for a while, and I need to find Jessie."

Cody shook his head. "No, I'll go. There's no reason to believe Marcus will return today."

"Thank you. Call me when you find her, okay?"

"Will do."

Chapter Twenty-Two

As Jessie washed her hands in the pub bathroom, she stared at herself in the mirror. Thinking of her morning with Zach, everything they'd done in her motel room, had her body flushed with warmth.

Being with him this morning had been so different than when they were at her condo. The way he slowed down and maintained eye contact was so intimate, like he could see her soul. She'd never felt so exposed with anyone. She never opened herself up like that to Dillon. But she was, without a doubt, falling for Zach.

After splashing water on her face, she stepped out of the bathroom. Beautiful photographs hung on the walls, showcasing scenes from the forests of the Pacific Northwest. She'd missed all the green when she was in Virginia. It was nice there, but it wasn't the same.

The image that grabbed her attention was called "The Hall of Mosses". Zach had never mentioned hiking, but that was what these photos reminded her of.

She pulled her eyes away from the pictures and kept walking. Just as she was about to round the corner and enter the main area, the front door opened with a creak. She stepped back.

"Hey, you remember our old friends the Bannons, right?" The voice was familiar. Marcus Beyers.

Why the hell are the Bannons here? Blaese said they were going to Davenport. Was he trying to ensure I wouldn't be here for this?

Straining to hear better, she wanted to know who Marcus was talking to about the Bannons. Had he brought someone else with him?

She stood at the edge of the hall and listened as Zach responded.

How does he know they're away from home? How the hell does he know who they are?

Something wasn't adding up. He seemed to have more information than she'd thought. But when she'd speculated that Marcus Beyers had only threatened Zach because his pub was on their delivery route, Zach hadn't corrected her.

"As I live and breathe, Jazz Murphy is alive!" a third voice she didn't recognize spoke.

Jazz Murphy? The missing Murphy son?

She wanted to bend around the corner to see who the new voice was speaking to, but she didn't have to. When Zach spoke up, saying he had no interest in the Murphy business, she knew. It was him.

She couldn't breathe. She had to get out of there.

Making her way toward the back of the building, she looked for another way out. Maybe there had been a clue in the files she missed. How the hell could she have been sleeping with Jazz Murphy and not know it?

Shit. Shit. Shit.

She had feelings for a Murphy? Why had he not told her? He should have told her. But he didn't. Why? What else could he be hiding? Her stomach rolled and nausea threatened but she took several deep breaths to calm herself. She had to get out of there and think this through.

After making her way out the back exit and around to her car, she drove as fast as she could to her motel. She ran in and grabbed her bag with the files, then got back in her car. If Zach was going to look for her, he would come here first.

During the entire drive to Davenport, she went over every word Zach had ever said to her. Had he tried to drive the investigation in the wrong direction? Is that why he'd refused to help the FBI at first?

Was that why Blaese had outed her? Did he know who Zach really was?

Zach sure as hell knew who she really was. An FBI agent investigating his family.

Pulling into Davenport, she noticed it was a lot like Fisher Springs, maybe a little bigger. It even had a hospital, which she drove by on her way to the new bar.

She parked a half-block down from her destination and then pulled the files out of her bag. The top one was the Cole Murphy file. She'd read through it and knew Cole had a son, Jazz, who disappeared.

She flipped the file over and opened it from the back. Just inside was a manila envelope containing photos she hadn't reviewed yet. *"Surveillance for Jackson Street bust. 6/29/2006"* was scrawled across the top. Ripping the envelope open, she dumped all the photos out onto the passenger seat. Then she looked through them one by one.

She recognized Marcus Beyers right away. He was skinnier and younger, but otherwise looked the same. Another one showed an older man that looked mean as hell. She knew from prior photos that was Cole Murphy.

She flipped the file back over to review the family tree again. Despite Cole's mean appearance, he was popular with women; he had at least six known kids, all with five different mothers. Five daughters and one son.

Shit. That's exactly how Zach described his family. If she'd been more familiar with this file, she would have picked up on that.

Nearing the bottom of the pile—and the end of her patience, because how had Jazz never been photographed?—she pulled up a photo with a new guy. Based on his build, he was likely a teenager. He was facing away from the camera.

That must be Jazz.

He was thin, not built anything like Zach. But based upon the date, Zach would have been a teenager. The boy was in the last few photos in her pile, two of which showed him arguing with Beyers. In one photograph, the boy was facing the camera, and there was a large, white bandage on his cheek. The moment she saw his eyes, she knew.

Nausea rolled through her. *No, it can't be.*

With each image, the boy looked more and more like a young Zach. She flipped the pile over. *"Jazz Murphy"* was written on the back of each one. The field notes stated that the boy had been sent to juvenile detention for a few months when he was seventeen. He was a known car thief. There were no other notes about him beyond that.

Jazz, what happened to you? And when did you become Zach?

A loud group of twenty-somethings walked by her car, laughing, jarring her back to reality. What she wouldn't give to feel that carefree right now. Hell, she was a twenty-something. Why was everything in her life so serious?

She watched the group walk down the sidewalk then cross to the other side. *They must be headed to the bar.*

Then she heard it. It was faint, but someone was whistling. That song.

Dillon…?

Glancing around, she spotted a shadow in the alleyway between the bar and a bail bonds business. She couldn't make out his face, but she knew it was her ex.

Goosebumps broke out all over. *No, it can't be.*

She got out of her car and walked to the alley. The man ran from her, and she gave chase. By the time she got through the alley to the next road, the man had disappeared.

Was she losing her mind or had that been Dillon?

Why would Dillon be here?

She pulled out her phone and called Carter.

"Carter."

"It's Doyle. Did you assign Harris to surveillance in Fisher Springs again?"

"I did. Why?"

Yeah, why?

"Oh, I just wanted to make sure someone has eyes there, since I'm in Davenport." She cringed, hoping Carter would buy it.

"Yep. Bases are covered. Anything else?"

"No." She ended the call and cursed herself for letting Dillon distract her from this case.

When she got back to the front of the bar, she watched a group go inside. Through the door, she saw the growing crowd. At least the crowd would help shield her from Marcus's eyes.

Stepping inside, all the seats were taken, and the place was packed. As she took in the big screens mounted on the walls, she realized everyone was there to watch the hockey game. She hoped Silas would be playing today.

I really need to call him and find out what's going on with him.

Playing pro had always been his dream. Whenever he got out on the ice, he was the happiest she'd ever seen him.

"Hey, you looking for a place to watch the game? Come join my table."

Jessie took her eyes off the television to take a peek at the man standing beside her. He was grinning and looking at her. She glanced around before figuring out that invite had been for her.

He motioned to a booth where four others were already seated. They appeared to be two couples, meaning the man had been the fifth wheel.

Then the front door opened, and Marcus came through. Behind him were two tall men who looked a little rough around the edges. Before he could spot her, Jessie turned her body to the new guy. "That would be great. Thank you."

"I'm Charles. What's your name?"

"Jacki," she said.

He led her to the table where his friends sat.

"Everyone, this is Jacki," Charles said.

"Jacki? Is that short for Jacqueline?" one of the women asked.

"No," she said as she sat down on the side that would keep her back to the door. Then she sat at an angle, tossing a glance to the bar now and again.

Charles ran through everyone's name, and she tried to appear like she was listening to him, when she was really straining to listen to Marcus.

But from here, she couldn't hear a thing. The crowd kept yelling at the television.

"Doyle, you suck!"

Jessie jerked her head toward the voice's owner, a man sitting with a group of friends. She took a couple breaths to keep her cool. When she glanced up at the nearest screen, she noticed her brother wasn't playing as well as he usually did.

"Get Doyle out of there!" the man yelled again.

"I'm afraid I have to agree with that guy," Charles said. "Something's off with Doyle."

"Give the guy a break. Maybe he's having a rough day," Jessie said. It was a reflex to defend her brother.

She snuck a quick glance over her shoulder and watched Marcus and his companions follow another man toward the back.

"Excuse me, I'll be right back," she said, standing up.

"Oh wait! Are you going to the bathroom? We'll go with you," the woman sitting on the other side of Charles said.

Shit. She needed to detach from these two as soon as possible. "Go ahead, I'll meet you there."

Before they could ask what she was doing, she walked up to the bar. The two women shrugged and continued straight to the bathroom, but Jessie turned to see Charles watching her.

"What can I get you?" the bartender asked without looking up.

Not wanting to bring attention to herself, she asked a question she was sure he'd heard a thousand times.

"Can you tell me where the bathroom is?"

"Round the corner over there." He roughly motioned to the hallway still not looking at her.

That was all she needed to give those girls a head start into the bathroom. She made her way down the hall she watched Marcus enter. The bathrooms were on the right, and as she passed the women's, she heard the two from the booth talking.

"What do you think of the new girl?"

"I don't know. She's kind of aloof. But you know Charles, he's not that particular."

They both laughed. Thankful she didn't have to try to converse with them, she focused on her surroundings, listening for Marcus.

At the end of the hall, she heard voices coming from behind a closed door.

That must be the office.

To her left, a door was ajar. She pushed it open slowly and peeked inside. It was a small room that held supplies.

She stepped in and closed the door. After finding an open spot on the wall that was likely shared with the office, she pressed her ear to it. The voices were slightly muffled, but she could still make it out.

"I told you already, I can't keep up. You said you had that other bar on board, the one in Fisher Springs."

"Relax. I just came from there. He's on board. He's family, he understands loyalty. Speaking of... you know, soon he's going to be just as busy as you are."

"Look, I appreciate the business, I really do, but having this size of a crowd all the time is drawing attention. When we first opened, we were the new, shiny thing. But I've had a couple of officers come in and ask how I stay in business with such low prices. I need to raise the prices."

"I'll think about it. You have the cash from last week?"

"Hey! What are you doing in here? Customers aren't allowed back here!"

Jessie turned her attention to the door to find the bartender.

She had to get out of there.

Pushing past him to go back into the hall, she yelled, "Sorry, just trying to find a quiet spot."

He yelled back, "Then don't come to a bar!"

"What the hell is going on?" another man asked.

She knew it was the man from the office.

"Some woman was in the supply room," the bartender said.

Once she turned the corner out of the hallway, she couldn't hear them. She bolted through the bar, heading for the door.

"Jacki!" Charles called.

She waved to him and kept going.

Once she reached her car, she jumped in and drove. She didn't slow until she was about two miles down the road. She glanced in her rear-view mirror. No one was following her.

Had they seen her? Did they recognize her?

After her adrenaline died down, she focused on what they'd said. *'He's on board.'*

She'd left Brannigan's Pub out the back after she heard the man call Zach 'Jazz'. Had he actually agreed to launder money for them after all?

She knew better than to get involved with him. She'd stayed away from men for a reason. First Dillon had lied to her, and now Zach was doing the same. How could he not have told her who he really was?

The sound of tires screeching behind her caught her attention. A light flashed in her rearview mirror. She glanced up to see a car behind her with its headlights on. She couldn't make out much, but it appeared the driver was alone. Just to make sure the car wasn't following her, she made a series of turns through town instead of getting on the highway.

But the car stayed with her.

She yanked her phone out of her pocket. "Call Carter," she commanded it.

"Calling Carter," the phone said back.

A moment later, he answered. "Carter."

"Carter, it's Doyle. I may have been compromised at Bucky's Bar, and now someone is following me around the town."

"Where are you? I'll call Agent Harris to find

you."

"Dillon?"

"Yes, he's a lot closer to you in Fisher Springs than any of us are. "

All this time, she had thought it would better for her career to not tell Carter about her past. But now, she felt she had to tell him.

"Carter, there's something I have to tell you about Dillon. We have a history."

A sudden crash on her left side caused her to lose her grip on her phone. She looked out her window to see that the car that had been following her was now beside her. And Dillon was driving.

"He's trying to run me off the road!" she screamed. She glanced down in search of her phone; it was on the passenger floorboard, and the call was still connected, thank goodness. "He's driving a black, four-door sedan."

Dillon slammed his car into hers again hard enough to force her off the road.

She held on as the car sped downhill, toward a field. A tree stump popped up in front of her, but she had no control to turn or stop. Upon impact, the car came to an abrupt stop, and her airbag exploded, forcing her head back.

"Doyle! Are you there?" Carter shouted from the phone.

Jessie tried to respond, but she couldn't get words to come out. She couldn't keep her eyes open and then everything went black.

Chapter Twenty-Three

Jessie woke with a start and sat straight up. Her surroundings were familiar. It was like a mirror version of her motel room, but it wasn't her room.

"Good morning sleepyhead."

She turned toward the voice. Dillon. He was lying next to her in the same bed.

Why the fuck was she with Dillon in a motel room? She pulled the covers around her, as if that would provide some protection. Checking, she was relieved to see she was fully clothed.

Her head was pounding.

"What the hell happened?" she asked.

"You got into some trouble in Davenport, and I saved you."

What was the last thing she remembered? She'd heard someone call Zach 'Jazz'.

That familiar punch in the gut came. He'd lied by not telling her who he really was.

"I drove to the Davenport bar for surveillance,"

she recalled slowly.

"Yes, that was what Carter said. I was doing surveillance in Fisher Springs since Blaese was unavailable."

There was no way she would have willingly gone with Dillon. She had to figure out what was going on, and fast.

"Why don't I remember more?" She rubbed her neck. "And why do my head and neck hurt?"

Dillon sat up and moved behind her, then began to softly rub her shoulders. "Does this help?"

His touch nauseated her, but her gut told her she needed to go along with him until she had a plan to get out of there.

"A little."

"From what we've been able to piece together—"

"We?" she asked.

"Yes, me and Carter. You called him while driving back to Fisher Springs and said someone was following you. He called me and ordered me to search for you. When I found you, your car was in a ditch, apparently stopped by a tree stump."

Why was none of this sounding familiar?

"As for your head, the airbag deployed and likely caused your head to jerk back, hitting the seat hard. I'm pretty sure you have a concussion."

She remembered parking in front of the bar and then… nothing.

"Hey, don't stress if you can't remember. You

need rest. It will come back in time," Dillon said softly as he continued to rub her shoulders.

"Who was following me? How did you find me?"

"We suspect it was Marcus Beyers. According to witnesses, you ran from the back of the bar, and Marcus was chasing you."

That meant she had been in the bar.

Charles. She'd met someone named Charles.

"When Carter called me, I drove toward Davenport and found your car off the side of the road. It was just luck I took the same route you did," Dillon said.

When he drove to Davenport? No, she'd heard him in the alley. He'd already been in Davenport.

"I need to get back to work." She tried to stand but felt dizzy. She sat back down.

"You need a day off to rest. I have everything here you might need." Dillon went to the mini fridge and opened it. "Your favorite, chocolate milk. I also have hard boiled eggs, cheese sticks, beef jerky, and trail mix."

He thought those were her favorite foods because she'd eat a variety of them during breaks in training. What he didn't realize was they were just easy to pack.

Well, maybe not the chocolate milk. She really did love that.

But wait, why is his minifridge stocked with my favorite foods? She knew he didn't like those things himself.

It didn't matter, she had to keep playing along.

"Thank you."

Then she remembered she'd *seen* him following her. She could have sworn it was him. But now he was acting nice and taking care of her. What was his endgame?

Dillon returned to the bed and continued to rub her shoulders.

"Where's my phone?" She glanced at both nightstands.

"I don't know. Maybe it's still in the car."

"Can I use yours?"

His hands stilled on her shoulders. "Who do you need to call?"

Why did this feel like a test?

"Carter. I need to check in and find out if there have been any developments."

Dillon jumped up. "No need. I've already spoken to him. He knows you need your rest."

The more he spoke, the more she realized she was trapped. She needed to get out of this room.

"Are you doing surveillance again today?" she asked.

Dillon smiled. "No. Carter gave me the day off to take care of you. Isn't that great?"

No! Shit. Now what?

Seemingly unaware of her panic, he continued, "We can stay here all-day, watching reality television like we used to. Remember that?"

Danielle Pays

They'd watched a few shows, but it was always after they'd had sex. That was what Dillon always wanted the moment he saw her, sex. He'd claim it had been too long since they'd been together. But it was Dillon who'd said he could only see her two days a week.

Now he was in Seattle and showing up in places she was.

Why was he doing this?

"Dillon?"

"Huh?" He had picked up the remote and was wiping it down with a disinfecting wipe. He glanced up and smiled. "Can never be too careful. They say the remotes in hotel rooms have the most germs."

Ah yes, how could she forget he was a germophobe? That was his explanation for why they only met up at her place. He had to have his bedding cleaned in just the right way. And that was why she couldn't stay the night at his place—he didn't let anyone in.

God, how could she have been so naive? If he were a true germophobe, he wouldn't have been willing to be in her bed.

"Why did you transfer to Seattle?" she asked trying to sound casual.

He stopped wiping the remote. His jaw ticked, and he tossed the wipe into the garbage a bit too hard. After a moment, she wondered if he was going to answer.

Finally, he said, "One of my students told my

220

boss we were having a relationship, and I was given the choice to transfer or resign. It had to happen fast, and Seattle had an opening."

Fortunately, he turned to the fridge, so she had a moment to school her features.

He was lying. He'd told Carter and Blaese he moved for his girlfriend. And now she was in his motel room with him with no phone.

She wasn't stupid. She knew he wouldn't let her leave. But why? What did he want?

"Here, you should eat." He placed a small carton of chocolate milk on the nightstand and handed her the bag of trail mix.

"Thank you." She opened the milk and took several swigs. She was hit with a sudden wave of nausea and had to take several deep breaths.

"You alright?" Dillon asked.

"I think I should wait on the food."

"Are you up for watching television?"

He turned it on, but trying to focus on it made her head hurt.

"No. I think I need to rest."

He turned the television off and sat in a chair near the door. Jessie laid down and closed her eyes.

"Jessie, do you ever regret our breakup?"

Her eyes popped open. Dillon was staring at her with an intensity she was not used to.

How the hell was she supposed to answer that? *'No, Dillon, I never regretted the breakup. I regretted ever dating you. You hurt me, and now I can't trust another man.'* She couldn't say that.

"Do you?" she deflected instead.

He leaned back in his chair and rubbed his eyes. "I do. I'm so sorry I wasn't fully committed to you. This will sound cliché, but I really didn't know what I had until you were gone."

She had no idea what to say. She certainly didn't want to encourage him, but she was trapped and didn't want to anger him either.

He took her silence as permission to keep talking. "I was thinking, now that we are both in the same town, we could give it another shot. But then I saw you with that man from the bar," his voice grew angrier with each word. "The way you looked at him in the park... You know, you used to look at me that way."

In the park? What the fuck? He'd been watching her since then? How the hell was he getting any work done if he spent his days watching her?

"But now that you know who he really is, you're done with him, right?" Dillon almost pleaded.

"Who he really is?" she asked.

How could Dillon know? She'd only just found out herself.

"Yeah, a damn Murphy," he spat. "He's probably been using you this entire time. That's how they've been able to keep one step ahead of the FBI. It all makes sense, doesn't it?"

"I only figured out who he was yesterday. I haven't had time to think it through."

A loud crack made her jump.

"Dammit." Dillon jumped up and stomped to the sink, something blue dripping off his hand.

While he was washing up, she glanced to the table, where he was sitting. He'd broken a pen in two.

"What is there to think about?" he demanded. "He's part of the Murphy family. Marcus is too, and he appears to be heading up the whole operation. It's clear your boyfriend is guilty. So unless you want to lose your job, you'll cut off all contact with him."

She narrowed her eyes. "What do you mean lose my job?"

Dillon smiled and sat back in the chair. "You can't very well date a suspect, can you? At least before, you didn't know. That was fine. But now that you do... Carter is very by-the-book."

There was no point in arguing. She'd had the same thoughts, that Zach could be involved and that he'd lied to her. She wasn't going to get any answers from Dillon. Plus, she needed to appease him.

"You're right. I'm going to rest now."

If he thought she was asleep, maybe he'd stop talking to her or expecting answers.

"Good. I'm glad we are on the same page. Get some rest. When you wake, we can discuss us." He walked over to the bed and planted a small kiss on her head. "Sweet dreams, my love."

Just get through the day. Hour by hour.

That was what she was trained to do, and that was how she was going to get through this.

Chapter Twenty-Four

"Where the fuck is she?" Zach shouted inside his truck.

He'd already been by Jessie's motel room. Since he'd been running the manager a tab for years at his pub, the man had agreed to do a safety check when Zach asked. That got both of them into her room, where he discovered her things.

She hadn't left town, but her car was gone, and her phone went straight to voicemail.

Now Zach was waiting to hear from Cody as to whether Jessie's boss had heard from her.

"Dammit!" He slammed his hand against the dashboard. As much as he hoped she was simply avoiding him, his gut said otherwise.

His phone rang beside him, and he grabbed it. "Hello?"

"Zach, it's Cody. Apparently, Jessie called her boss, Carter, while on the road. She said someone was following her. Carter said he heard a loud bang and then silence. He sent another agent to look for her, but that agent, Dillon Harris, stated he didn't find her. I'm not familiar with him. He's fairly new to the Seattle office."

"Fucking Marcus must have gotten to her. Do you have any idea where he's staying?" Zach asked.

"Zach, calm down and let me handle this. You need to open your pub soon."

Open his pub? He couldn't even think straight.

"I'm afraid I can't do that until I find her."

"I'm on my way to Davenport, and I'm checking the roads she likely drove. I need you to go home and — What's that?"

Zach sat up straighter. "What's what?"

"I think I just found Jessie's car. I'll call you back."

"Where are you?" He asked. The desperation in his voice clear.

Cody had already hung up.

"Fuck!"

He was going to go stir-crazy if he had to wait another moment. But what choice did he have?

Ten minutes later, Zach was halfway to Davenport when Cody called back.

"What did you find?" *Please let her be all right.*

"Her car is in a ditch. It hit a stump, and the driver's airbag deployed. She's not here, though. But I did find her phone and FBI badge on the passenger floorboard."

She's not in her car, and she doesn't have her phone or her badge? "Marcus took her. If anything happens to her, I'll kill him."

"I'm going to see him next."

"Wait. You know where he is?" he probed.

"Agent Blaese gave me some idea. And no, you're not coming with me."

Zach pulled off to the side of the road. "And exactly what the hell am I supposed to do?"

"Go home or to the pub, wherever she would most likely show up if she could."

If she could. Those were the key words.

"I'll call you as soon as I know something," Cody promised.

All this time, he'd thought Jessie was avoiding him, but it turned out Marcus likely had her. But why now? Marcus hadn't sent a delivery yet, so Zach hadn't had a chance to accept or refuse.

Unless he wanted her as leverage.

Zach texted Gina, asking for Bethany's number. Of course Gina didn't simply text back, she called.

"Why do you want her number? You thinking of getting back in touch?"

Zach sighed. "Marcus kidnapped my girlfriend."

"What the fuck is going on?" Gina demanded.

"Too much."

"You outed yourself? After fourteen years?" she asked incredulously. "Why the hell would you do that?"

"I didn't out myself so much as Marcus found me. He thought I'd jump back into the business, so

226

when I said no, he took Jessie."

"Shit. Need me to help?"

No one would know from looking at her, because she was small, but Gina was a badass bounty hunter that could probably take down a man faster than Jessie. She had a black belt in Jiu Jitsu; that was why Zach didn't worry about her when she chased after a skip. Of course, she chose some of the worst to go after. *'They pay the best,'* she would always say.

"No. The FBI is involved," he told her. "But I need Bethany's number to make sure Marcus doesn't do something stupid before I can get to him."

"Okay. I'll text it to you. But you call me once you know more, and if you change your mind about me helping, let me know. I'll be there as fast as I can."

"Thanks."

He ended the call, and the text with Bethany's number came through. He called her, hoping she'd be honest with him.

That was one thing he had always been able to count on in the past—Bethany was a straight-shooter.

"Bethany's phone," Marcus answered.

"Motherfucker, where is she?"

"Who the fuck is this?"

"Jazz." He flinched, hearing himself say that name. "Where's Jessie?"

"Who?"

"The FBI agent!"

Marcus laughed. "You mean your girlfriend? I don't know, but I'm looking for her. She came to

Bucky's Bar, trying to overhear something she shouldn't."

"Are you saying she's not with you?"

"That's what I'm saying. But wait. How do you have Bethany's number?"

"I got it from Gina."

"You sure about that? Maybe Bethany knew you were alive… She's been keeping secrets from me, I can tell."

"Yeah ask Gina if you don't believe me. I've got other issues to deal with." Zach ended the call.

If Marcus didn't have her, then who did? Maybe some kind stranger picked her up and brought her to the hospital.

After verifying she wasn't at the hospital and seeing no new messages on his phone, Zach decided to drive back to her motel and check again. Maybe there was something he'd missed.

As he was driving down Main Street, the car in front of him stopped suddenly, and a man in a suit ran across the street, into the diner. That was not something seen every day. Hell, he looked like another FBI agent. He'd have to ask Kate what that was all about.

After parking, he went to Jessie's room and knocked on her door. Suddenly, the door next to hers opened, and a woman ran out. No, *Jessie* ran out.

"Macushla?"

She stopped and turned, eyes wide. "Zach?" She had a cut on her forehead, and dried blood in her hair.

"I thought this was your room," he said, confused.

"It is. I have to go. He'll be back any minute."

"Who?"

"My crazy ex."

If that man so much as hurts her…

He didn't have time to think about that now. They needed to leave.

He grabbed her hand. "I've got my truck. Let's go."

He helped her into the passenger side, then got into the driver's seat and took off down the road.

After several blocks, it was clear Jessie wasn't going to be forthcoming with information.

"What happened?" he asked.

Her voice shook. "He tried to drug me, gave me pills to help me sleep. He only left because he thinks I swallowed them. He said he was going to grab us some lunch."

"What will happen when he realizes you're gone?"

Jessie shook her head. "I'm not sure. But he's been following me for a while. He saw us together at the park that day."

"He's stalking you?"

"Yes. And he knows who you are. He probably knows where you live too. We can't go there."

"I know where we can go."

He turned down the familiar streets until they arrived at Harmony's apartment building.

She practically lived with Chase, staying over every night, so when she'd heard Jessie was staying in a motel, she'd offered her apartment. Anything to get Zach matched up. But now he was thankful for the offer.

Once parked, he turned in his seat to face Jessie. She was trembling. He put his arm around her, but she stiffened. He pulled it back.

"What happened?"

She stared out the window. "I don't know. I remember going to Davenport, but I don't remember much after that. Dillon told me what happened, but my gut says he's lying. I swear I saw him following me."

"Who exactly is Dillon?"

"I told you. My crazy ex. I found out he transferred to Seattle after I broke it off. Then he managed to get me transferred here, too. I thought I saw him watching me a few times, but when I would look again, he'd be gone. I thought I was paranoid."

"An agent?"

"Yes."

"I'm pretty sure I saw an agent running into the diner. Wait, you said Dillon… Dillon Harris?"

Her eyes swept to his. "How did you know?"

"You aren't paranoid. Cody found out that

Agent Harris was sent to locate you, but when Cody checked in, Harris reported he couldn't find you. I think he ran you off the road. And if you've lost your memory, you might have a concussion. We can stay here for now until you feel better."

"Where is here?"

"A friend's apartment."

Her gaze turned down. "One of your girlfriends'?"

He chuckled. "No, it's Harmony's, Chase's girlfriend. She works in the diner. She's practically living with him. She actually offered this place to you, but I hadn't had a chance to tell you yet. Let's go inside."

"Wait. I'm not sure that's such a good idea."

"Why not?"

"You're Jazz Murphy."

Chapter Twenty-Five

Neither of them had spoken the entire time he'd cleaned and bandaged her cut. Now she was lying on the couch, and he was pacing the floor, trying to figure out where to start.

"You lied to me," she spoke softly.

He turned to her.

"You purposely didn't tell me who you were." She pinned him with her gaze. "Are you part of the operation? Is that why you lied? By getting to know me, you could stay a step ahead of the FBI?"

He fisted his hands, trying to control his anger before he spoke. "Are we back to this? You think I'm a criminal?"

She looked away. "That's just it. I don't know what to think of you. I thought I knew you, and then I find out you're someone else."

When he heard her sniffle, he moved to her side and sat on the coffee table. "No, I'm not someone else. I'm exactly who you think I am. I was always myself with you. What you heard in the pub was just a name. A name I abandoned a long time ago. It was the only way I could get away from them."

"Why did you want to get away from them? Weren't you a part of the Murphy family car-stealing operation?"

"Not by choice."

He stood and paced again. Memories of his father flooded him. Memories he had never wanted to remember again.

"Explain to me what happened. Make me understand. Please," she said.

He turned to her again.

The pain in her eyes was his fault, and he hated it. He cared about this woman. The only way they could ever be together was if he told her everything, all the dark, ugly truths. He just had to hope like hell she'd still wanted him.

"I grew up with my mom," he began. "I didn't really know my dad, and my mom wouldn't tell me much. But when I was fourteen, my dad showed up and said I would be living with him for the summer. I went willingly because I thought my mother was too strict."

Jessie sat up and patted the couch next to her.

Zach took a seat. "The summer turned into four years. He wouldn't let me go home."

"How did he keep you there? You seem a bit rebellious."

Zach laughed. His father had knocked his

rebellion out of him that first week. "When I told him I didn't like what we were doing, and I wanted to go home, he laughed. Then he said if I tried to leave, he'd tell my mom I was a worthless piece of crap and stealing cars."

He could remember the conversation clearly.

"But I was a punk, and his words didn't scare me. So I told him to tell her." He rubbed his scruff. "Then he changed his threat. He said he'd hurt her if I didn't stay with him and contribute to 'the family business'."

"I'm so sorry."

"I knew he would do it. At that point, he'd already slapped me around enough, I knew he'd keep his word in that regard."

Zach shook his head. "But then I got caught on a job. My dad was furious when they impounded the car I was trying to steal. It was a Porsche. He said I'd lost him a lot of money. I was more pissed about getting sent to juvie. When I got out, I thought my days of stealing cars were over — they weren't. He insisted I steal a car the very day I got out. He said I had to make up for that Porsche."

Jessie pulled the blanket tighter around her. He could feel her eyes on him, but he couldn't look at her. Not for the next part.

He took a breath. "I refused his order. Unfortunately, I did it in front of everyone. My father wasn't used to anyone saying no to him, so he took out his pocketknife and before I knew what he was doing, he'd sliced my face." He pointed to the scar.

"Your dad cut you?"

"Yeah, he said some stuff about me being a pretty boy and thinking I was too good to be a Murphy. I'll spare you the details. But he said if I refused again, he'd keep on cutting."

His eyes grew wet as he remembered the fear and hatred he'd felt.

"That's why you called it a manmade dimple?" she asked gently.

He nodded. "After that, I stole more cars. But a month later, my father dropped dead. They said it was a heart attack."

"They said? You don't believe it?"

Zach shrugged. "He was thirty-nine. It's possible. But a lot of people hated him."

"Then you were free?"

Zach laughed. "That's just it. I wasn't. My father had business associates counting on his income. They came up to me at the funeral and made it clear they expected me to carry on in my dad's footsteps."

"You were trapped."

He nodded. "A week after the funeral, I turned eighteen. Marcus and Bethany came to me and said it was time to get the business going again. But I knew if I was caught at that point, I wouldn't be going to juvie. I'd do hard time."

He turned to her. "You have to understand, I never wanted any part of that life. So I left early the next morning. I drove down south of Boise and stayed with an old friend just long enough to change my name. Then I started to drive to the coast. I didn't make it very far, though."

"Toppenish," Jessie said.

Zach raised his eyebrows. "How did you know that?"

"From the background check."

"You said you ran that check because you saw that truck outside my pub… Is that the only reason? Or did you suspect who I was?"

"No, I ran the check because if there was any chance you were involved and we were dating, I could lose my job. Yes, when I heard you were actually Jazz, I wondered if you were in on it, and if you'd been lying to me. But now that the shock has worn off, I know deep down you could never do that. The man I know couldn't be a part of this."

She took his hand in hers, and his anger cooled. It was nearly impossible to stay mad when he was just grateful she was still there.

He turned and took her into his arms, holding her tight. "I'm sorry I didn't tell you, but I'd put Jazz behind me a long time ago."

"Was Jazz your legal name? You said you had it changed."

"Jazz was a nickname. My legal name was James Zachary Murphy."

"Zachary. Where did you get Brannigan?"

He kissed the top of her head. "It was my grandmother's maiden name. I wanted to embrace my

Irish heritage."

Holding her in his arms felt right. They'd let so much come between them, but now he was sure this was where he was supposed to be.

"I'm hungry," he said. "How about I order a pizza? We are actually close enough to Timmy's that he'll deliver."

"Sounds great. I'd like to take a shower, if that's all right." She rose from the couch and glanced around.

"Of course. Let me show you the bathroom."

★ ★ ★

By the time she came out of the shower, Zach had everything ready for dinner. He was about to open a bottle of wine, but then he remembered she had a concussion, so he grabbed two cups of water instead.

"You set the table?" she asked.

"I did. Maybe we can call this a date."

She laughed. "Sure. Hey, so I was thinking about everything you told me, and I have a question."

"Sure." He pulled a couple of slices of pizza from the box and set them on their plates.

"Why Toppenish?" She took a bite while watching him.

He chuckled. "Because I got a flat tire on the highway there and had no spare."

"Really?"

"Really. A guy pulled over to help me. He took

me back to his family's house, and everything clicked. It felt right being there. I helped out on their farm, and they let me stay. I ended up becoming really good friends with that guy. We used to brew beer, but then he took it a step further, and now owns his own brewery and grows some of the most sought-after hops right there on his farm."

He took a bite of his pizza as he remembered the first time he saw the farm. It was an oasis in the middle of what looked like a desert.

"Wow. That sounds… free."

"It does." He grabbed another slice. "Want another?" He nodded toward the box.

"Not yet. Why didn't you stay there?"

"Honestly? It was too damn hot in the summer."

She laughed.

"One day, I took a ride on my motorcycle and came over the mountain into Fisher Springs. I realized how much milder the weather is on this side of the mountains. Then I drove by the pub, and it had a for sale sign in the window. I had never seen a pub for sale before, so I talked to the owner. Then I bought the place."

"What about your friend? Does he ever come to visit?"

Zach let out a breath. "He hasn't in a while. He keeps growing his business and gets busier with every year. But I go see him now and again. I serve a lot of his beers in the pub. You should try one when you're feeling better. They're a lot better than what I've seen you drink."

"I will. Your friend sounds cool."

He hadn't thought about Liam in a while. He hadn't seen him since the previous summer. But now talking about him, he felt nostalgic.

After they'd finished the pizza, they both sank back onto the couch.

"Feeling better?" he asked.

"Yes, thank you."

"Good, because now I want to know more about this ex and why he was holding you against your will."

"It's a long story, but what's important is that I'm okay now."

He closed his eyes and braced for her answer to his next question. "Did he—"

"No, he let me sleep and he had the mini fridge packed with snacks. Though he ate most of those. Like I said earlier, he gave me some pills, claimed they were for my headache. He said after I took them, he'd go get some lunch."

Thank god. He looked at her curiously. "What did you do with the pills?"

She smiled. "I hid them in my bra. But I was certain they were sleeping pills, so I pretended to fall asleep."

"And then he left?"

She nodded. "I waited until I heard a car start and leave. Then I put on my shoes, searched for my phone—which I never found—and ran out of there. That's when you found me."

"He's probably looking for you."

"I'm sure he is."

"Why did you two break up?"

She squirmed in his arms.

"If you don't want to talk about it, I'll understand."

"No, you opened up to me. I can do the same. Besides, I understand why you want to know."

She took a breath to calm her nerves. "I met Dillon during training in Virginia, and we started dating. I was naive and thought things were good, but then I discovered he was cheating on me. So I ended it. That was last year. Then I transferred here, and discovered Dillon had been working in the Seattle office for months. I only recently learned he had pushed for my transfer to get approved."

"You mean he pushed for it after you had broken up?"

"Yes. I didn't want to tell my boss about our past, but when I realized Dillon was trying to run me off the road, I was already on the phone with Carter, and I tried to tell him." Her eyes widened. "I remember the accident and how I ended up in Dillon's hotel room." She shuddered. "God, I need to call Carter. I think Blaese might be dirty, too. What a mess." Jessie glanced around. "And I don't have a phone."

He stroked her cheek. "Rest tonight. We can

deal with all of this tomorrow. Okay?"

"Okay."

They held each other on the couch until he heard her breathing slow. When he was sure she was asleep, Zach carried her to the bed and tucked her in. He debated whether he should sleep on the couch, but decided if she woke in the night confused, it would be best if he were next to her.

He climbed in beside her and fell asleep.

Chapter Twenty-Six

Jessie woke with a start.

"You all right?" Zach asked from behind her.

She turned to find him lying next to her; his arm had been around her waist.

"I am."

That sexy smile of his was enough to keep her in bed. That, and the delicious feel of being pressed up against him. She scooted back to get even closer, settling in so her ass was nestled against his groin.

"Jessie," his voice was gravelly, "as much as I want to attack you right now, you have a concussion. You need to take it easy."

"I'm not going to break." Jessie scoffed and sat up, and a searing pain shot through her head. "Shit." She lay back down. "Maybe you're right."

"Trust me, I want you, but I did some research. You need to rest and heal for a couple of weeks."

"A couple of weeks?" She didn't have time to rest. "Wait. You researched when we could have sex?"

He shrugged. "I'm not going to deny that I want you. But you need to heal first."

That was the sweetest thing.

"But wait, a couple of weeks for sex, or for everything? Because I can't keep missing work. I've already missed too much."

Zach pulled her into his arms. "Don't worry, Macushla. Cody spoke with your boss and explained what happened. Carter is fully aware you need time off right now."

Jessie relaxed into Zach's arms. "Explained? Did he mention Dillon?"

"He did. According to your boss, Dillon is missing."

She tried to sit up again, but he held her tightly. "Missing?" She frowned. "He has a room at the motel."

"Apparently, he was the man I saw running into the diner yesterday. According to Kate, he picked up two lunches and left. Cody went to his room, and a maid was cleaning it. She said no one was in that room. Dillon left."

She knew very well that wasn't true. "He's looking for me," she said.

"Yes, he likely is." Zach ran his hand up and down her back in soothing strokes.

She turned and snuggled into his chest. He smelled like fresh soap with a hint of peppermint.

"Did you shower and brush your teeth?"

He chuckled. "I did. I also called Gina back. Then I climbed back into bed with you."

"What time is it?"

"Just after noon. You need a lot of sleep right now."

She nodded.

A pounding at the door made her jump.

"Do you think Dillon found us?" she asked.

Zach hopped out of bed and put his jeans on.

Jessie couldn't help but stare. The man had more muscles than she'd ever seen in real life, and his tattoos added an element of danger and sexiness she couldn't resist.

"It's Cody. He said he would bring your phone by. Also, he's going to stay here with you today. I need to open the pub, but Ariel agreed to come in later and close, so I'll be back soon. In the meantime, stay here with Cody."

She continued to stare.

"Hey, I know that look. Two weeks."

Jessie laughed. "All right, we'll wait. But you can't just keep me locked up here. I think you forget who you're talking to. I've been trained to kill a man five different ways."

She had a point.

"But you have a concussion," he reminded her, "and apparently, a possible psycho looking for you. Please, stay here? For me? You need rest. Just sleep as much as you can. I read that helps too."

"Okay, but I'm calling Carter to discuss Dillon."

"Deal." He left the room to let Cody in.

When she pulled her eyes from where his

tempting form had been, Jessie noticed a robe laying across the bed. She got up carefully, put it on and slowly walked out to the living room.

"It's all clear. No one followed me," Cody said as she walked in. "Here's your phone and a charger. I picked one up in case you didn't have one." He handed the items to her.

"Thank you."

Zach turned to Cody. "I'll be back in a few. Call me if anything comes up."

"Will do."

Then he turned to Jessie. "Stay here."

"Yes, sir!" She stood up on her tiptoes to give him a kiss—just an innocent peck, since Cody was there.

After Zach left, she sank onto the couch. Her head hurt more than she wanted to admit, and she was feeling a bit dizzy.

"How are you feeling?" Cody asked.

"I've been better." She gave him a weak smile.

"Why don't you take a nap while your phone charges?"

"Okay." She was too tired to argue.

Damn, Zach had been right. She needed rest. She wouldn't be able to deal with Dillon in her current condition.

She made her way back to the bedroom and plugged in her phone then curled up in bed.

When she woke a couple hours later, her phone was charged enough to call Carter.

"Doyle? What the hell happened? You called, it sounded like some car hit yours, and then nothing. Agent Harris said he searched everywhere and couldn't find you. Then I get a call from a man named Cody who said Dillon took you to a motel room against your will?"

Her head was pounding. Telling her boss about the relationship she had with Dillon was something she hoped she'd never have to do.

"Yes, it's true. I have a history with Dillon."

"You mentioned that when you called before your accident."

Jessie took a deep breath and filled him in. Since he was her boss, she gave him the short version, just the facts. Then she had to tell him the events of the last twenty-four hours.

"Dillon was outside Bucky's Bar, in an alley. I heard him whistling, but when I followed him, I lost him. I thought maybe I was losing my mind. But then when I woke up in the motel room, I knew he'd followed me. And he wouldn't let me leave. He said he'd told you I was there and that I needed the rest."

"That's a lie. Agent Harris was assigned to do surveillance in Fisher Springs because Blaese wasn't available. Then after your call, I sent him to locate you. The last I heard from him was yesterday when he said he hadn't been able to find you. He hasn't answered his phone since."

A wave of nausea hit her, so she lay back down on the bed.

"I wish I had known about Harris sooner," Carter said. "He was out looking for you because I ordered him to. I'm sorry about that. As soon as he answers his phone, I'll tell him to return to Seattle. I don't want him to know we've talked until I can locate him. Understand?"

"Yes."

"In the meantime, you have the next few days off to rest and heal. I had Blaese drive to Davenport before his surveillance shift to take photos of your car. Based on the scratch marks on the side of the car, it was clear you were run off the road."

"Carter, there's more. About Blaese... I saw him in a car with Bethany Murphy. I don't know what they said, but it looked like it got heated."

"Dammit."

"I'm sorry, I don't mean to be the bearer of all bad news."

Shit, she felt her chance at that promotion slipping away.

"No, don't be sorry. Bethany is the informant, but she only agreed if no one else knew. She was worried there might be a leak at the FBI."

Jessie was willing to bet that leak was Blaese. "Yeah, after seeing Bethany in his car, I was pretty sure she was the informant."

"Doyle, if Marcus Beyers or any of the Bannon family find out, they'll kill her. The fact she's a Murphy won't save her."

"Who all knows?" *Does Zach?*

"Just me and Blaese. And, well, now you."

"Why would she turn on her husband?"

"Because he's an abusive shithead. At least, that's what she told us. She said she wants to get her kids out of the family business, but she can't as long as Marcus is around."

Well, that she didn't expect. That was good, though, if she was on their side. That also explained the meeting she saw between Blaese and Bethany. Although it didn't explain the kiss… But Blaese did end it.

Please don't let Blaese be crooked.

She had too much to deal with as it was. Even if he was on the straight and narrow, being involved with an informant was a big ethical issue.

Just like being involved with a Murphy. Shit.

Who was she to judge?

"Why does Bethany think there is a leak at the FBI?" she asked.

"No idea. I've been looking into that but haven't found anything yet. I think she's paranoid."

She wondered what he meant by 'looking into it,' but knew he wouldn't tell her even if she asked.

She didn't have time to dwell on it before he spoke again.

"Doyle, take the next few days off. That's an order. I'll get Harris to Seattle, then I'll talk to Blaese. If he needs another agent, I'll send someone else."

"Okay, thank you."

Carter ended the call before she could say

anything more.

She sat up, trying to ignore her headache, and walked out of the bedroom to find Cody. "You told Blaese about my car?"

The man narrowed his eyes. "Of course I did. A crime had been committed, he needed to know. We thought Marcus had you."

A memory of Marcus chasing her out of Bucky's Bar flashed in her mind.

"He might be looking for me too."

"That's why you are staying put. Two psychos, I can handle. But I can't risk you going out there and ticking off any more."

She laughed. "You made a joke."

He didn't even break a smile. "I can do that."

Her stomach growled.

Cody gave her a measuring look. "Zach said there was leftover pizza in the fridge if you want it."

As if on cue, her stomach growled again.

"Yes, thank you."

He followed her to the kitchen.

"Don't worry about me," she waved him off. "I'm good here. But I'm curious, do you know Blaese well?"

Cody nodded. "I've worked with him in the past."

"Is he known to cross the line? Like, have a relationship with an informant or suspect?"

Cody raised a brow. "You mean like what you're doing?"

Damn. Guess he has an opinion on this. "Zach isn't a suspect or informant," she hedged.

The man nodded. "Fair enough. No, Blaese wouldn't do that."

Jessie stared at him. *How can he be so certain?*

As if reading her mind, he responded, "Blaese is my cousin. That's how I know him. Why are you asking about this, anyway?"

Well, shit. Family drama was the last thing she wanted to be in the middle of. She needed to redirect this conversation.

"Blaese outed me in front of Marcus at the pub last week. I don't understand why."

Cody grabbed the pizza box from the refrigerator and placed a slice on a plate. "Yeah, I was there. I remember. When I grilled him about it later, he told me he was concerned for your safety. But I'm not sure I buy that." He placed the plate in the microwave.

She bit her lip. "Why do you think he did it?"

Cody leaned against the counter. "Honestly, I don't know. But Blaese is ambitious. I don't think he liked being out in the car while you were in the pub where everything was going down."

The microwave dinged, and he pulled the plate out and put it on the table. She sat down to eat and thought about what he'd said.

Blaese might be ambitious, but what he'd done wasn't right.

After she finished the pizza, Cody took her plate away.

"You should try to sleep," he said. "A buddy of mine had a concussion recently. He slept fourteen hours a day for a while. Now he's fine."

Fourteen hours a day?

No, that wasn't going to work.

Chapter Twenty-Seven

Apparently, she did need to sleep fourteen hours a day. Now after several days of sleeping then sitting in the apartment, doing nearly nothing, Jessie was going out of her mind. Her head still hurt, but the dizziness was gone.

The nights with Zach were great. They just held each other in bed, and she slept so soundly in his arms. But then during the days, he had to go to the pub, and she was left bored.

After turning on the recap of her brother's hockey game, she discovered he hadn't played. Between that and the distracted way he was playing when she saw him in the bar, she knew something was wrong.

With all the time on her hands, she did something she had been meaning to for days. She called Silas.

He picked up immediately.

"What's wrong?" he asked.

She laughed. "Nothing's wrong. Can't I call my brother?"

After a moment of silence, he spoke. "My workaholic sister is calling me in the middle of a workday. What's going on?"

"Fine. I have a concussion and have been ordered to rest."

"Shit. How bad it is? What happened?"

He practically got beaten up for a living, and he was worried about her? She resisted the urge to roll her eyes.

"I'm fine. It was work related. But I want to know what's going on with you. Why did you miss your last game?"

"I'm not sure you do."

"Silas."

"It's Hunter. He was having some trouble at school, so the coach let me take a few personal days."

"What the hell is going on with Hunter?"

"Nothing. I handled it. Don't mention it to him. Promise?"

Dammit. He'd better not be hiding anything serious from me. "Promise," she grumbled.

"Okay. I have to go to practice. You rest up and check in with me tomorrow. I want to make sure you aren't pushing yourself."

"Okay, *Dad.*"

He chuckled.

"Bye, sis."

"Bye, Silas."

Well, she felt better knowing Silas wasn't doing something to throw his career away. He'd worked hard to get where he was, but he did have a temper that sometimes got him into trouble.

She checked the time on her phone; the call had only taken a minute, and she was still bored out of her mind. Maybe Carter needed her after all. It was worth a shot to ask.

"Carter," he answered.

"It's Doyle. I'm feeling better—"

"No. You need a couple more days at least."

"With all due respect, sir, how would you know?"

"Last year, another agent got a concussion from an explosion."

"An explosion? That sounds a lot more serious than a minor car accident."

"After a few days, he said he was fine. Turns out, he wasn't. He got dizzy during a confrontation, and now he's dead."

Well, shit.

"That's horrible."

"It is. So don't ask me for permission to go out in the field."

"I won't, but can you at least tell me what's going on? Where's Dillon? Where's Marcus?"

"Dillon is MIA. I've left messages, and he hasn't returned them. I'm sorry. I understand you are safe and there is someone there to protect you? Stay put. As for Marcus, he's taking a delivery containing money to

Brannigan's Pub today. Blaese will be doing surveillance, and there are still listening devices in place in the pub. We are all set."

"Today?" Why didn't Zach tell her? *Because he's trying to protect me too. Dammit!*

Why the hell were all these men trying to protect her? Couldn't they see she was perfectly capable of taking care of herself?

"Yes, today. Rest up, Doyle. We can talk again in a few days." Again, he hung up before she could say anything more.

That was a really annoying trait of his.

When her phone buzzed a moment later, she hoped maybe Carter had more to say.

But it was a text from an unknown number.

Unknown Number: *Princess, come out, come out wherever you are, or your boyfriend is dead.*

A photo came through. It was the front of Brannigan's Pub.

Princess. Dillon's pet name for her.

Dillon was at the pub. He was close to Zach.

Cody would be there; he needed to know Zach was in danger.

Thank god Zach programmed Cody's number into my phone!

"Hello?" he answered.

"Cody, it's Jessie. Dillon just texted me a really creepy message and sent a photo of the front of the pub. He's outside, and he's threatening to kill Zach if I don't show up."

"Listen to me. Whatever you do, do not leave the apartment. I can protect Zach. But Marcus is about to show up, do not come down here. It's too dangerous." Cody hung up.

What the fuck was wrong with all of these guys? She was tired of them trying to run her life.

Cody was too busy looking for Marcus; how the hell could he protect Zach if Dillon snuck in and shot him before they even knew he was in the pub? Neither Cody nor Zach even knew what he looked like. Plus, Dillon was a trained FBI agent.

But she knew exactly what skills he was trained with. He had been her instructor after all. She had no choice but to stop him.

Fortunately, Harmony's apartment was a short walk to Main Street. From there, it was just a few blocks to the pub.

God, I wish I had my Glock. Cody had said he'd searched her car but didn't find it.

As she walked closer to the pub, she spotted Blaese's car several blocks away. Empty.

Where the fuck is he?

If Marcus was inside, she couldn't go in through the front. She'd have to use the back door.

Picking up her pace, she turned down the alley that led to the back entrance.

"Hey!" someone called behind her.

She turned. *Marcus! Shit!*

She ran toward the door, but before she got there, a large hand grabbed her shoulder and turned her around. The jarring movement made her dizzy, and she lost her footing.

"Jessie, is it? This is perfect timing! You see, my asshole brother-in-law is still trying to refuse my business."

This man didn't make sense to her. "Why the hell do you keep showing up here? You know there are two FBI agents hanging around," she asked, confused.

Marcus grinned then jerked her up to her feet, and she held back her whimper. Her head was now pounding, and her neck hurt too.

"None of your business. Let's go," he ordered.

She tried to untangle herself from him, but she felt like she was moving in slow motion.

"Bitch, stop fighting me!" Marcus shouted, and then it felt like her eye exploded.

When she opened her eyes, she winced; her head hurt even more, if that was possible. Her hands wouldn't move, they were pinned behind her back.

She was sitting in a chair in what appeared to be a warehouse. There were boxes everywhere. Liquor boxes.

What the hell? How long have I been out?

The sound of feet shuffling behind her made her jump. She tried to turn to see who was coming toward her, but her sore neck wouldn't obey.

"Good. You're awake. I was wondering if you would wake up. I need you to talk to Zach so that he takes me more seriously."

"No."

A hand hit her face before she saw it coming.

"You will not fuck up my plan. My brother-in-law will pay for what he's done. God, look at him living freely all these years. Who the fuck does he think he is?"

She knew Marcus was setting Zach up for something, but what? She needed to keep him talking.

"He just wants to live his life. Just leave him alone," she said.

Marcus leaned over her. "And he has you ready to defend him. You're very pretty, you know that? I see why he likes you." He stroked her hair and leaned his face down close to hers.

She turned away.

"Aw, not going to give me the time of day? Is that how it is?"

He reached for his back pocket, and then a shot rang out.

Jessie tried to shrink into herself, but it did no good, she was a sitting target. However, she didn't feel like she'd been shot. Then her eyes were drawn to Marcus's chest as his shirt turned from gray to red. Blood.

She watched as Marcus fell to his knees. Her heart was beating so hard, it dimmed her hearing. Where was the gunman?

"Who the fuck are you?" Marcus barely got out.

His surprise meant it couldn't be a Bannon brother. Who, then?

There was no reply.

Marcus collapsed to the ground.

Jessie tried to calm her breathing while taking in her surroundings. In front of her, Marcus was likely dead, and he didn't appear to have any obvious weapons. Behind her was someone with a gun and a possible grudge against Marcus. And she was tied to a chair and had no weapons—but her feet weren't tied. She could push back or kick.

The footsteps behind her grew louder. Still, whoever it was didn't speak.

She tried again to turn, but still no luck. *Damn sore neck.*

"You know, if you hadn't run from me, you wouldn't be in this pile of shit."

Jessie froze. "Dillon?"

He stepped into her line of vision. "I'm going to free you, and you're coming with me."

"You killed Marcus," she said cautiously.

"He was going to kill you. Now we have to go. Understood?"

She nodded reluctantly. Arguing with him would not be in her best interest right now. Not until she could figure out how to get his gun or get away.

He stepped behind her, and she felt her hands get released from their bonds.

"Come on, we need to go. There are two more

men at the other end, up by the gate, and they likely heard the gunshot." Dillon took her hand and practically dragged her as he ran.

She tried to keep up, but it took all she had.

Once they were outside the warehouse, Dillon stopped running. He edged them to the corner and peered around. "Come on," he ordered.

They slowly walked along the length of the warehouse. A loud door slammed inside, making her jump.

"What the fuck happened here?" someone shouted from inside the building. His voice echoed.

"Where's the woman?" another familiar voice asked.

Dillon was pulling her along faster now.

"Look, she must have gone that way," the first guy said.

The sound of heavy footsteps running echoed through the warehouse.

"We have to run *now*!" Dillon broke into a full sprint.

She kept up, despite the fact her head hurt and she was about to throw up, and they made their way to his car. As they approached, she recognized it was in the same place she had parked when she was doing surveillance here and had first spotted Marcus.

They both dove into the car, then Dillon started the engine and peeled out. The sound of gunfire as they sped away had her ducking down in her seat.

"Hold on," Dillon said as he took a corner

almost too fast.

He continued to speed down the roads until he hit the highway.

Glancing in his rearview mirror, he said, "I think we lost them."

Jessie let out a sigh of relief, but then immediately tensed. She was in a car, alone with Dillon.

"Where are we going?" she asked.

He shot her a smile. "Somewhere I can keep you safe, Princess. I'm not going to lose you again."

Chapter Twenty-Eight

Zach was antsy to get back to Jessie. Especially after what had happened with Marcus. If only Cody would check on her and confirm she was okay, but he refused to leave Zach's side.

"Marcus doesn't know where she's at. If I go there now, I'll lead him right to her," Cody explained.

He was right. Hopefully, with the way Zach had left things, Jessie would be the last thing Marcus was thinking about.

Agent Blaese walked in the door. "Great work, Zach. I was in the van and heard everything. Now we have proof Marcus and Hawthorne Distribution are behind the money-laundering scheme."

"Are you going to arrest them now?" Zach asked.

"No."

"Why the hell not?"

"This was just the first part, to get leverage. Our goal is to take down the Bannons—without their meth money, Marcus and Hawthorne Distribution would be out of business."

He shook his head. "When you refused to give him any money, I was about to shit my pants. That is not what we discussed." Blaese glanced at Cody then shot Zach a sly smile. "But I would have loved to have seen the look on Marcus's face when you said Jonny Bannon had offered you the chance to take over Marcus's role. I bet it was priceless."

"Marcus is paranoid," Zach shrugged. "Even hinting that the Bannons would rather work with me than him would have him riled up. But why aren't you following him? He's probably on his way to see them now."

Blaese smiled. "I hope he is. Our informant planted some listening devices in the warehouse for us, so we will be able to record whatever is said. According to our source, Marcus usually meets the Bannons there."

"Can you use that against him?"

Blaese shrugged. "Maybe not in court, but we can use it to get a confession."

Lauren walked in the door. "Sorry, Zach. I came as soon as I got your message. I can take over now."

"Thank you!" Zach had never been so happy to see her. "I really appreciate you helping these last few days."

Lauren had been taking over the bar, and helping Ariel close the last few nights so he could be with Jessie.

"No problem. You're lucky it's a slow week for accounting." She winked.

"That I am. Let's go," Zach told Cody.

As they walked back to the apartment, Zach was struck by the fact that Cody had not left his side since all this began. For a solid week, Cody had been focused solely on keeping Zach safe.

"Thank you for sticking by me. I want you to know it might take me a while, but I'll pay you for all your time."

Cody frowned. "Already covered."

Zach stopped. "What? How?"

Cody turned to him. "Nick. I'd do anything for him. He has my back, and I have his."

"I understand loyalty, but you've been by my side for several days. I have to pay you something for your time."

"No. You don't. Nick covered it."

Zach was about to argue, but then Cody cut him off.

"If you have a problem with that, you can take it up with Moore." He walked ahead, leaving Zach feeling like shit.

"I'm sorry," he called after him. "I didn't mean to offend you."

"I'm not offended."

Well, okay then.

Cody was a mystery to Zach. The guy was like a tomb. He never showed emotion and was always calm. Hell, *he* probably never had a tell like an accent turn on at the worst times.

Zach decided he would do as Cody said and take it up with Nick. Although, he was pretty sure Lauren had paid this bill. After inheriting all the Chanler money, she had more than she knew what to do with.

"Are all your jobs like this?" Zach asked.

"Like what?"

"You've been with me for a week and I've never seen you so much as take a personal call. Do you always block your life out on jobs?"

"It helps me stay focused. Besides, I don't have anyone to call right now."

Zach wanted to ask more but when Cody picked up his pace, he took that as a sign he was done talking.

When they got to Harmony's apartment, the door was unlocked. Cody motioned to Zach to wait outside.

A few minutes later, he returned, alone. "She's gone."

"What do you mean she's gone?"

"Jessie is not in that apartment. Neither is her phone."

"But where would she go? She doesn't have a car."

"Maybe the diner," Cody suggested, and he started to walk to the parking lot.

Zach followed him, hoping like hell he was

right. But as they approached the diner, he looked inside and saw Harmony at the counter, talking to the establishment's only customer. Which wasn't his favorite FBI agent.

"She's not in there." Zach glanced around the street while Cody entered the diner. *Where could she have gone?*

The other man returned. "She's not in the bathroom, and they haven't seen her."

"Maybe we passed her, and she went to the pub?" Zach took off at a run, heading back to the pub.

The only one there was Lauren.

"Marcus has her. I can feel it," Zach said. He called Bethany and put the call on speaker. "Bethany, where's Marcus?"

"Hey, I'm doing well, thanks for asking," she replied.

"Cut the shit. He has Jessie. Where is he?"

"I don't know, but he if he has her, he likely took her to the warehouse out on Zucker."

"I know the spot," Cody said.

"Thanks Bethany," Zach said then pocketed his phone.

They were about halfway there when Zach's phone rang.

"It says Bethany. Want me to answer it?" Cody asked from the passenger seat.

"Put it on speaker again."

Once he did, Zach called out, "What's going on?"

"He's dead!" Bethany cried. "Marcus is dead, and your bitch killed him."

Zach glanced over to Cody, who looked as confused as he felt.

"Are you sure?"

"Yes, I'm sure. She shot him."

"Bethany, where are you?"

"At the warehouse. Oh my god, what am I going to do? Marcus ran everything." She cried into the phone.

"Bethany, it will be all right. I know all the contacts. I can keep the business going," a male voice said.

"Tony? You do?" she asked.

"Hell, Marcus didn't do shit. Jonny and me have been running this thing since the beginning. We won't let anyone come after you."

"Thank you, Tony."

The call ended.

"Is it just me, or does it feel like we were set up to hear that little performance?" Zach asked Cody.

"Yeah, something about that wasn't right." Cody agreed. "Also, Jessie doesn't have her Glock. She told me she hasn't seen it since the accident. Let's go to the warehouse, but don't drive straight up to it. This could be a trap."

By the time they pulled onto Zucker, it was blocked off with a police car. Cody got out and talked to the officer. On the way back to the car, Cody answered a call.

Zach watched as Cody nodded a couple of times and then ended the call.

Cody returned. "They have the sheriff's office and the FBI up there. According to the officer, they received a 911 call from a neighbor, who reported a shot was fired. But when they arrived, someone shot at them. Now they have three dead men and one missing woman."

"Three men?"

Cody nodded. "Tony and Jonny Bannon and Marcus."

"And Jessie is still missing," Zach said.

"Yes," Cody confirmed.

Chapter Twenty-Nine

Jessie kept looking back as they sped down the highway.

"I don't think they followed us," Dillon said calmly.

Jessie turned around and relaxed into the seat. One threat down. Now she had to figure out how to get away from Dillon. For now, he was heading west, and she hoped he was taking her back to the Seattle office. But when he turned to go north on the main highway instead of south, she knew that wasn't the case.

"Where are we going?" she asked.

"Like I said, somewhere I can keep you safe."

"I can keep myself safe," she said.

He laughed. "You always were stubborn. You think you can keep yourself safe when the Bannon family thinks you killed off their main money source?"

"But I didn't kill him. You did."

He glanced over at her with a sick grin. "You've

always been so easy to manipulate. You know that? That's one of the things I really like about you."

She had a sinking feeling. "What are you talking about?"

Dillon switched three lanes to his left in one swift move. Jessie glanced behind her. The car he'd just cut off flipped her off.

She gripped the seat and tried not to show fear, but she was sure Dillon could smell it.

"Am I scaring you?" he asked.

"No," she lied.

"I should."

"Why?"

"Because, Princess, I used *your* Glock to kill Marcus. If you don't do exactly what I want, I'll tell the police that Marcus was dead when I entered the warehouse." He shot her a smirk.

Her Glock. Cody had said he couldn't find it in her car. Her brain had been so muddled from the concussion, she wasn't thinking clearly. How could she not have figured out that Dillon had her Glock?

Because she was still wrapping her brain around that fact that he was crazy.

Then his words sunk in. Not only would the Bannons think she killed Marcus, but *everyone* would. But even if they didn't believe her that it was Dillon, they'd have to believe it was self-defense.

"I see your wheels turning. I'll speed it up for you. I'm the only one who saw you tied up. To everyone else, it will look like you killed the man trying to force your boyfriend to do something illegal. You need me, Princess."

He reached for her hand, and she pulled back.

"Is that how you're going to be?" he snapped.

The evidence would indicate she was alone in the warehouse with Marcus. No one saw him take her near the pub. The last anyone knew, she was in the apartment. Then she was at the warehouse. But she didn't have a car, how would she have gotten there?

"I can see it now. You were pissed at Marcus for threatening your boyfriend. You'd do anything for him. You went to stop Marcus, but an opportunity arose. He was sitting in his car outside the pub, alone. You jumped in the passenger seat and forced him to drive you to the warehouse at gunpoint."

Who the hell was this man?

"You've obviously spent some time thinking about all of this," she said, shocked he would set her up.

"You have no idea," Dillon said. "Then you got to the warehouse, and Marcus wouldn't listen to you. He probably said one of those phrases that sets you off. You know, like 'you're just a woman'." He grinned at her again.

She'd confided in him how much that bothered her. Her dad had always said to her, if only she was a boy, she could have been a major league baseball player. Then when she'd joined the FBI, she found that choice assignments were handed out to her male coworkers. She heard the same excuse many times.

'Sorry, Doyle, but we can't send a woman in there. Too dangerous.'

One time, she'd lost her temper. She'd made such a scene, she'd had to meet with human resources, so it was likely in her file.

Based on how much thought he'd clearly put into this, she'd bet Dillon had seen that report.

"What do you want?" she asked.

Dillon started whistling, the same song he would when they were dating. It was usually a sign he was happy or had gotten his way. It was the same song she heard in the alley next to Bucky's.

He'd been watching her. How long had he been watching her?

Since he apparently wasn't going to answer her about his goal, she thought through what had happened at the warehouse.

They had exited before the Bannons came in. When they were running to the car, she'd looked back, but they hadn't exited the warehouse yet.

They never saw Dillon.

"What I want is for you to understand I really am trying to keep you safe. We'll hide out for a while until Carter tells us it's clear for you to come back," he ordered.

"Carter?"

"Yes, hiding you was his idea."

He was lying. Dillon hadn't called Carter since they'd left the warehouse. Plus, there was no way her boss would agree to that, knowing what he did currently.

"Carter told me Marcus had been threatening you," Dillon continued. "He asked me to keep you safe."

Carter wouldn't put them together. No, he said he would bring Dillon back to Seattle. He also said he hadn't been able to locate him.

Every word out of Dillon's mouth was a lie.

She reached down to scratch her leg. Good, her phone was still in the side pocket of her cargo pants. Marcus hadn't thought to check there. If only she'd gotten her hands free before Dillon showed up, she wouldn't be in this mess. But now, she needed to talk to Carter.

"I need to go to the bathroom. Pull over at that rest stop," she pointed to an upcoming sign.

"We can't. You're going to have to hold it."

"How long?"

"Thirty minutes."

Thirty minutes north? *Holy fuck.* "Are we going to Canada?"

"We are."

"I don't have any ID, they won't let me cross the border," she said, hoping he'd turn around.

She didn't have her wallet or FBI identification. Cody had found both in her car, but she'd left them at the apartment.

"I've got you covered. Don't worry."

Don't worry?

"You have my ID?"

"Better. Your passport."

She tried not to react. How the hell could he have gotten her passport? It was locked up in her apartment. *He's bluffing. He has to be. Has he been in my apartment?*

Those thoughts ate at her for the next thirty minutes until she noticed the signs for the Canadian border. There was a line of cars waiting to get through. She considered jumping out and running or causing a scene.

"Don't even think about it," he said.

She turned to him and he pinned her with his gaze, a mix of anger and disgust on his face.

"If you get out of this car, I'll blow up your boyfriend's bar."

Her eyebrows shot up. "Dillon, you don't mean that."

"Don't believe me?"

He pulled up a photo on his phone that looked like the hallway of Zach's pub. Then he swiped. The next photo was an open shot of the office. The next showed explosives taped to the underside of Zach's desk.

"I put that there early this morning. It is controlled remotely. All I have to do is activate it from my phone, then *boom*. No more Zach."

Her heart was beating out of her chest. Who the hell was this man? "I'll go. Just leave Zach out of this."

Now Dillon laughed. "I tried to leave him out of it, but every chance you got, you ran to him. What, was the sex so good you couldn't resist? Fucking made you blind to the fact you were fucking a Murphy? And now the Bannons probably want you dead. Was the sex worth all that?" He was yelling, and spit was flying.

She sat quietly as they inched their way forward. Dillon took her hand, startling her. When she looked at him, the anger was gone, replaced by something else.

"I'm sorry. I didn't mean to scare you," he said, softly. "Just thinking about that man's hands on you makes me crazy. I get it now. I get why you were upset in Virginia."

It took all her control not to scream. He was comparing her dating Zach while single to his numerous affairs? The man was delusional.

When they finally made their way up to the booth, Dillon handed over two passports.

"Please state your names," the border patrol asked.

"Dillon Harris."

"Jessie Doyle," Jessie answered when the woman looked at her.

"Just a minute." The border patrol officer typed something on her computer then turned back to Dillon. "Pull over there. You've been randomly selected for inspection."

Dillon pulled out his FBI badge. "You don't understand. I'm taking her to a safehouse."

"Pull over there," the border agent pointed

again, ignoring his credentials.

He did as he was told, swearing the entire time. "Don't say a fucking word," he said to Jessie. "I have my phone ready to go if you do."

Before he had a chance to turn off the ignition, his door swung open.

"Sir, please step out of the car. You too, miss," A large border patrol man said.

Dillon stepped out. "There's been a mistake. I'm taking this woman to a safehouse."

Jessie got out of the car but stayed on her side.

The agent spun Dillon around and handcuffed him. "A safehouse in Canada? Where?"

"Why the fuck are you handcuffing me? She's in danger."

A female patrol officer came up behind Jessie. "Jessie Doyle?"

She turned. "Yes?"

"Please come with me," she said.

"Don't you dare!" Dillon shouted at Jessie. "You know what I'll do!"

"Take his phone from him," she told the officer. "He has threatened to detonate a remote bomb with it."

Dillon's face turned bright red as the border agent found the phone and pocketed it.

Jessie followed the female agent away from Dillon and into a building. Once inside, she said, "I need to call someone about that bomb."

The agent pointed to a phone. "You received a

call. You can tell him."

Jessie froze. *A call? How?* She picked up the phone. "Hello?"

"Doyle?"

"Carter?"

"Thank god," he said in obvious relief. "Are you safe? Where's Dillon?"

She turned to the window. "He's being detained. I'm safe now. How did you know where I was?"

"You said you had a history with Dillon on the phone. When I couldn't reach him, I had a talk with the agent he worked with on his last case. He hadn't wanted to come forward at the time, but since I was asking about strange behavior, he had a lot to say. The more he talked, the more concerned I became for your safety. Then Blaese called in to say you'd gone missing. I had your cell phone pinged, and Dillon's. Both were going north to the border. I knew it wasn't a coincidence."

"Yes, that's where we are. They made him pull over."

"That was my doing. I alerted them that he was likely holding you against your will."

"Thank you, Carter."

Dillon was practically dragged past the window next to her. He was cursing the entire way.

"Oh, Carter, Dillon planted bombs in Brannigan's pub, under the desk in the office. He was going to remotely detonate them with his phone.

Please have Blaese get everyone out of there."

"Got it. I'm calling him now. In the meantime, you should rent a car and go home. I'll call you when I know something." He ended the call before she could object.

She'd rent a car, but she wasn't going home.

Chapter Thirty

Jessie had picked up the rental car that Carter arranged for her and was about to pull out of the lot when her cell phone vibrated in her pocket.

"Carter, I got the car. Thank you."

"Good. Now drive to the Seattle office. Mackenzie will debrief you."

Seattle? Oh hell no. That was two hours out of her way in getting back to Fisher Springs. "Carter, please can't this wait until tomorrow? By the time I drive back, it will be evening. All of my things are in a motel in Fisher Springs. I just want to get some sleep and pack up."

Carter let out a sigh. "You're right. I'm sorry, I forgot about your concussion. You're probably exhausted."

"Thank you. I am." That was the truth. Good thing her adrenaline was keeping her going.

"Jessie, you should know that Marcus Beyers, Jonny Bannon and Tony Bannon are all dead. I'm on my way to Fisher Springs to find out where the fuck Blaese was during all of this," he said with uncharacteristic venom. "I'll check on the bomb situation too, then likely stay the night so we can talk in the morning."

She wasn't used to hearing Carter angry. She didn't want to add to it, but she had to make sure he knew the truth about the events.

"Dillon shot Marcus," she told him.

"I know."

"What? How? Did he confess?"

Carter sighed into the phone. "Our informant planted listening devices inside the warehouse, and I heard the recording. I know what happened."

"Then how did the Bannon brothers die?"

"According to the deputy I spoke with on the phone, they got a call about a shooting at the warehouse. They arrived before any of our agents got here, and someone fired at them. In the end, one officer had been shot, and Tony and Jonny were found dead inside the warehouse."

Jessie considered his words. The warehouse was in the middle of nowhere; there weren't any houses for miles. It was the kind of area where people shot tin cans for practice, and no one raised an eyebrow.

"Who called the police?" she asked.

"I don't know, I'll be looking into that. But I have to go. We'll talk tomorrow morning." And just like always, he ended the call with no goodbye.

She checked her screen and saw twenty missed calls and five voicemails, all from Zach.

She called him back.

"Jessie? Where the hell are you?" Zach asked.

"Canada. Zach, please tell me you aren't at your pub."

"Canada? Are you okay?"

She let out a breath. "I am now. It's a long story but Dillon drove me up here against my will but I'm safe now. I'm heading back to Fisher Springs. Where are you?"

"Dillon? If he hurt you—"

"He didn't. Zach, where are you?"

"I'm in my truck with Cody. We've been looking for you."

He wasn't at his pub. She relaxed back in the driver's seat. "Stay away from your pub. Dillon planted a bomb there."

"What the fuck? A bomb?"

"Just stay away. I'll call you when I get to town."

Zach sighed heavily into the phone. "Alright, please drive safe."

After ending the call, she pulled out onto the road. By the time she made it to Fisher Springs, it was getting dark. She tried to drive down Main Street toward Zach's pub, but it was blocked off. She had to find Carter and get an update to make sure Zach was safe.

After parking one block over, she made her

way through the crowd gathered in front of the diner and found her boss talking to two men. "Carter," she called out.

He waved her through the barricade.

"What's going on?" she asked.

"There's no bomb," he told her.

"But Dillon showed me photos on his phone, photos of the pub's hallway and the office."

"I have a copy of those photos here." Carter pulled them up on his phone. "This is the pub's hallway, but that's not the pub's desk. It turns out that photo was from a prior case he'd worked. Here is a photo of the actual desk in the pub's office."

She took Carter's phone and stared at the office photo. She couldn't help her smile. Of course... it was minimalist and masculine. It screamed *Zach*.

"We had the bomb squad go through the entire building just in case. They just cleared it."

"Dillon lied."

"Yes. And from what I understand, this isn't the first time he's done something like this."

"Excuse me? He's kidnapped another FBI agent before?" she asked.

"Not exactly. We can discuss that tomorrow. Right now, there's a more pressing matter. Let's go to my car for privacy."

Carter led her one block up to his SUV and used the fob to unlock the doors. Once they were inside, he stared straight ahead. "I don't know how to say this, so I will just come out with it. I like you,

Doyle. I think you're a damn fine agent with the potential to go far. But your personal life and choices are shit, and they're going to fuck up your career."

She'd suspected she might get reprimanded for dating Dillon. He had been her instructor and she knew better. But she'd hoped Carter would be lenient after all she'd been through. He wasn't holding back, though.

Her hands shook, so she clasped them together, hoping Carter wouldn't notice. "I'm sorry. I know dating Dillon was a poor choice. I didn't—"

"Yes, it was. But you were young, and it turns out he was manipulating a lot of his students. That we could overlook. What I can't overlook is what I learned today. Doyle, you're dating Zach Brannigan, aka Jazz Murphy."

Shit. He knows. Her chest tightened as she struggled to calm her breathing.

She'd hoped it wouldn't get back to him. Zach was innocent, but because of his name, Carter likely wouldn't believe that. But she had to say something.

"When I first started dating him, I had no idea he was anyone other than the owner of a pub. I only found out the truth just before Dillon ran me off the road."

"I understand that. Blaese said he didn't know until one of the Bannons called Zach 'Jazz Murphy' on the recording. But you see, the problem is two-fold. First, you brought this case to Jazz and allowed him to manipulate you. Second, you just admitted you found out who he really is, but you stayed with him for days after that."

He was right. This looked bad. How the hell was she going to explain? Anything thing she could think of to say only made her sound naive. But hell, he had to know where she stood.

"He did not manipulate me. Zach's innocent. You've heard him on the recordings. He wants nothing to do with that business."

Carter leaned back in his seat and stared at the ceiling. "You're not being objective. What you've said is one take. Another is that he is very much involved and found a way to direct the FBI's attention off him."

"No, that's not true."

"Doyle, you have to make a choice. Do you want to stay with the FBI, or date that man? Because you can't do both. He is, at best, a suspect, and at worst… well, you know what the Bannons and Murphys have done."

She had to choose? She couldn't give up the career she'd worked so hard for. But the idea of not seeing Zach gutted her.

Carter didn't wait for her to speak. "Tomorrow morning, we'll talk about Dillon. You can give me your decision then. But you should know, if you stay, there will be a reprimand in your file. You are off this case."

A reprimand? He might as well just hand the promotion to Blaese.

He sighed. "Go to the motel and get some sleep. I'll see you at eight a.m."

She had been dismissed.

She got out of the car, her headache back in full force. But instead of going straight to her car, she walked around Fisher Springs.

She'd loved this place, but now it only reminded her of Zach. God, how could she end it with him? Once she was away from the crowd, she let the tears roll down her face.

Without realizing, she made it back to her rental car, but just stood beside it in a daze.

"Jessie?"

She jumped, startled to see a woman so close. She was tall, with curly brown hair.

"Sorry, I didn't mean to scare you," the stranger said with a gentle smile. "You're Jessie, right?"

"Yes. Who are you?"

"I'm Kate. I'm good friends with Zach." Her smile vanished when she got a good look at Jessie's face. "What's wrong?"

You're going to hate me soon, too. She sobbed. "Everything. Sorry, I'm not a crier. I'm sure it's the concussion making me emotional."

"Zach told me about that. You need to rest."

"I was heading to my motel to sleep."

"The one just two blocks over? We can walk, or I can drive your car? You don't look like you're in any shape to drive."

Jessie handed her the keys. "Thank you."

Normally, she wouldn't be so trusting of a stranger, but Zach had mentioned that Kate was one of his best friends.

As Kate drove, she said, "You know, in all the years I've known Zach, I've never known him to *date* a woman. You're really special to him."

Jessie couldn't hold back her sob.

Kate pulled into the parking lot and turned off the engine, then turned to her. "I'm sorry, you didn't want to hear that?"

Jessie shook her head. "Did you say he's never dated a woman? I find that hard to believe."

"I'm not saying he was a saint. I'm saying he never liked anyone enough to pursue."

Jessie burst into tears again. "I have an impossible choice to make."

"Let's go inside so you can lay down while we talk."

Even though Jessie didn't really know Kate, she wanted to talk to her. Kate knew Zach, so maybe she could help him understand after Jessie was gone.

It was in that moment she realized she'd already made her decision.

Chapter Thirty-One

Zach knocked on Jessie's motel door, frustrated they hadn't spoken last night. While he was happy she left him a voicemail the night before letting him know she'd made it to town, he was upset she didn't respond to his calls after that. He was about to storm her door last night but Kate stopped him, telling him she probably needed her rest. But nothing was stopping them from talking this morning.

When she opened the door, he immediately knew something was wrong. Her eyes were red-rimmed, but Jessie didn't strike him as a crier.

"What's wrong?" He reached out to her.

She stepped back. "Come in. We have to talk."

Dread filled him.

Jessie sat on the bed and motioned for him to join her. He took a quick glance around and noted that everything in her room was packed up. That's when he spotted her suitcase by the door.

"You're leaving."

"Yes."

His mind raced. The case was far from solved. Why would she be leaving now?

"Are you leaving because Dillon kidnapped you? Is he still out there?"

She frowned and shook her head.

The quieter she stayed, the more nervous he became.

He paced the room. "When I discovered you were missin' I was out of my mind. I thought Marcus had you. But then Cody and I discovered Marcus was dead and you were still missin'. Thank you fer callin' yesterday, but when you didn't answer last nigh', I was almost stormin' your door. Kate stopped me and said you were probably tired."

Jessie stood and took his hands in hers. "I was. I like Kate, I had a chance to talk to her yesterday. She's a good friend to you."

"What's goin' on? You're scarin' me here."

Fuck. His damn accent. He couldn't play it cool if he tried. But dammit. He had to know.

"I can tell. I'm sorry." She reached up and touched his chin.

"Sorry, I haven't had a chance to shave with all that's goin' on."

She laughed, then her eyes welled with tears. "I like the stubble."

He grinned. "You do?"

"Yeah. But that doesn't matter." She stepped away as a tear fell down her cheek. "My boss found out about us."

Her boss? She was crying over that?

"Is that a problem? We're both adults."

She stared at the ground instead of meeting his eyes. "He believes you are, at best, a suspect, and at worst, a criminal. He knows you're a Murphy."

He had to sit down.

After making his way to the bed, he sat with his head in his hands. "Fer so many years, no one knew my past, and in this last week, it seems everyone does. It's not somethin' I'm proud of, but I swear to you, the man before you is not that boy from years ago. I was a Murphy, but I haven't been fer fourteen years."

She got down on her knees in front of him. "I know, Zach. Believe me I know. Which makes what I have to say that much harder."

"No." He pulled her up on his lap and kissed her hard.

This felt like goodbye. This couldn't be goodbye. Not after everything they'd been through to get to this point.

She kissed him back, hard, then she pulled back. The look in her eyes said it all.

"Zach, I can't see you anymore." Standing, she turned her back to him.

No, he couldn't let her do this. He couldn't let her give up. Where was the tough Jessie who fought for what she wanted? There had to be a way for them to be together.

"I get that your boss could see this as a conflict

of interest." He stood and grabbed her hand. "Let's take a break, and then when the case is wrapped up, we can talk."

We can get back together, he wanted to say.

Jessie spun around, releasing his hand. "Zach, this case is just the tip of the iceberg. After this, we'll go after the next person in the operation. Today, it was supposed to be Marcus. Tomorrow, the Bannons. After that? Probably the Murphys. It doesn't end. There is no 'later' for us."

Fuck. He felt weak.

He sank back onto the bed. *No 'later' for us?*

She'd gutted him. And there was nothing he could say that would change her mind. Numb... he felt numb all over.

"So you're choosing your job over us?"

"Zach—"

He shook his head.

He didn't want to hear it. Her career came first. Of course it did. They'd only known each other a couple of months. What else did he expect? But why the hell did it hurt do much?

"I should go," he managed to say.

He stood and stumbled his way to the door, though each step felt like he was walking in quicksand.

His heart begged him not to leave. He couldn't let it end like this.

He turned and marched back to her. "I've never felt this fer anyone before. And I don't think I will again. Goodbye, Jessie." He kissed her forehead and then got the hell out of there before she could see him shed any tears.

When he closed the door, and heard her sobs, it took all his strength not to go back in there and hold her and tell her they'd figure it out. But Jessie was stubborn. And she'd made her choice.

Zach stumbled to his truck. The last thing he wanted to do was leave, but he had to. He couldn't watch her put her suitcases in her car and drive away.

Instead of going home, he drove to the pub. He'd find some way to keep busy. He had to.

When he arrived, Kate was sitting outside the pub door.

"What are you doing here?" he asked her.

"I talked to Jessie last night, remember?" She stood and pulled him into a hug.

"You knew?"

"I'm sorry, Zach. I tried to talk her out of it, but she's really stubborn."

He laughed. "Yeah, she is."

After unlocking the pub, he led her inside, then immediately poured a shot for himself.

"Want one?" he offered.

"Zach, it's not even noon yet."

He shrugged. "Doesn't really matter, does it?"

"Is Ariel opening?"

He nodded.

She lifted an eyebrow. "You're closing?"

He nodded again.

"I'll close for you."

His eyebrows shot up. "You? Have you ever worked a bar before?"

Kate's hands went to her hips, and suddenly, Zach was reminded of Jessie. The tears came, he couldn't stop them.

Fuck, why bother trying?

"Kate. I can't do this," he swallowed back a sob. "It's too much."

Immediately, she was by his side, pouring another shot. "You'll get through this. We'll take it one day at a time."

Zach drank that shot. Then another and another. It was only him and Kate in the pub.

Cody had told him the Bannons had been killed during a shootout with the FBI at the warehouse. With the immediate threat removed, that meant Zach no longer needed Cody, so the other man had left for good the night before.

The place felt so empty. No, he wouldn't go there. Today, he would get drunk. Tomorrow, he would go back to focusing on his business.

Chapter Thirty-Two

Jessie stared out the window of her office. Seattle was experiencing a gray and rainy early June; the weather was miserable, and so was she.

Nearly two months had passed since she last saw Zach in that motel room. Breaking things off with him had been hard, but she'd managed to not cry until he had left. Then she cried for a week straight every night as soon as she left the office.

Just when she thought she could get through a night without breaking down, Zach had sent a couple of texts. She never responded. What could she say? Instead, she spent all her time in the office, trying to earn back Carter's respect.

After being taken off the Hawthorne case, she'd been stuck at her desk doing paperwork. Carter had said he was giving her time to rest until her concussion healed, but she knew the truth. This was punishment.

She turned in her chair when she heard a knock on her door, expecting to see Sam. It was Carter.

"We need to talk." He walked in and closed the door behind him.

This was it. Since she'd been back, he'd barely looked at her; he was going to fire her, she could feel it.

"Dillon escaped."

That was not what she was expecting.

Dillon had been held in Canada for a brief time, and then transferred to a hospital in Seattle for an involuntary hold and an evaluation. His partner on his last case had come forward with some very disturbing stories, and those, combined with what Dillon had told the Canadian authorities, had earned him a stay in a low-security mental health facility.

"What do you mean escaped?"

Carter shoved his hands in his pockets. "Apparently, he just walked out the front door during a shift change this morning. No one noticed until they served lunch, but according to footage, he'd left five hours prior."

He's free?

She tried to calm her nerves.

Dillon was out there somewhere. Would he come after her? She hadn't spoken to him since Canada.

"Jessie, I know this is personal, but I have to ask. Did you break it off with Zach Brannigan?"

What the hell? He was asking this *now*?

"Yes, the last morning I was in Fisher Springs. Are you telling me my rosy disposition hasn't been a clue?" she snapped.

Carter smiled.

"Sorry," she grumbled. "It just really sucks."

"You really care for him."

She nodded, because if she spoke, she might not be able to control the tears.

Every time she thought about Zach, she cried. She had gone from being a tough agent to an emotional mess.

Despite her best efforts, a tear escaped. She quickly wiped it away.

"I'm sorry I had to ask, but Dillon's therapist thinks he's going after Zach. Apparently, Agent Harris has it in his head that Zach is what is standing between you and he being together." Carter shook his head. "I don't know how he passed any of the FBI tests. Though, his therapist said sometimes issues like his get worse as people get older."

"Zach's in danger?"

"As soon as I heard, I sent Agent Blaese out to Fisher Springs to check on Mr. Brannigan."

"When did he leave?"

"Ten minutes ago. Why?"

Blaese had wrapped up the Hawthorne case the previous week and returned to Seattle, so that meant he was two hours from Zach.

"Dillon has been loose for five hours. It might be too late."

She grabbed her phone and called Zach.

He answered on the first ring.

"Jessie?"

God, she missed that voice.

She took a deep breath to calm herself. "Zach, Dillon escaped from a mental health facility five hours ago. We believe he's on his way to harm you. Agent Blaese has been sent to help you, but he's two hours away. You need to get out of there. Drive to Seattle. We can protect you here."

"So this is a business call then?" His voice was cold.

"Please, Zach. You're in danger."

"I'm not worried about Dillon. He can't hurt me any more than I already have been." He ended the call.

She dropped the phone on her desk, barely able to breathe. He'd been so harsh.

"Is he coming in?" Carter asked.

She shook her head. "I need to go." She grabbed her phone and purse and made her way to her door.

"Doyle, No." Carter made it there before her. "Dillon is likely looking for either you or Zach. You need to stay here until we have him in custody."

Jessie turned away from Carter and wiped her eyes. She hadn't expected she would have to call Zach, but she never could have prepared herself for his words. She had hurt him, and he was still angry. Too angry to protect himself.

"I understand," she said finally.

There was no point in arguing with Carter now. It would only delay her from saving Zach.

Once Carter was out of the office, she looked up

the number to the Fisher Springs Police Department. Fortunately, Nick answered. She briefed him on the situation.

"How long have you been off the Hawthorne case?" he asked.

"Since I left Fisher Springs, why?"

"Jessie," Nick sighed. "I'll take care of Zach. But it's best if you don't show up here."

She fell back onto her chair. "Are you saying I'm unwelcome in your town, detective?"

"You really hurt him. He's a miserable fuck who's still in love with you. So unless you plan to fix that—which, based on what you told him, it doesn't sound like it—please stay away." His tone had grown harsh.

"Based on what I told him?"

"You said you guys couldn't date because of your case. You've been off your case for, what, a couple of months, and yet you still haven't contacted him? That's all I need to know." Nick ended the call.

She couldn't breathe. Zach was in love with her? Had he told Nick that?

She'd never know, since what she'd said to Zach hadn't changed. She couldn't date him. Not while the FBI was investigating his family. Yes, the Hawthorne case was closed, but as she'd suspected, it was the tip of the iceberg, and they were moving up the chain.

She couldn't be with him. But at least she could keep him safe.

Carter had gotten enough of a head start he wouldn't spot her leaving. She walked briskly to the elevator before anyone could stop her.

The moment the elevator door opened to the garage, the hair on the back of her neck stood up. Making sure to have her key fob in one hand, she put her other hand over her Glock.

Halfway to her car, she heard the familiar whistling. That song. It echoed off the concrete walls so she couldn't pinpoint where it was coming from.

"Princess, don't look so scared."

"Where are you?"

"Near," Dillon said simply.

Jessie slowly moved toward her car.

"You're getting colder."

"What do you want?" she shouted.

"You, Princess. Always you."

Another step toward her car.

"Why me?"

"You have to ask? Because I love you. I'm sorry I didn't appreciate what I had in Virginia, but trust me, I do now."

His voice was coming from near the elevator, but she couldn't see him. Damn the dark garage.

She moved closer to her car, and spotted movement between the trunk and the structure wall. She stilled. Carter stood just enough for her to see him with his finger to his lips, urging her not to say anything that would alert the other man to his presence.

"Dillon, this isn't love," she pleaded.

"Princess, I thought I'd go crazy in that hospital. But then I got out, and do you know where I drove to?"

Instead of responding, she took another step toward her car.

"Fisher Springs," he answered for her.

She stilled.

He'd gone there long before she even knew Zach was in danger.

"What did you do?" she demanded.

"I went to that guy's pub. I couldn't stand the thought of him being with you, but you know what I saw?"

"What?"

"The guy looked miserable. His hair wasn't combed, he had a scraggly beard. Hell, he looked like hadn't showered in weeks. That's when it hit me. He was heartbroken."

Imagining Zach in that condition gutted her. What had she done? She was miserable, and he was miserable. She barely managed to hold in a whimper.

"You left him for me." Dillon stepped out from behind a car with a gleeful smile. He was only twenty feet from her now. "Once I realized that, I had to come see you. I've missed you, Princess."

"You drove? How did you get a car?" she asked.

Dillon laughed. "I charmed a nurse for her keys. Wasn't hard to do."

He was halfway to her when Carter and another agent closer to Dillon's location popped out.

The next few minutes happened in a flash. Dillon was taken into custody. She was whisked back upstairs to safety, and Carter ordered her not to leave.

She sat in her office, but she couldn't concentrate or get any work done. There were too many questions swirling around in her head. But the loudest one was about Zach. She wanted to know how he was doing but there was no one she could call. Everyone in Fisher Springs was his friend, not hers.

After an hour of nearly pulling her hair out, she went in search of Carter and found him in his office.

"You said you were going to Fisher Springs," she said accusingly from his doorway.

"I lied. I was pretty sure Dillon was in contact with someone here, so I made certain that agent overhead me telling someone else that you left for Fisher Springs on your own."

"But you told me not to."

Carter chuckled. "I know you, Doyle. You're stubborn, and while you normally follow rules, you don't when you think you're right. I wasn't sure if you would defy my order, but we figured if you didn't, Dillon would show himself eventually."

She was stunned. Carter had set her up, and she fell for it. Her emotions had blinded her.

She furrowed her brow. "Who was Dillon in contact with?"

He waved her in. "Come in and shut the door."

When she did as he asked, he continued. "What I'm about to tell you stays in this room. Do you understand?"

"Yes."

"I think you should be aware how deep Dillon's obsession is. Last week, Dillon's case manager, Sheila, contacted me. Apparently, Dillon received phone calls from his girlfriend during his stay in the facility. Dillon was told the calls were recorded yet he still gave out what Sheila thought might be classified FBI information."

"What kind of information? And why would he do that?"

Carter opened a file and slide a paper across the desk. Jessie scanned it.

"Those are some of the notes from his counseling session," he explained.

"Aren't these confidential?" She didn't care for Dillon, but she didn't want to invade his privacy.

"Read it. He lost the privilege when he violated his oath to this office."

Jessie read it closer. She saw her name, Zach's name, and Bethany's. "This is from the final report in the Hawthorne case."

"Exactly. Between this and some other things Dillon said, specifically that he felt bad you were stuck at your desk now, Sheila realized he was obsessed with you and Mr. Brannigan, and had someone inside our office feeding him information."

"He knew I was doing desk duty? If he had a

spy, wouldn't he know I broke up with Zach?"

"I never put that in the report, or told anyone. He wouldn't know."

Jessie shivered at the idea someone was reporting her actions to Dillon.

"There's more. It turns out Dillon has been dating two female agents from this office."

"Two agents? He hasn't changed," she mumbled.

Carter gave her a questioning look before he went on. "He asked them both about you. One told me she broke off her relationship with him because Dillon seemed more interested in all the other women in the office. I only found out about their connection because Dillon's partner had mentioned her when he gave his statement on Dillon."

"Is she the spy?" She tossed Dillon's counseling notes back on the desk.

"I don't think so."

"Can you tell me which agents he was dating?" Carter leaned back and studied her. He'd already shared confidential information with her so she wasn't sure why he was hesitating now.

"I can only tell you about one. The other is under investigation for the leaked evidence."

Jessie thought of all the single female agents in the office, coming up with a very short list she didn't like. She looked at him expectantly.

"The one who said he was creepy and broke up

with him is Sam."

There was no way she heard him correctly.

"Can you repeat that?"

Carter stood and came around his desk. He sat on the edge of it and faced Jessie. "I'm sorry. I understand you two are friends. But she dated Dillon. When asked about it, she stated he suggested she befriend you, since you were new to the office. But she claims she didn't know that you and Dillon knew each other beforehand."

Jessie closed her eyes. "I never told her. I spoke of an ex, but I never used his name."

"Sam also said that after she befriended you, Dillon wouldn't stop asking about your conversations. You should ask her yourself exactly what happened, though."

She wasn't sure that was such a good idea. She had confided a lot in Sam, even though she'd never said Dillon's name. But if Dillon had asked Sam to be her friend and then grilled her about it, how would Sam not be suspicious about his interest?

There had to be more than she was admitting.

Jessie's head started pounding. She had the concussion to thank for her now regular headaches. That and the shitstorm that was her personal life.

It was one thing to have misjudged Dillon. She'd been young and naive. But to misjudge Sam? How the hell did she miss that?

Fuck. One wrong assessment after another. Maybe she wasn't cut out to be an agent.

She thought about her conversations with Sam. Jessie had said a lot more about herself than Sam ever shared. But Sam asked a lot of questions, so to divert, Jessie would talk about her brothers. She was proud of all of them, and Sam and Kaila loved to hear about Silas — and if he was still single. That was her default safety topic.

God, why hadn't she grilled Sam more about the man she was dating? Hell, she had asked his name a couple of times, but her *friend* had never given it up.

Sam had asked Jessie a lot of questions about her dating life since her breakup with Zach. It didn't seem odd at the time, but now it felt like Dillon had been digging for information. Had the clues been right there all along? If she hadn't been so caught up in her own problems, would she have seen it? What else had she missed?

There were still some things that didn't add up.

"Dillon had my passport when he took me from the warehouse. How did he get it? It was in my apartment."

"Jessie, did Sam have a key to your apartment?" Carter asked.

Nausea overtook her as she put the pieces together.

"I think I'm going to be sick."

Carter moved fast and handed her his wastebasket. Jessie vomited with her mind swirling.

Growing up, she had been a tomboy. Having four brothers didn't help that. She played sports, and always found herself hanging out with the guys. She'd never been good at having female friends. That didn't change in adulthood.

That was probably why she had been so easy for Dillon to manipulate in Virginia. She had been a loner. But then she came to Seattle, happy to be near family even if she could only see them now and again.

When Sam introduced herself on Jessie's third day at the office, Jessie had been relieved. And she and Sam had bonded immediately. They shared many of the same interests.

Dillon must have told her everything.

Carter handed her a Kleenex, and she wiped her mouth, then stumbled back to her chair.

Did Sam let Dillon in my apartment or did she take the passport herself?

"But this doesn't make sense. Why would Sam befriend me and feed Dillon information if she wanted him?"

"I don't know. But I will find out. In the meantime, I need you to not act any different around her."

"Ha! You're kidding right? I'm sorry. I can't do that."

"Then go home. After everything that has happened today, you should go home and process it all."

"Home?"

"Don't worry. Dillon's in custody. You're safe."

She avoided rolling her eyes. Even Carter

didn't think she could take care of herself.

"I'm not worried about Dillon," she told him.

It's Sam who should worry about me.

Chapter Thirty-Three

"Zach, we need to talk."

Kate sat on a stool at his bar while he mixed drinks for a couple at the other end of the bar.

Shit, not this again. "I'm busy."

He already knew what she was going to say.

She scoffed. "No, you're not."

He handed the drinks off to the couple and glanced around. Only three people were in his bar, and it was fucking *happy hour*. Where was the crowd? Oh yeah, still in Davenport. Bucky's didn't get shut down like he thought it would.

Turning back to Kate, he crossed his arms and leaned against the counter behind him. Might as well get this over with.

"Go ahead," he swept an arm toward her.

"You can't keep wallowing."

"I'm not wallowing."

She arched a brow. "No? Look in the mirror. Did you even shower today?"

All right, she might have a point.

The door opened, and for a moment, he was excited to see more customers. Until he saw it was Nick and Chase. While he appreciated their business, he knew they were here out of concern for him more than anything else.

"Hey guys, what can I get you?" Zach asked.

"A couple of beers would be great," Chase said as he and Nick took their seats at the bar.

"I know she hurt you," Kate began.

"No, we are not talking about this." Zach pointed at Nick and Chase. "And that goes for you two as well."

"That's not why we're here," Nick said.

"Nope. We have a better idea," Chase said.

Zach stared at them. He knew when they were hatching a plan, and he also knew he wasn't gonna like it. "What are you up to? And why the hell aren't you on your honeymoon?" he asked Nick.

"My wedding was two weeks ago. We're already back. Although, I understand why you might not really remember it," Nick said.

"Yeah, he was pretty drunk," Kate said.

"Thanks for keeping an eye on him that night," Nick said.

As Zach poured their draft beers, a few memories from the wedding came back to him.

Aw, shit. Zach rubbed his beard. He vaguely remembered getting shitfaced at their reception and going on to Kate that he should be marrying Jessie.

Holy fuck. Marrying her? He did have it bad.

Over two months had passed since she'd told him they couldn't be together, and he still struggled to function. He had no idea what day it was half the time; he was lucky to get into the bar to open and close it.

Although, one more month of Bucky's stealing all his business, and he wouldn't have to open the pub doors ever again.

The only thing that kept him from getting drunk every night was that old guitar he'd pulled out of storage. He thought maybe if he could play like he used to, maybe he could put on a show and attract some customers. Fuck, he had to do something to save this place.

"Between you being shitfaced at my wedding, and Chase disappearing in the middle of it, you're both lucky I don't hold a grudge. It's a good thing I really like you guys."

"Hey, I told you why I had to leave, and I was back before the reception was over," Chase reminded him.

Nick laughed. "If you count going off to one of the bedrooms with Harmony as being 'back,' then sure."

"Wait. Why would you leave his wedding?" Zach asked.

"It had to do with Joey."

Zach grunted.

Their friend Joey had been arrested for murder. He didn't know all the details, since he'd been so caught up in his own life, but Joey was not only the Police Chief's son, but had once been the detective in town, and was good friends with almost everyone. Word around town was he'd started using meth shortly after his mom died.

All Zach knew was it was hard watching his friend ruin his life.

Chase slapped the counter, pulling him out of his thoughts. "Lauren and Harmony are joining us shortly, and they are bringing a new friend."

Someone new? *Don't they think I've already tried that?*

Shortly after the breakup, a woman had spent the entire night flirting with him. She made it clear what she wanted, and he tried to let his mind go there, but he couldn't even feign interest.

"No," Zach said.

"Hear us out," Chase said.

Kate shook her head. "Can I get another beer? This just got interesting."

Zach growled as he grabbed another bottle, popping off the top before handing it to her.

"Harmony met her at a wedding last weekend," Chase explained. "She was one of the bridesmaids and helped Harmony with the photos of the wedding party. They got to talking, and Harmony came home screaming she'd found the perfect woman for you."

"No," Zach repeated.

"She likes tattoos and beards. You wouldn't

have to change for her the way you changed for Jes—"

Zach slammed a bowl down on the counter, sending peanuts everywhere. "Don't you dare say her name."

The pub fell quiet. Then the squeak of the door opening caught their attention. In walked Harmony, Lauren, and another woman.

"Shit." Chase was up and off his stool in record time, pulling Harmony aside.

Zach knew exactly what he was saying. *Abort mission.* But no one told the new brunette, who sashayed up to the bar, staring at Zach like he was being served up on a platter.

"You must be Zach. I'm Penelope."

Not in the mood to entertain any of this, he gave her a nod then asked, "What can I get you?"

"A glass of red wine. For now." She grinned at him, then her eyes moved down his arms and took in his tattoos.

Yep, she was one of those. He could tell. All she wanted was a night with him to check off her bucket list.

"Do you ride a motorcycle?" she asked.

And that confirmed it.

He poured her wine and after sliding it across the bar to her, he leaned in. "I don't know what Harmony told you, but I'm not up for any *Sons of Anarchy* fantasies you have going on in your head."

Her eyes widened, and he thought for a minute he'd misspoken.

"I'm not sure what you're talking about exactly, but yes, I'd love a night with a man like you."

He grabbed the edge of the bar tightly, trying to control his anger. At this point, he was angry at Harmony, at this woman—hell, at everyone.

"And exactly kind of man do you think I am?"

Why the hell did he bother to ask? He knew what was coming.

Her eyes moved up and down his body. "You look like you like control and you know how to please a woman. I'd let you tie me up anytime." She bit her lip.

Jesus. That might have turned him on before he met Jessie, but now his cock couldn't retreat fast enough.

"Sorry. Not tonight," he bit out.

She recoiled, and part of him felt bad. It wasn't her fault he was being a prick.

"Oh. No, I'm sorry. I think I misunderstood." She picked up her wine glass and made her way to the booth in the back where Lauren and Harmony waited for her.

"Ouch," Chase said.

"Yeah, you sure shot her down," Nick added over the top of his beer glass.

"I told you before she came in here, I'm not interested."

Nick and Chase looked at each other.

"What? Do you have a problem with that?" He was practically yelling.

Chase grabbed a handful of peanuts, eating them one by one while staring at Zach.

"What? Stop starin'. You're makin' me uncomfortable."

Chase grinned. "I can tell. Accent's out again."

If Ariel were here, Zach would leave these fools. He was in too foul a mood for this.

"Look," Chase said. "It's clear you're still hung up on Jessie. You just had a gorgeous woman throw herself at you, and you had no interest."

"Okay, Captain Obvious. Are you goin' to stand there tellin' me what I already know?"

"You have a choice. You either win Jessie back, or finally move on. You can't keep wallowing like this."

Zach ran his hands through his hair. "Fer Pete's sake, I'm not wallowin'."

Nick arched a brow at him. Chase grinned.

Zach took a calming breath before speaking again. Sometimes deep breaths keep the accent at bay. "All right, maybe I'm wallowing a little."

Kate snorted. "You bypassed 'a little' weeks ago."

Chase pointed to Nick. "I had to watch this guy wallow. God, he was a messed-up fucker. But now look at him. He took charge and got his woman back."

Zach remembered hearing that Nick had gotten so drunk, he had to miss work. Now that he knew the guy, he knew how out of character that was for him. He'd moped around town until Lauren finally took him back.

"Jessie won't come back," he said grimly.

"That's a defeatist attitude," Nick said.

"She didn't just break up with me over one case."

"Oh shit, what did you do?" Nick asked.

"Nothing."

"Is she dating someone else? Is that why you're so pissy?" Chase asked.

"No. I don't know. Why would you bring that up?"

Now he was picturing Jessie out with some other man.

He shook the thought away. He couldn't go there. "She won't date me because I'm a Murphy, and according to her, the FBI will always be investigating some Murphy or Bannon. Therefore, she can't date me and keep her career. As you all can tell, she chose her career over me."

Chase ate another handful of peanuts. His chewing was the only sound Zach heard.

He grabbed the bowl and put it out of Chase's reach.

"Hey!"

"I'm baring my soul and don't need your jaws grinding those peanuts as background music."

"I thought Marcus led the family business. With him gone, who's really left?" Nick asked.

"When I was still in Idaho, there were cousins and long-time family friends that were considered family. I assure you someone took over the business," Zach said. "So Jessie won't be coming back. She values her career more. Hell, she called earlier—"

"Wait, she called? You didn't mention this," Kate said.

Three pairs of expectant eyes stared at him.

This was exactly why he didn't mention anything. The hope in their eyes mirrored exactly what he'd felt when he saw her name come up on his phone.

"It's not what you think. She called to warn me that her ex might be coming for me."

Nick nodded. "She called me about that too."

"Yeah, well, then you know. The call was only to warn me. Nothing else. It's been months. If she wanted me back, she'd have said something."

"Aw shit. That might be my fault," Nick said.

All eyes turned his way.

"What did you do?" Chase asked.

"When Jessie called me about Dillon, I told her not to come here unless she was ready to get back together with Zach."

"Sounds like you did me a favor," Zach said. "She didn't come because she made her choice."

Kate shook her head. "I wouldn't be so sure. Remember, I was the one she talked to the night before she called it off. She didn't want to do it. Feelings like that just don't go away. Plus, you're forgetting all you did to help the FBI after she was taken off the case. There's no way her boss would still view you in a negative light."

"Kate's right," Nick agreed. "Plus, I can tell you that, as much as I wanted Lauren back, it took a while for me to get up the nerve to do anything about it. But the gift I gave her really helped."

"What was that?" Zach asked.

"A pen and letter opener set engraved with *Harrow Accounting*. I wanted her to know that not only did I love her, but I believed in her."

"Damn, that's romantic," Kate said.

Zach wanted to believe they were right about Jessie. Hell, he'd give anything to win her back at this point, but he wasn't so sure he could.

Kate jabbed a finger at him. "You need to do something like that and show her how much she means to you."

"Yeah? How do I do that?" he asked.

"I know," Chase said. "We'll get her to show up here, and you will have the place decorated in hundreds of roses and balloons. She'll love it."

Zach tipped his head back. "Do you remember Jessie? That woman that tackled me just down the street from here. She's not going to be impressed with that cheesy idea."

"Hey, I think you're on to something," Nick cut in. "You met when she tackled you, right?"

"Yeah."

"Go full circle and bring it back to the beginning."

"What the fuck are you talking about?" Zach was growing impatient with this group.

"Tackle her. Or invite her to a gym and see if she can take you down again," Nick suggested.

Kate laughed. "Damn, Nick. I guess you only get one good idea in this life. Those options suck."

"Oh yeah?" Chase said. "You got a better idea?"

Kate finished her beer then spun on her stool to face them. "As a matter of fact, I do."

Chapter Thirty-Four

Carter had been right, Jessie needed to get out of that office in order to process everything he'd told her. Her mind kept going back to Sam. That deception hurt the most. She truly believed they'd been friends.

Crawling into bed, she put her hand under her pillow, hoping to curl up and sleep and try to forget the rest of the day. But her hand touched something. The charm Zach had given her.

Last night, she'd tried to take her mind off of everything by listening to music, but that didn't work. The Ed Sheeran song they'd danced to in her motel room came on. Their song. That led to a glass of wine and her falling asleep clutching the revolver charm. She was amazed she hadn't broken down when she called him earlier. God, she missed him.

Zach's memory still hurt like hell. At one time, she'd thought she cared for Dillon, but it was nothing like what she felt for Zach. From the moment she'd met him, it all felt different. And not having him in her life now felt wrong. But how the hell could she let him back in? With his ties to the Murphy family and her being in law enforcement, it would never work.

Someone knocked at her door.

She sat up. *Please be Zach.*

Then she chided herself. Zach was too angry with her to show up. He'd probably moved on by now. A man like that wouldn't stay single. He'd texted her twice after the first week of their breakup. She never responded, and he didn't try again. She hadn't heard anything about him until Dillon painted her a picture of Zach's state.

He'd probably exaggerated Zach's appearance. He was probably just tired from being up all night with some other woman.

She squeezed her eyes shut. She didn't want that image in her head.

"Jessie! It's Sam. Open up."

Jessie stuttered to a stop a foot from the front door. *Sam?* Why the hell was she here? Anger consumed her. *How dare she!* She swung open the front door.

"Jessie, how are you doing? Oh my god, I'm so sorry about Dillon. I had no idea he was your ex until the entire Canada thing, and then I wasn't sure how to tell you. I wasn't with him anymore, and I just wanted to forget."

"You knocked. I'm surprised you didn't let yourself in," Jessie snapped.

"What are you talking about?" Sam looked

down the hall. "Can I come in? We should talk."

What the hell. Maybe Sam would fess up to what she'd done.

Jessie stepped back to let the other woman in.

Sam dropped her purse by the door and took off her shoes. "I don't have much time. I'm on a late lunch break."

Jessie turned to face her, clenching her jaw.

"Carter said he sent you home. What happened?"

"Like you don't know."

Sam wore a pinched expression. "Jessie, what is going on? Are you mad at me? I told you I had no idea your ex was Dillon."

Jessie walked away before she did something she regretted. But then she turned back. "Did you and Dillon laugh about me? Did you go to him after our happy hours and tell him you befriended me just as planned?"

Sam's eyes widened. "What are you talking about?"

Jessie guffawed. "That's rich."

"Seriously, Jessie, why would you think that?"

"Carter told me!" she yelled.

Sam frowned. "I told Carter that Dillon had suggested I be nice to you when you first transferred. I was going to introduce myself anyway. I didn't befriend you because of Dillon."

"Do you deny that Dillon asked about me?"

Sam opened her mouth to speak then shook her

head. "He did ask. And at first, I answered. But then it got weird."

"Weird how?"

"I thought he was interested in you. Around that time, I noticed he flirted with everyone, even the waitresses on our dates. Remember that one happy hour I said he wasn't a relationship kind of guy? That's how I knew and why, not long after that, I dumped him."

Jessie walked to the kitchen for water. She needed a moment to think this through. When she returned, Sam was sitting on the couch, bent forward with her head in her hands.

"Answer me this," Jessie said. "If you weren't using me for Dillon, then why didn't you tell me you were seeing him? Why keep it secret?"

Sam shook her head. "Because I didn't want anyone to know. We work together, and you know Carter—he wouldn't be okay with it. Dillon and I agreed to keep it quiet to protect our jobs."

Jessie snorted as she sat on the other end of the couch. "Yeah, I know all about how Dillon likes to keep things quiet. And it's not just to protect his job."

"I wish I had told you. Because you're right. I wasn't the only one he was seeing." Sam shrugged. "It shouldn't have bothered me because I didn't go into it thinking long-term. But I at least thought he'd be exclusive for a little bit. But like I said, he started to openly flirt in front of me, and ask me about other women in the office. It was getting creepy, so I ended it."

"Was that before or after you took my passport?"

Sam shook her head. "What? I don't know what you're talking about."

"My passport. Dillon had it when he took me to Canada, but I kept it here. You're the only person besides me who has a key."

"Jessie, I've never been in your apartment except when you invited me in. I didn't take your passport, I—Oh no." Sam jumped up and raced to her purse.

She returned holding a set of keys. "One night, Dillon asked me what all these keys were for. I told him this one was for your apartment."

Jessie stared at the key. It had a pink rubber cover around it, which made it stand out from the rest. Was it possible Dillon had taken it from Sam, and her friend was really innocent in all of this?

She wanted that to be true. But how could she trust it?

"You have to believe me, Jessie. I would never knowingly hurt you. You've been a good friend."

Sam looked sincere. But Jessie was too tired to figure it all out right then.

"Thank you for coming by. I need to be alone now."

Sam shook her head. "You want me to go?"
Jessie nodded.
"Are we okay?" Sam asked.

"I don't know. I need time to think."

Sam stood and clutched her keys. "I'll give you space. But, Jessie, don't shut me out. You know I wouldn't do this."

Jessie stood as she watched her friend leave. When Sam was gone, Jessie walked back to her water glass on the kitchen table, waiting for the sadness to overtake her. But it didn't.

She had shut Zach out, and now she wanted to call him, hear his voice, get his opinion. She wanted him there with her now. She'd never longed for a man like this. He'd only been to her place once, but still she felt his presence everywhere.

Scanning the room, remembering the fun they'd had on her couch, her eye caught on her bookshelf. "What the hell?"

On the shelf was a stuffed dog Dillon had given her on one of their first dates. But she'd packed that stuffed dog, along with a few other items he'd given her during their time together, into a box and shoved it into his arms.

She remembered the day clearly. She stood on his doorstep in Virginia, holding the box. When he opened the door, she felt weak and thought she missed him. She had been about to suggest they go out for coffee when a tall blonde came up behind him, possessively put her arms around him, and asked who she was.

Shaking her head, Jessie realized she'd forgotten that. He'd had a woman in his place. The place he said he didn't allow anyone in because of germs.

Shit. Jessie had been the other woman all along. Well, knowing Dillon, the *other*, other woman.

Jessie had shoved the box into Dillon's chest, and looked to the woman. "This is what your future looks like."

She *knew* the stuffed dog had been in that box. So how the hell was it on her shelf now? She walked over to it and grabbed the dog. It was definitely the same one. How long had it been here? Why had she not noticed before?

She closed her eyes. She likely hadn't noticed because she had been putting in ten-hour days since she had transferred to Seattle, only coming home to eat and zone out while watching a little television.

Had Dillon put this here when he'd taken her passport? Did he ask Sam to?

Turning the dog in her hand, she noticed a rip in the seam. That was new. Pulling it open, something fell out... a small camera.

What the fuck?

The camera had been sticking out of the seam and was pointed... She followed its line of sight and found herself looking at her couch.

Dillon had been watching her? Her body went numb. This was too much. Had he watched her every night on her couch? Oh god, had he seen her and Zach here that night?

A bitter taste filled her mouth, and she felt

nauseous. She dropped the dog, grabbed her keys, and left. Her apartment was the last place she wanted to be. She needed a long drive.

Without thinking, she found herself halfway to Fisher Springs. What the hell was she doing? She couldn't pop in and see Zach. That wasn't fair to him. But she longed to see him, even if at a distance.

But what if he's with another woman? The thought tore at her heart.

Well, if he was, there was nothing she could do about it. It was bound to happen sooner or later.

While her mind knew this, her heart wished it weren't true.

After another hour, she drove down Main Street. A few people strolled the sidewalk. The diner was full of smiling customers. Brannigan's Pub was open, but of course she couldn't see inside.

Being this close yet so far away was more than she could take. The tears started to fall. But she couldn't let herself fall apart on Main Street. Someone would see her and tell Zach.

No, she wouldn't do that to him. Instead, she made her way to Harmony's apartment building and parked in the lot. There, she let herself cry.

Between Dillon's obsession with her, and losing Zach, she was stretched beyond her limits. Carter had been right, she needed time to figure out how the hell to deal with all of this.

One day. She would allow herself one day to weep and wallow. Then tomorrow, she'd put on her brave face and get back to business.

With that settled, she opened her window to get some fresh air, and wiped her eyes. A woman's laughter caught her attention.

"You like that, don't you," a man said.

Jessie squeezed her eyes shut. The last thing she wanted to see was a happy couple.

"I do. I like everything about you, Sean."

Jessie's eyes popped open. *That voice.*

She scanned the lot and then spotted the couple. They walked hand in hand toward her. She was too shocked to move, even to squat down.

The man stopped his companion at the car parked in front of Jessie's. Then he spun her around.

"I love you, Sean," she said. "I can't believe we did it. I've wanted nothing more than to be with the father of my kids."

"Me too, baby. Soon we will have it all."

Jessie sat still as they made out against the car.

Wait, what was she doing? She needed photos.

She quickly snapped a few, checking to make sure she could see each of their faces in some of the images.

As their make out session wound down, Jessie reclined her seat. Now that the shock had worn off, she didn't want to be spotted.

"I'll see you in an hour," he said.

"I can't wait. Any special requests for dinner?" she asked.

"Whatever you pick up is fine. Here's my key.

You'll probably get back before I do. Are you sure the kids are all right?"

"Yes. My mom has them."

Jessie stayed reclined as she listened to more lip smacking, and then finally, one car drove off, and she heard footsteps going upstairs.

When she sat up, she sent the photos to Carter with a message. *"Carter, I'm in Fisher Springs. I needed a drive. Saw this. Bethany and some guy named Sean. I overheard them talking. He's the father of her children, not Marcus. Who is he?"*

After she hit send, she saw the man walking back down the stairs. Damn, she should have paid more attention to figure out which apartment was his. Sean walked to a truck and got in.

She quickly snapped a photo. "Gotcha."

The truck was property of Russet Burbank Construction. A search on her phone didn't pull up a list of employees for the company, but it did tell her they were based in Portland.

Now she needed to get back to Seattle. She'd know who this guy was soon enough.

Chapter Thirty-Five

"You're serious?" Zach asked as he stood across the bar from Blaese.

"I am. Your services are no longer needed. As you know, Marcus Beyers is dead, and Jonny and Tony Bannon died in the shootout with the FBI that same day," the agent said.

"And I'm not a suspect?" Zach asked.

Blaese laughed. "No. I'm sorry we treated you like one. But with the Murphy name… you understand."

"Unfortunately, I do. That's one reason I changed it."

"Probably for the best. But you should know, we shut down Bucky's Bar last night."

"Please tell me they are permanently closed."

Blaese nodded. "We found over one hundred thousand dollars that can be traced directly to the Bannon's meth business."

Zach frowned. "How the hell did you do that?"

"I can't give you details, but I can say it helps when someone on the inside is willing to used marked bills." He straightened his tie. "I hope that means more business will be flowing your way soon."

Zach couldn't hide his smile. "You and me both. Business was great until they opened up."

Blaese rapped his knuckles on the bar top and stood to leave.

"Hey, did you drive all the way out here to tell me this?" Zach asked.

Blaese shook his head. "Sorry to disappoint, but I actually stayed in the motel last night, since the Davenport case went late."

"Why didn't you stay in Davenport?" Zach asked.

"Let's just say there are a few things I like about Fisher Springs. Oh, one more thing. You'll probably find out soon enough, but we've arrested your sister, Bethany."

"Bethany? For what?"

"It turns out she and Sean Bannon tried to play the FBI in order to get Marcus and the other Bannons out of the picture."

Sean Bannon? What the fuck? "Are you sure?"

He wasn't surprised about his sister. She'd always been the one in charge, although she'd never gotten the credit. But to try to use the FBI to do it? That took balls. What shocked him even more was Sean Bannon's involvement. He'd moved away before Zach had, claiming he wanted nothing to do with the business.

"I am," Blaese confirmed. "We have a recording of them discussing their plans. Bethany had been staying at Sean's place here in town. When we arrived at his apartment to arrest them, Sean cooperated, but your sister…" He laughed. "She ran out to the back deck and tried to shimmy down to the one on the second floor. Her pants got stuck on some nail, and she was literally hanging there, waiting for us when we got around back."

Sounds like Bethany. "She's not one to give up without a fight."

"That's for sure."

Kate walked into the pub just as Blaese leaned over the counter.

"Maybe in time, she'll tell you what the hell she was thinking." Blaese winked and stood up straight. "You have a great little town here. I'm going to miss it."

"You won't be back?" Kate asked.

Blaese turned to her, and for the first time, Zach saw the man smile.

The agent reached out and rubbed Kate's shoulder. "I wish I could, but I'll be assigned a new case soon, and who knows where that will take me. I'm glad I got to know you, Kate."

Blaese bent down and kissed her lightly on the lips. Then he slipped out while Zach's jaw was practically on the floor.

Blaese had been all business any time he'd seen

him. He'd questioned if the man was even human.

"You and Blaese?" he asked, dumbfounded.

Kate shrugged. "Mitchell. His name is Mitchell." Then she sat in the stool he'd vacated.

"Another one-night stand?" Zach asked.

Kate looked like she might cry; it was not typical for her to get emotional over men. She had a rule that she'd *only* do one-night stands. Zach had asked her why once, and she'd changed the subject.

"One that turned into a few weeks," she admitted. "But it's fine. We both agreed it was just a fling. Time to move on."

He heard her words, but Zach knew that look on her face. "Did you tell him you got attached?"

Kate's eyes darted to his before she barked out, "No. I'm not attached."

Zach nodded. "Whatever you say. Can I get you a beer?"

"Sure."

He grabbed her a bottle of her favorite and opened it.

"It wasn't him I got attached too. He just reminded me of someone I miss."

"I'm sorry. Want to talk about it?"

She took a pull from her beer, then shook her head. "Don't worry about me. I'll be fine. You, on the other hand, have been a wreck. But there must be good news... If Mitchell is leaving town, the case must be complete, right?"

"He said I'm no longer considered a suspect."

Kate laughed. "You were more than cooperative with the FBI. They had no reason to still treat you like a suspect."

Zach shrugged. "It doesn't matter now."

"You're right. It doesn't. Woohoo!" she yelled, making Zach jump. "You know what this means? Project Get-the-Girl-Back begins!"

He shook his head, then grabbed the bag of peanuts from under the counter and refilled the bowls. He didn't respond further to Kate's crazy idea.

The moment Blaese had come in, he had a feeling it was good news, and his mind had started going in circles.

He wanted Jessie back, there was no question. But what if she'd moved on?

"You'll get her back," Kate said.

"How did you do that?"

"I can see your worry all over your face."

"It's been months. She's probably seeing someone else by now," he said.

He tossed the peanut bag back under the counter a little too hard, causing several items to fall to the ground.

Kate reached for his hand. "Hey, you'll never know if you don't try. Start now."

She was right. If he didn't try, he was sure to stay miserable. At least if he found out he didn't have a chance, maybe his heart could move on.

That was a big maybe.

He nodded. "All right. I'll start, but if this goes

badly, I'm blaming you."

"Fair enough. Here's to phase one!" Kate held up a peanut to toast.

He couldn't help but laugh as he grabbed a peanut and tapped it against hers.

Phase one was simple enough. He would text Jessie each day, hoping she hadn't blocked his number.

Shit. What if she'd blocked his number?

"We didn't think this through," he said.

"What?"

"What if she blocked my number, or what if she blocks it after I text her?"

Kate finished her beer. "Zach, stop worrying. If that happens, we'll figure it out. Just text her already."

She was right, again.

He typed up his text and hit send. Then he tossed the phone on the bar, knowing he was going to drive himself crazy, staring at it every few seconds, hoping she'd responded.

The phone vibrated on the bar. Kate grabbed it before he could.

Her eyes lit up, and she started to jump up and down. "She responded! This is great! Now control yourself, and don't send another one until tomorrow. Got it?"

"Okay."

She handed Zach his phone, and he opened up the messages.

Zach: *Agent Blaese said I've been cleared. I miss you.*

Jessie: *That's great news.*

He stared at it again. "What the fuck?" he asked. "Which is great news? Me being cleared, or me missing her?"

Kate shrugged. "You can ask tomorrow. You haven't texted her in months. Let your news sink in."

Sink in. Yeah, easier said than done.

Jessie stared at Zach's message. She was sitting in her office, trying hard not to cry. But that's exactly what she wanted to do when she saw his words.

He missed her.

All the emotions she'd tried to stuff down came back with just those three little words.

She wanted to write back that she missed him too, but then what? Did they have a chance?

How could they? She still worked for the FBI, and yes, he might be cleared of this case, but he was still a Murphy. As much as she hated it, she had to acknowledge that fact would likely hold her back in her career if they were together.

Her career. She'd been thinking a lot about it lately. When she'd first started with the FBI, she was excited about the cases and looked forward to work. Now she wasn't sure this was even what she wanted to do.

But if not this, then what? She'd never seen

herself doing anything else.

She pulled the familiar card out from her desk. Zach's sister Gina had reached out to her right after their breakup. That woman was relentless and wouldn't give up until Jessie had agreed to meet with her.

The entire meeting was a sales pitch. Gina wanted Jessie to work with her as a bounty hunter; it was her attempt to find a way for Jessie and Zach to be together. Jessie had accepted her card but told her the idea of hunting down some of those bail jumpers sounded scary even to her.

But meeting with Gina had pushed her into looking at other opportunities. She'd been meeting weekly with a local private investigator she'd worked with before. After she found out he was a former FBI agent, she grew more intrigued.

"Hey, Doyle, you have a minute?" Carter stood in her doorway.

"Yes, come in. I was just working on the last file you gave me." She dug it out from under some papers.

"I'm not here for that." Carter closed the door then sat down in the chair across from her desk.

She swallowed. This couldn't be good.

"Zach Brannigan was officially cleared this morning," he informed her. "He's helped us tremendously."

"That's good. He's a good man. Now he can move on with his life," she said. Tears threatened to fall from her eyes. She stared down at the papers on her desk, hoping Carter wouldn't notice.

God, why couldn't she get out of this emotional funk?

"I was wrong," Carter said gently.

That caught her attention. She glanced up to see a look of concern on his face.

"When I told you to cut things off with Brannigan," he clarified. "I didn't realize…"

"Realize what?"

"That you were in love with him."

If she hadn't been sitting, she probably would have fallen over. Suddenly, it was hard to breathe, and she found herself coughing for air.

"Easy," he soothed. "Take slow, deep breaths. I'm sorry. I thought you knew."

She still couldn't speak. She focused on her breathing. The last thing she needed was to pass out in front of her boss.

"You think I'm in love?" she finally asked.

Carter smiled. "Doyle, you've been a shell of yourself these last few months. I thought it was disappointment, and time would heal, but it's clear that's not the case. I'm sorry I made you choose your career over him. While it was wrong to get involved with someone affiliated with an ongoing case, there's no reason you shouldn't be with him just because of what his last name used to be."

"What are you saying?"

Carter leaned forward. "If you love that man, then go make things right. Love like that doesn't come around very often. Don't lose your person like I did."

Her boss never opened up about himself. No one really knew much about his personal life.

"I'm sorry. Did you lose your wife?"

He shook his head. "I never got that far. I walked away from the love of my life for this job, and I regret it every day." He stood and walked to the door. "That was all I wanted to say."

After he left, she sat frozen. There was nothing standing in her way with Zach? Well, except that maybe he had moved on. But then why would he have sent that text?

Another knock on her door. This time, it wasn't Carter.

"Sorry to bother you," Sam said meekly. "I just couldn't walk by without saying hi."

"Hi, Sam. I'm glad you did. Come in," Jessie said.

"I still feel so sick about everything that happened," the other woman lamented.

"It's all right. I've had time to think about it, and I believe you. Dillon was very manipulative. I mean, he tricked me too. I'm sorry I doubted you."

Jessie had missed her friend. Dillon had really done a number on her life, and she was finished letting him have any control.

"Can we be friends again?" Sam asked.

Jessie smiled. "I'd like that."

"How have you been? You've looked unhappy since you split from Zach."

Jessie's eyes welled with tears. She couldn't hold back any longer. She had to tell someone. "I love him. I ruined the best thing that ever happened to me."

Chapter Thirty-Six

Jessie tossed and turned most of the night. Hell, she'd been doing that all week. Zach had texted her each day. Just like that. Like they hadn't been apart for months.

She wasn't sure what he wanted. To be friends? To try again? What?

Dammit. She knew what she wanted. But could she let herself go there? As wonderful as her time with Zach had been, she couldn't help but think of how she'd once thought that about Dillon.

No. This was different. Zach was different. And this might be his way of opening the door.

Her phone buzzed. Another text from Zach.

He had started by saying he missed her. Then the next day, he told her Nick and Lauren had gotten married, and it was a beautiful ceremony. The next day, he told her about a new shop opening in town.

She hadn't responded because she didn't know what to say. Every day, he sent another text telling her about something going on in his world. Every day, she read those texts and missed him more. Time was supposed to heal the pain, but instead, her longing for him deepened.

Jumping out of bed, she padded to the kitchen and made coffee. It was Saturday, which meant she was scheduled to play in a softball game. All she wanted to do was stay in bed, but she knew getting out would be good for her. Plus, Sam would be there, and she'd promised her friend she'd go.

Just before she left, she checked her phone again. Another text from Zach.

That was new. He had only been sending one per day.

The second text stopped her midway out the door.

Zach: *I want to see you.*

That was it. Plain and simple.

Was he asking her out on a date? What else could it be? She would have to answer this one. What would she say? She wanted to see him, but no, that would make it worse.

Hell, it couldn't get much worse than how she felt without him.

Jessie: *Okay.*

Well, there. No turning back now.

She didn't check her phone again until she got to the game. When she did, she found no new messages.

For reasons she couldn't explain, she was

disappointed. Part of her wanted Zach to be pushy like he had been when they first met. But then again, less than hour had passed. Why did she expect so much?

Because if he'd been as miserable as her, he'd have done more.

The more she thought about it, the angrier she became. It was a good thing she had an excuse to swing a bat right now, because she was quite worked up.

Every time she was up, she hit the ball hard, earning her two home runs and three doubles. They were crushing the other team.

"Hey, Doyle, we're heading out for lunch after this. Want to join us?"

She turned to see the new agent in their office smiling at her. He was nice-looking, but he didn't do anything for her. Too clean-cut. The opposite of Zach.

Damn, now she was thinking about him again.

"No thanks. I have plans," she lied.

"Next time." He turned to walk away, but stopped. "Hey, is that truck driving onto the field?"

Jessie turned and saw a truck that looked very much like Zach's drive up to, but not quite onto, the grass. Another car pulled up next to it, and two guys got out.

Wait, she recognized those guys. Nick and Chase. They pulled what looked like an amp out of the trunk of the car.

The agent who'd just asked her out ran over to them. After they exchanged a few words, he ran back to their dugout.

"Well, I guess you do have other plans, Doyle."
He winked.

Oh no, what are they going to do? Her skin
prickled as she felt everyone's eyes on her.

Chase was setting up a microphone, and he
turned on the amp. "Can I get everyone's attention
please?"

Everyone was already looking his way, since
their intrusion had interrupted the game. Although,
they only had half an inning left, and to be honest, the
other team was unlikely to catch up.

"My boy here has something he needs to say to
Jessie Doyle."

Chase stepped back, and Zach got out of his
truck.

God, he looked good. His beard had grown
back, and he was wearing a T-shirt that fit tight across
his chest and showed off all his tattoos. It looked like
he'd spent the last three months working out.

He walked up to the mic. "Jessie?"

"Over here!" half her team shouted.

Zach glanced her way, and they locked eyes.
"Hi," he said, smiling.

She stood frozen. What was he going to do?

"I'm not good with words," he continued, "and
I realize I've probably done a shit job of tryin' to tell
you how I feel over those texts, so I've decided I'll let a
song do it for me."

Holy shit. Was he really going to sing?

Zach walked back to his truck and grabbed something. A guitar.

He plays guitar? How did she not know this?

He plugged it into the amp and began to strum. Then he launched into the song.

At first, she was in awe; he could really sing, and his eyes remained locked with hers the entire time. Then she recognized the song. Their song from the motel.

When she let herself listen to the words, her heart fluttered. Was this really how he felt? He sang that it felt like falling in love.

Love. Was that what this was? Carter thought so.

It had been months since she'd broken it off, and every day, she longed for this man. The hole he'd left couldn't be filled. And now, he was here, singing about his love.

Her chest swelled with so many emotions. Tears fell from her eyes, and she was wearing the biggest grin.

He sang "kiss me" over and over. Not once did he take his eyes off of her. It wasn't just the words making her swoon… love emanated from his gaze.

After he sang the last note, everyone clapped and cheered.

Sam gave Jessie a push. "Go get your man."

Zach handed the guitar to Chase, but he stood in place. Waiting for her.

It was her turn to put herself out there.

Jessie took a step forward. Then another. Normally, she couldn't stand to be the center of attention, but knowing Zach had put his heart out there for her in this way was frankly overwhelming.

As she closed in on him, she could see he was balling his fists. He was nervous.

Well, she had no doubt how she felt now, and it was time to show him.

She broke into a run and jumped when she got to him.

He caught her and was all smiles. "Hi."

"Hi." Then she crushed her lips to his.

Their chemistry was stronger than ever, and the kiss took on a life of its own. Her hands tangled in his hair, and his hands cupped her ass, holding her in place.

Someone behind her wolf-whistled.

Zach released her legs and slowly lowered her, but he kept his arms around her. "I meant what I sang. Jessie, I've fallen fer you. We had a rough start." He chuckled and shook his head, "And a rough middle. But these last few months have been miserable. I know you were worried about your case, but I've been cleared. Just… hell, Jessie, just give us a chance." His eyes were glassy.

This big, strong, mountain-looking man was near tears. It made hers fall all the more.

"Yes, Zach. I've been miserable too. I've never felt the way I feel about you."

"I'm so happy to hear you say that, this could

have gone a completely different way. It's a little risky, interruptin' a bunch of FBI agents." He was grinning ear to ear.

She laughed. "Do you have to go back to the bar?"

He shook his head. "Ariel's got it covered. Kate said she'd help out too. I think they are both hopin' I don't come back to Fisher Springs tonight."

She smiled up at him. "Good. Let's grab lunch then we can go to my place." She ran her hand over his beard. "It grew back."

"It did. I thought about shavin' it, but I really don't know what you like."

"I like it. But I like seeing your face too. Both. My answer is both."

"So diplomatic," he growled.

"Only about that."

He grinned. "Trust me. I know your not-so-diplomatic side."

"Hey." She tried to tickle him, but instead, he moaned. The fire was back in his eyes.

He pulled her flush against him and kissed her hard.

Again, there was a wolf-whistle behind them.

"Okay, guys. You should go be alone now," Nick said.

"You're one to talk," Zach said to him. Turning back to Jessie, he said, "When Nick and Lauren don't have their hands all o'er each other, they're eye-feckin' each other."

"Hey, don't make our love sound so crass."

"Shut it," Zach said told him. Then he grinned at her. "Let's go."

He took her hand and led her to his truck.

"Wait, my car is here," she remembered.

"We'll take it back to your place," Chase offered.

"See? We've got it all figured out," Zach said.

"Yes, you do."

Chapter Thirty-Seven

During the entire ride back to Jessie's, Zach held her hand tightly, thankful she'd said yes to giving them another try.

"How did I not know you can play guitar?" Jessie asked as they parked at her place.

He grinned.

He'd been practicing that song for the last three months. To him, it had been torture, playing it over and over. While he'd hoped to play it for her someday, as the months wore on, his hope had dwindled.

"It never came up," he shrugged.

Jessie turned to him, arching a brow.

"Seriously," he insisted. "I hadn't played in a long time. But these last few months, I picked it up again. It was therapeutic."

It really had been. If it weren't for his guitar, he'd probably have drunk himself into a stupor after closing each night.

"I loved it," she smiled.

It had started to rain on their drive to her house, and now that rain was falling harder.

"What do you say? Want to make a run for it?" he asked.

"A race. I like it."

She was out of the car before he could respond.

"Hey!" he shouted, hoping to slow her down so he could catch up.

It didn't work. Despite her shorter legs, she was fast and beat him to her door.

"I win," she taunted as she unlocked and opened the door.

He grabbed her and walked them both inside, kicking the door closed behind them. Then he whirled her around and pressed her against the door.

"No, I'm pretty sure I won."

She rolled her eyes. "Nice line."

Does she still not get it? Just to make certain, he leaned his forehead to hers and locked eyes. "Jessie, it's no line. I love you. And if you need me to tell you that every day, I will. You're it for me, Macushla."

She blinked several times, and he realized she was trying to blink back tears.

"I love you too, Zach."

He hadn't realized how much he wanted to hear those words until that moment.

Not able to hold back any longer, he kissed her hard. When she opened up and let him in, he knew it was more than just a kiss. She was letting him into her heart and soul. A place he would cherish.

Fuck Dillon and what he had done to this wonderful woman. He may have damaged her, but Zach would do everything he could every day to show her he would never betray her, never leave her. The last three months had taught him that he needed her. Without her, his world was black and white and felt empty. But with her, he felt alive.

As he kissed her, she moaned, and he couldn't help but grind into her, pushing her harder against the door. Her hands moved down to his hips, and then she was lifting his T-shirt up, trying to get it over his body.

"Take this off now," she demanded.

"Yes, ma'am."

He set her down and ripped off his T-shirt. While he was occupied, Jessie pushed past him and yanked off her shirt, tossing it to the floor. She then removed her bra.

He followed her and her clothing trail to her bedroom, where she was wearing nothing but a blue, lacy thong. He quirked a brow. "You play softball in a thong?"

"It was all I had. Now get over here before I decide to do my laundry instead."

He laughed as he quickly undressed. "You know, your carpets do look awfully clean, now that I'm noticing." He climbed onto the bed and pulled her up against his body.

"You think those are clean, you should see my makeup brushes."

Now that made him laugh.

"Careful," he warned. "You sass me too much, I might have to teach you a lesson." He leaned in for a kiss but instead, found himself being flipped over onto his stomach.

This was too familiar, as Jessie sat on top of him, holding him down.

He laughed again. "You aren't going to make this easy on me, are you? I knew the moment you first tackled me that I had to get to know you."

"You like bondage or something? Cause I hate to disappoint, but my handcuffs are for work only."

"Damn. Are you saying there are no cuffs in my immediate future?"

Her mouth was on his neck, kissing lightly up to his ear. "If I cuff you, you wouldn't be free to touch me."

"Oh honey, I'm sure I could convince you to let me use those handcuffs in other ways," he growled, imagining Jessie sprawled in front of him and cuffed to the bed. "Serious, though, can I tie you up sometime?"

She sat up, allowing him to flip over. "We'll see."

It was his turn to grab her and flip her over. But before she could complain, he kissed her and ground himself between her legs, causing her to let out a moan.

"Jessie, I haven't had sex with anyone since you. I know I'm safe. I'm not sure how you feel about it, but I want to be with you. No barriers."

Her smile lit up her face. "You haven't been with anyone? In all these months?"

He looked at her and shook his head. "I didn't want anyone else."

"I haven't been either," she promised. "I'm safe." Her hands roamed down his back and cupped his ass. "And I'm on the pill."

The need to be inside her was strong.

He reached down and swept his fingers between her legs. "Damn, you are so wet."

"I want you so bad."

He couldn't wait. With one tug, he ripped off her lacy underwear. She gasped. Then he lined up at her entrance and plunged in.

They both stayed very still as she adjusted to him. He had forgotten how good she felt, and he was trying everything he could to not lose it like his teenage self would have.

"Fuck, Jessie. I swear to god you were made for me."

"I need you to move. Oh god, Zach, I think I'm going to come already."

He'd intended to try to take things slow, but as soon as he slid back, he couldn't. He slammed into her again. "I can't go slow. I'm sorry."

"Don't. Go faster."

He did, and just when he didn't think he could hold on any longer, her entire body quivered in his arms.

"Zach. Oh my god!"

He thrust harder as his own release overtook him, and he pushed in as far as he could, reveling in the sensation of her orgasm pulsating around him.

When they finally came down from what had easily been the most incredible sex of his life, he held her tight.

"Each time we're together, I think it's the best I've ever had, but then it gets better," he grinned.

She turned in his arms and propped up onto one elbow. "Well, good thing we have all day and night to keep testing that theory."

"Sounds good, but I need food."

"We can have something delivered," she said. "First, tell me about your tattoos. What made you get so many of them?"

He shrugged. "My first one was this eagle." He pointed to the ink that wrapped around his entire right bicep.

"That's pretty large for a first tattoo," she commented.

He nodded. "It was my symbol for being free. It was important to me that it stood out."

Her fingers traced the lines of his other tattoos.

He watched her movements. "The other ones are all based on what was important to me at the time."

Her fingers glided up his left arm. "What's this?"

He glanced down. "Beer brewing equipment, and then up here, that's a hops plant. Liam and I were really into brewing for a while. Like I said, he made a career out of it."

"Why didn't you continue to pursue it?"

Zach laughed. "Because everything I made tasted like shit. I knew it wasn't the career path for me. That's when I started taking business courses online."

"Oh yeah?"

"Yep. It was a good thing, because then I was ready to run the pub when the opportunity came along."

Jessie pulled away and fell back onto the bed. "You know, there's something pretty important we haven't discussed."

Now it was his turn to sit up. For the first time today, he swore he caught a flash of fear in her eyes.

"What's on your mind?" he asked.

She stood up. "Maybe we should have lunch and a drink first."

Jessie already had her robe on and was heading for the door when he stopped her.

"What's wrong?"

"You own a pub in Fisher Springs. I work mostly in Seattle, which is a two-hour drive from you."

Yeah, he'd thought about it, and it sucked. But after being apart for all that time, he'd drive any distance, even if it meant only seeing her a few times a month. At some point, they'd have to find common ground.

"It is a bit of a drive, but one I'm willing to make to see you. You mean too much to me to let a little distance get in the way. I thought we'd take some time to figure out how we might get into the same town."

"Same town?"

He grinned. "Yeah. I mean, I'd like to live with my wife when the time comes."

Her eyes widened. "Your wife?"

After a soft kiss, he looked her in the eyes. "I have no doubt in this world that you are the one for me. If I have to sell the pub and move to Seattle, I'll do it."

Tears fell from her eyes. She wiped them away. "I swear I'm not normally this weepy. You seem to bring it out in me."

"I don't mean to make you sad."

She shook her head. "You don't. But I don't want you to sell your pub. It's who you are."

Tightening his grip on her, he leaned his forehead to hers. "Macushla, I can't be running a pub all hours of the night after we have kids, so eventually, I'll have to figure out something else to do."

"Jesus, Zach. Marriage, kids? You do come on strong."

He kissed a trail from the corner of her mouth down her neck. "Tell me you've never thought of those things with me."

"Mm. That feels good. But I'm pleading the fifth."

He pulled back and quirked a brow.

"All right," she relented. "I might have looked into the possibility of becoming a private investigator. It's not uncommon for FBI agents to move into that line of work."

"I thought you loved being an agent?"

She shrugged. "I did, but I've discovered I don't do well with authority. It might be good for me to work for myself."

Zach laughed. "You recently discovered this, did you?"

"Shut it and kiss me."

She was using his words, but he loved it.

Lunch could wait a while longer.

Chapter Thirty-Eight

Two months later.

"Relax. You look like you might punch someone," Jessie said.

"I'm not goin' to punch anyone. I'm just nervous to see my nephews. One was just a toddler when I left. And now they are about to be in my home."

"They've had a rough couple of months. I'm sure they are nervous too," Jessie said.

Zach had been shocked to find out that Sean Bannon was the father of Bethany's kids. So shocked, he'd gone to visit her in prison to ask her why the hell she'd stayed with Marcus.

Of course she wouldn't answer him. She was too busy demanding he get revenge on Sean. He couldn't blame her. While he didn't like what Bethany had done to her sons, she had been blindsided by Sean's betrayal.

"I know you're on the fence when it comes to

Sean, but I like him," Jessie admitted. "It might have taken him a long time, and you may not agree with the way he did it, but he got his sons out of the family business."

She was right about that. If they'd stayed with Bethany, she would have used them the way his father had used him. No doubt about it. Bethany was a chip off the old block.

After his visit to Bethany, her oldest, Aiden, finally came forward and said he'd lied for his mother, taking the blame for shooting an FBI agent last year. Apparently, Bethany had convinced Aiden that because he was under eighteen, he wouldn't do any time, but if they knew *she* had killed him, she'd go away for years.

Jessie was right. Sean had put his kids first, something Bethany had never done.

Jessie pushed up on her toes and gave him a kiss. "I'm going to finish making sure everything is set up. You need to take some deep breaths."

She took a step away, but he grabbed her wrist and pulled her back flush against his body.

"I'm fine," he rumbled. "Do you hear my accent now?"

Jessie studied him. "No."

He smiled. "There you go." He bent down and kissed her, and it quickly grew heated.

Damn, he wanted her. Maybe they had time before any guests arrived.

"You two can't be left alone, can you?" Nick

had somehow snuck up and was standing behind Jessie.

"Goddammit! Don't sneak up on us like that," Zach snapped.

"Sneak up? You invited us over. You should be expecting us," Nick grinned.

Zach glanced over at Lauren, who was also grinning.

"Whatever, like you two can talk."

They both laughed.

Zach couldn't count the number of times he'd walked in on them kissing or making out. Hell, one time, Nick had his shirt off, and Lauren was pressed against his office wall at the pub. He'd told them to get the hell out of there.

If anyone was getting any in his pub, it would be him and Jessie.

Nick was lucky he was a good friend; anyone else going into his office would meet a worse fate. Yeah, he was a bit paranoid after hearing about Dillon's threat of a bomb beneath his desk. Thank god that had been a bluff.

"Zach? You around?" Chase's voice called from the doorway.

"Come on in," he called back.

Chase walked in with Harmony, but apparently, they hadn't checked a mirror in the recent past.

Nick was the first to bust out laughing. Then Zach. Lauren was the next to go.

Jessie tried to maintain a straight face, and held out long enough to ask, "Did you two have a good time?"

Harmony's faced flushed a bright red, and Chase's eyebrows shot straight up.

"What are you talking about?" he asked.

Zach jerked his head toward the bathroom. "Go look in the mirror."

Chase was still holding Harmony's hand as he led her down the hall.

"Shit," they heard him say, which caused another fit of laughter.

Chase closed the door, but they could still here them.

"Harmony, how could you not say something about my hair?"

"Your hair? Did you see mine? What the hell? Were you fisting it the entire time?"

Nick was laughing so hard, he started to cough. "Stop, please! I can't take anymore."

Their friends walked out of the bathroom.

"Fuck you all. Like you don't all do the same thing." Clearly, Chase had decided to take the defensive path.

"Your fly is down too," Zach couldn't help adding.

Chase opened his mouth, likely to tell them to shut the hell up, but a knock at the door interrupted him.

"They're here," Jessie singsonged.

Zach glanced around; everyone was watching him. They all knew his new friendship with Sean had been an important part of putting his past behind him. It was important to Sean too, as he'd had a similar struggle with his name while remaining in Idaho. That was why he'd finally moved to Portland: for a fresh start. Both of his sons had been more than happy to move.

Zach opened the door to find Gina standing on the front porch holding two large gift bags.

She smiled wide. "Surprise! I was able to make it after all. Are my nephews here yet?"

Zach sighed. "No."

She smirked and gave him a hug. "Good to see you too. I'm glad you grew the beard back. That photo you sent clean shaven was startling." She gave it a tug.

He was too. Once Jessie admitted she found it sexy, he'd resolved to keep it. It was too much a part of him to let it go. Plus, he hated shaving every day.

"Sorry, I am happy to see you," he said.

"Me too," she said.

Kate walked in behind her.

"You two came together?" Zach asked.

"Yep," Kate said.

"I didn't realize you were friends."

"We talked a lot during those months you were wallowing," Gina said.

He wasn't surprised they had become friends. He'd always thought they were an awful lot alike. But still, he said, "I wasn't wallowin'."

"Yes, you were," half the room responded.

No sooner had he closed the door than someone knocked.

This had to be them.

"I'll get it," Jessie offered.

A moment later, Sean walked in, followed by both boys. Although, calling them *boys* was a stretch. They both looked like grown men.

"Wow. You look so much like Zach," Jessie said to the older one, Aiden.

"That's what Sean says. Oh, sorry, I meant 'Dad'." Aiden's cheeks flushed red.

"Don't worry about it. I know it will take time," Sean said.

The boys kept their gazes turned down and their mouths shut.

It reminded Zach of himself as a teenager. His goal had been to go unnoticed because being noticed by his dad wouldn't have been a good thing.

"Thank you for having us," Sean said. "This tall guy is my oldest, Aiden. And this here is Caden."

"We are so happy you could make it," Jessie enthused. "If you want, we can eat in the dining room and kitchen. I hope you don't mind, but we kept it casual and ordered pizzas from Timmy's."

"Oh, I love that place!" Chase said as he led the way toward the kitchen.

After everyone had gotten their fill, Sean and the boys appeared more relaxed.

"So, you knew my dad when he was younger?"

Caden asked.

Zach nodded. "I did."

"How did neither of you get forced into the family?" Aiden asked.

Zach told them how he had essentially run away to avoid taking over. Sean's story was different, in that he had two brothers who wanted to take control of the business, so they were happy when he wanted to pursue something else. Sean was able to stay in contact with everyone yet keep his distance.

"Look, boys," Zach said. "Your mom is a lot like my dad. He was hard and viewed his kids as workers more than anythin' else. Frankly, I'm happy you have this chance to get to know your father. Marcus was—" He stopped himself. As much as he hated Marcus, they had known him as their dad.

"He was an asshole," Aiden said.

Zach chuckled. "I can't disagree with you."

"Sean, how did you get released?" Nick asked. "I'd heard you and Bethany were both going away for a while." He shot a look to Aiden and Caden.

"It's okay, they know. I told them I'd never keep secrets from them. That was what their mother and Marcus did."

"Good, because I'm really curious. Last I heard, you both intended to take over the business," Nick asked.

"No. I've never wanted anything to do with it. Six months ago, Bethany came to me saying she wanted our family to be together. At first, I thought she was trying to fix us, but I quickly learned it was all about business for her. She had this crazy scheme to get Marcus and my brothers out of the picture and marry me. She thought that would let her run both the Murphy and Bannon family businesses. Again, I didn't want any part of it, but she used my sons to get me involved."

Fuck Bethany. Zach grimaced. "Sounds like somethin' my dad would have done."

"It was. And I wasn't going to let her do it. I went to the FBI and made a deal—if I told them what was going on, I'd go free."

Nick shook his head. "Are you saying you were the informant?"

Sean nodded.

The detective turned to Jessie. "I thought Bethany was the informant?" He glanced back to Sean, "As a courtesy, the FBI filled my chief in on what was going on after Marcus and the two Bannons died."

He nodded in acknowledgment.

Jessie shook her head. "She was *an* informant, but with help from Sean, it was discovered she was using our agent for her gain. I didn't even know Sean was working with the FBI until he was released."

"Was your arrest part of the deal?" Nick asked.

"Yeah, I was taken in with Bethany so she wouldn't suspect me, but I was released twenty-four hours later."

"And the business?" Nick asked.

"I was approached by a couple of men claiming

to be business associates of my brothers. Once I convinced them I wanted nothing to do with any of it and they could have it all, they left happy."

"I don't recall seeing that in the file," Jessie said.

"It happened after everything wrapped up. But there is something else that wouldn't have made it into the file. Marcus figured out Bethany was helping the FBI."

"How the hell do you know this?" Nick asked.

"She told me. He confronted her after he saw her get out of some agent's car. He threatened her and told her to get him immunity too."

"Did she tell him to go to hell?" Zach asked.

Sean shook his head. "She said she went to the agent she was working with, and he agreed."

"He never would have done that," Jessie said. "He couldn't. It wouldn't have been up to him."

"I figured she was lying, but according to her, Marcus believed her, and that was really all that mattered."

"Huh," Jessie said. "I wonder if that's why Marcus kept going to your pub even though he knew there were agents there. I never could make sense of that."

"What, you think he believed he could get his money *and* immunity?" Zach asked.

"Greed tends to make people stupid," she reasoned. "It's possible."

"Why don't we move on," Harmony suggested.

"We have some celebrating to do."

Zach glanced around the room and realized his nephews probably didn't want to hear all the details of the case. "Sounds good," he nodded.

"Sweet, I'll be right back." Harmony jumped up and returned a few minutes later with a cake.

"Did you make this?" Nick asked.

"I did."

He reached out to grab a fingerful of frosting.

Lauren slapped his hand away. "This is for Aiden's and Caden's birthdays."

The boys' eyes widened. "It's not our birthday," Aiden said.

"No, but I've missed far too many," Zach told them. "I'd like to start makin' up for that today."

"Wow. Thank you. No one has ever made me a cake before," Aiden said.

"Me either," Caden said.

Zach had to look away to hide the anger he felt toward his sister in that moment. Goddamn. She should have known better, after being raised by their dad. How could she not want better for her children? But maybe she didn't know how to achieve that. He'd had the benefit of being raised by his mom until he was fourteen.

"Well, you're going to have to share it, but we'll make sure you get the biggest pieces," Nick told the boys.

Then the group sang happy birthday. Zach actually didn't know when their birthdays were;

something he intended to correct.

After everyone enjoyed cake, Sean and the boys left. It had been a short visit, but Zach understood they had a long drive back to Portland.

He closed the door behind the departing family, and noticed Jessie standing back, taking it all in. He walked up to her and took her hand. "Everything all right?"

"Yes. I'm just so happy everyone can come together. Did you ever imagine Bannons and Murphys would be sharing cake with an FBI agent and a couple of police officers?"

"An officer and a detective," Nick corrected.

Jessie laughed. "I just never thought this was possible. That was why I thought we couldn't be together."

Zach pulled her into his arms. "I'm glad I was able to change your mind."

"Me too. And we have an announcement we'd like to make," Jessie told the room.

Lauren jumped up. "You're getting married?"

"No," Jessie said.

"You're pregnant?" Harmony squealed.

"No."

"What's left?" Lauren asked Harmony.

"I'm leaving the FBI," Jessie said. "I'm going to be a private investigator."

Zach held back his chuckle as the room fell silent.

"And she's moving in!" he finally added.

Harmony and Lauren cheered and pulled Jessie in for a hug, while Nick and Chase slapped Zach on the back.

"Jessie, I'm so happy you are back in Zach's life. I've never seen him as happy as he is when he's with you." Kate gave her a big hug.

"I'm glad to be back."

"Hey, if you need any leads for clients, let me know. I have a few connections." Gina smiled.

"Thank you, I'll probably call you," Jessie said.

Zach watched his friends and the love of his life, and wondered how the hell he'd gotten so lucky. He wasn't sure, but he wasn't going to waste any more time. He had a ring hidden in his dresser… now he was just waiting for the right moment.

"I see you watching me," Jessie said as she snuggled up to him.

"I was. I love you." He bent down until his forehead touched hers.

"I love you, too."

Danielle Pays

Playlist

Kelly Clarkson – "Heartbeat Song"
Kane Brown – "Heaven"
Foo Fighters – "Everlong"
X Ambassadors – "Unsteady"
Lewis Capaldi – "Someone you loved"
Rihanna, Paul McCartney, Kanye West –
"FourFiveSeconds"
Post Malone – "I Fall Apart"
Ed Sherran – "Kiss Me"
Maren Morris – "The Bones"

Other books by Danielle Pays

The Dare to Risk series
Deceived
Pursued
Played
Consumed
Captivated – A Holiday Novella

The Dare to Surrender series
Chasing Her Trust
Taking Her Chase
Saving Her Target
Trusting Her Hero

Saving Her Target

About the Author

Danielle Pays writes steamy romance novels with a touch of suspense. She enjoys romance as well as mystery and suspense and blends them both using her beloved Pacific Northwest for inspiration with its mix of small towns and cities.

When she's not writing her characters into some kind of trouble, she can be found binging Netflix shows, trying to convince her children to eat her cooking, or drinking wine after battling said children at dinnertime.

Follow her at www.daniellepays.com or on Facebook at https://www.facebook.com/daniellepays/

Saving Her Target

9 781737 004424